GARDENS OF THE QUEEN

AJ BAILEY ADVENTURE SERIES - BOOK 2

NICHOLAS HARVEY

Printed in the United States of America

First Printing, 2019

ISBN-13: 978-1082763458 (Amazon only)
ISBN-13: 978-1-959627-02-9 (IngramSparks)

Cover design by Wicked Good Book Covers

Mermaid illustration by Tracie Cotta

Author photograph by Lift Your Eyes Photography

This is a work of fiction. Names, characters, businesses, places, events and incidents are either the products of the author's imagination or used in a fictitious manner unless noted otherwise. Any resemblance to actual persons, living or dead, or actual events is purely coincidental. Except Jen and her Greenhouse Restaurant – you can't make up Jen, who kindly provided her permission to fictionalise her character.

DEDICATION

For Cheryl, my mermaid.

Reaching for the bottle of beer he'd just opened to enjoy with dinner he took a large swig.

'Yes,' he lied in his reply.

Another bite and another swig gave him time to ponder his dilemma. He could make sure he was at work early enough to tie them down and the bastard would never know. But with his luck the boss would go in extra early or, worse still, this storm over to the west of them would blow this way and they really would need to be lashed down.

With another swig he got up, grabbed his car keys and left with lukewarm burrito in hand.

Silvio pulled into the empty car park of a modern brick building by the ocean to the west of the small town. The sign on the building read 'Instituto de Estudios Geológicos', Jucaro, Cuba. Tall wire fencing stretched from either side of the building down to the water, securing the facility and making sure anyone arriving by land had to go through the front door.

He unlocked the door and disarmed the alarm, careful to close the door behind him. He walked through the small front reception room that rarely received anyone, past a few more offices, flicking lights on as he went. Next was a larger room with multiple computers and several benches scattered with microscopes and various scanning and analysis equipment. At the back of that room he unlocked another door leading outside to the concrete piers surrounding a manmade inlet cut into the coastline from the open ocean. With another switch on the outside wall, a couple of floodlights illuminated the inlet and a seventy-foot converted trawler tied to the cleats on the pier. The wind was blowing a bit but so far no other sign of the storm and he shook his head, figuring he could've stayed in his chair.

He lifted the lid of a waist-high container on the deck and dragged out some ropes, throwing them over by the boat. It was then that it struck him. Where was the damn seaplane? He ran down the pier and desperately searched the inlet. How could that thing break loose? He knew he'd tied it off when Carlos flew in earlier that afternoon from Jardines de la Reina, the island chain off the coast. He recalled watching Carlos top it back off with petrol while they chatted. They'd stood where he was standing now. He kept replaying it in his mind but every time it ended with a seaplane tied to this dock.

He slowly took his phone out and stared at it a while, summoning up the courage to make the call. Being caught in the lie about the extra tie lines was now the least of his problems – how could he explain to his Russian boss that he'd lost a whole float plane? Maybe Carlos, the pilot, had a trip Silvio didn't know about or came up late, he thought, but Carlos had left long before he had tonight. He dialled Carlos's number, hoping to God he had the answer. Straight to voicemail. "Damn it."

He had no choice, he had to call the Russian. He dialled the number and paced the pier, hoping the plane would magically reappear before he answered. No such luck. "Mikhail? We've got a problem here."

The voice on the other end of the line was calm, even, and with surgical precision spoke Spanish with only a hint of his native Russian accent. "What kind of problem?"

"It's the float plane, it's gone…" Silvio cringed, expecting the monotone tongue-lashing he knew was coming. His boss had a way of demeaning people while never raising his voice. He'd been admonished by him and seen it happen to everyone working there and not once had the man shouted. But he could verbally strip you down and whip you to pulp with his words. Always logical and usually correct, he had a way of exposing every vice, fault and mistake until you felt like a helpless fool.

"How can a complete aeroplane disappear Silvio? Are you telling me you didn't tie it down at all and it's drifted into the sea or has someone stolen it in which case one of you left it unlocked?"

Before Silvio could muster an answer Mikhail carried on, this time with a hint of urgency in his voice. "Go back inside. What is missing?"

Silvio stammered as he started back into the building, "Nothing,

I think, I didn't see anything out of place when I came through. The front door was locked and the alarm was on." He burst into the electronics room, scanning for anything out of place.

"Shit!"

Mikhail was almost a whisper. "The computer is gone, correct?"

Silvio put his hand to his forehead, "Well, yeah, the main computer is pulled out and it looks like the hard drive has been taken."

"Check the survey maps," the Russian continued. Silvio rummaged on the benches and threw his hands in the air. Returning to the mobile, he reluctantly confirmed, "All of them, cases, everything, it's all gone."

Mikhail was silent for a moment but Silvio dared not say a word.

He finally spoke. "Check the alarm log. Someone logged in after we left tonight. I'll be there in ten minutes."

3

———————

Sydney grabbed Carlos's shirt as the plane heaved over again and they both slid uncontrollably to her side away from the opened door. She wished she could see his eyes. Those beautiful dark eyes that made her heart skip when he looked at her. Those eyes full of life, adventure and laughter, the eyes of the young man she adored. The eyes she was sure she'd never see again.

Without hesitation or pause the plane rolled over and crashed upside down into the water with the powerful wave washing over it like a giant hand shoving them under the surface.

They fell head first to the roof of the plane as it inverted before being slammed by the wall of sea water rushing through the open door that had been ripped from its hinges in the melee. Sydney instinctively took a gulp of air as she scrambled to get upright again and find the door. Carlos was pinned under Sydney with his face shoved against the roof lining. A burning sensation in his cheek suggested all was not well. His head pounded and swirled hazily.

Sydney felt like she was clawing through mud – she tried to reach out and grab the door frame but it didn't seem her arms were responding. It was completely dark and suddenly became terrifyingly quiet. She quickly realised she'd been fighting against the fire hose of water pouring in and, now the cockpit had filled, she was under water and could move again. But move where? She had no idea where anything was, especially Carlos. She desperately searched around her until she found his body beneath her. He was still.

Her lungs burned for air and panic rose quickly. She grabbed at Carlos with one hand and fumbled for the door opening with the other. She had to have air. The feeling of panic overwhelmed her and she pushed hard with her legs, driving herself upwards where her brain told her air should be. Her head smashed into the inverted floor of the cramped cockpit and she gasped in pain. She screamed and the noise echoed around her head in a strange dampened way. She could breathe. She sucked in the precious air and calmed herself, her mind clearing and slowly able to assess the situation.

Carlos was below her – in fact she realised she was standing, or more accurately crouching, on him. He'd seemed unconscious... or was he dead? She forced the idea from her mind; it was too unfathomable that in the midst of doing something so right and so courageous he'd be dead. She physically shook her head to banish the thought and focus on next steps. She had to get Carlos, the unconscious Carlos, find the door opening and swim them both to the surface.

She drew in a smooth, deep lungful of air and ducked back into the water reaching down and fumbling for a way to pick her boyfriend up. With her feet to either side she found his armpits and heaved him upwards. A sudden thud forced her to drop Carlos as they both slumped against the roof. They'd hit the sea floor. She shot back up to get another breath of air but the pocket had gone. Panic washed over her again and she fought it back, she knew she had to think clearly. She reached her hand out along the floor of the plane that was now her ceiling. The bubble was probably still there but the plane had now settled over so the bubble must have shifted, moving to the highest spot.

Her hand broke surface to her right and she quickly stuck her head up in that direction. Her shoulder bashed against something and as her head found the air pocket her forehead jammed on something else. Wincing, she felt around as she drew in more of the valuable air. By touch she could make out the shape of a foot pedal – that's what she'd hit her head on and the thing now wedged into her back was the yoke. She reached straight out to her right and touched nothing. She'd found the door opening. Her thoughts turned back to Carlos who'd now been out for maybe a minute although it felt like ten. With a gulp of air she reached down again and found his armpits. Dragging him up she heaved him towards the air pocket but his limp body bounced and caught on various things in the confined space. And then he moved in her arms.

Carlos had no idea what world he was in. Everything was a dense fog and he felt like he was floating. His body seemed to be a separate entity from his mind. In his thoughts he was light as a feather and could fly like Peter Pan. His body didn't appear to agree and had no reaction at all to his requests. The fog was thickening as his body finally seemed to react, and he felt himself slowly rise. He wasn't sure why he was doing that but instinctively it felt right so with all the might he could muster he pushed with his feeble legs.

Sydney thrust Carlos's head up so his mouth was in the air pocket and he coughed and choked as air slowly replaced water in his throat. Sydney babbled incoherently as she struggled to hold him up. Slowly he regained control and use of his limbs and supported himself, gulping lungful after lungful of air. He took hold of her face and pressed his lips against her cheek.

It was ink black inside the sunken plane but she felt his hands on her face and his lips pressed against her. She pictured those pretty eyes. We're God knows how deep down on the ocean floor, she thought, and still completely screwed, but I got one more look into those eyes. She turned her head and kissed him.

4

Silvio heard the key turn in the front door and nervously looked around his desk to make sure there was no mess or anything else that he could be yelled at for. He really wished he'd put some clean jeans and a nicer shirt on instead of the torn tracksuit pants and scruffy tee shirt he'd planned to lounge around at home in.

Mikhail entered. A tall, firmly built man with short, fair hair greying around the sides, wearing black slacks and a button-down shirt. He was always perfectly put together, even in an emergency. Silvio wondered if he slept in business clothes. Closing the door behind him he spoke first, "Carlos, correct?"

Silvio looked surprised. "Yes, he came back in about thirty minutes after we left. How did you know?"

Mikhail looked disdainfully at the Cuban. "Who else can fly the plane and has the access code we change every two weeks?"

Silvio kicked himself; that one didn't take Sherlock Holmes to figure out and he just let his boss point out his stupidity once again.

Mikhail continued, "Besides, based on his social media and online activity recently, he was the most likely to cause a problem."

Two things bothered Silvio about that statement. The first was the casualness with which the man explained how they're watching every move the employees made and the second was the fact that they were watching every move the employees made. He was born and raised in Cuba, so being observed and controlled by the government wasn't new but they didn't have the technology or resources to track people in depth like this. He was glad he didn't use social media.

Mikhail pulled his mobile from his pocket, commenting to Silvio as he did so, "He wasn't flying alone either; I guarantee he had a passenger." With that he stepped into his own office, closed his door and began barking orders into his phone in Russian.

Silvio wasn't sure what was expected of him now so he stayed at his desk and brought up Carlos's social media page on his computer. Most Cubans didn't have the luxury of the Internet; it was expensive and solely available through the government provider ETECSAN, which made it easy to monitor. They were fortunate to have access at the office at a reasonable connection speed.

Nothing struck him as odd. There were pictures of Carlos with various aircraft – no surprise, he was a pilot. A few pictures of himself with family – that was nice, nothing seemed out of place. He clicked on his profile and read a few details: went to university at Ciudad Universitaria Jose Antonio Echeverria in Havana, studied in Miami for a semester, he's in a relationship… Silvio sat back, surprised. He's in a relationship? He had never heard Carlos speak of a girl. The two worked together for over six months now and not once did he mention a girlfriend.

Mikhail burst out of his office, startling Silvio, who quickly closed his Internet browser and stood up. "Prepare the boat," Mikhail ordered. "Make sure it's full of fuel, with provisions for at least a week and ready to go at midnight."

Silvio bumbled, trying to process the change of plan. "Provisions for a week? By midnight? But sir, the markets are all closed…!"

Mikhail stared blankly at him, his eyes unblinking, and Silvio could sense the disdain radiating from the Russian's mind.

"Then have one open for you. This is government business, a matter of state. Find the market owner and do it fast; we're leaving at midnight with or without food."

Mikhail turned to leave but hesitated and turned back to the still stunned Cuban, adding, "I'll have two other officials with me, so provision accordingly." He pointed a menacing finger at Silvio. "Breathe a word of any of this to anyone and you'll spend the rest of your days as a guest of the G2, understand me?"

Terrified at the mention of Cuba's Dirección de Inteligencia agency, their equivalent of the KGB or CIA, Silvio vehemently nodded with his voice escaping him.

Apparently satisfied, Mikhail turned and left.

Silvio slumped back in his chair. He knew his boss carried some weight in official circles but it seemed he'd underestimated just how far up the food chain his influence ran. G2 were a scary bunch: they made people evaporate, never seen again, and he wanted nothing to do with them. Freshly inspired by a solid dose of fear he nudged himself into action. He needed to get organised if he was to be ready by midnight, and sleep, apparently, was not in his foreseeable future.

5

―――――

Carlos's head began to clear enough for him to consider their options for escaping the plane, since they'd turned it into a submarine. They were both gulping down as much air as they could from the little bubble that had formed in the foot well.

"We need to make a move, Sydney, we're using all the oxygen out of this little bit of air and we'll be taking in our own carbon dioxide soon – that won't be good."

Sydney nodded, precariously keeping her mouth above the water line. "We sank a while but I've got no clue how deep we dropped, it felt like forever." She thought for a moment, "You know, if we were inside the sound it's twenty feet deep at most, I'm pretty sure we went down farther than that."

Carlos converted that to metres in his head. "Okay, so that wouldn't be bad, about six or seven metres to the surface."

She frowned. "Yeah, but if we're outside the reef then it's more like thirty to eighty feet deep."

The math on that didn't seem so appealing and he cringed. "We should hope for the shorter side of that."

Sydney hesitated before continuing, "And if we're farther north the wall drops off to hundreds of feet…"

Carlos wriggled to keep his mouth in the air. "The pressure would have reduced this pocket to nothing at that depth. I don't think we're off the wall, we'd have nothing to breathe off. Speaking of which, this air is starting to taste really stale. We don't have much time."

He shuffled again. They were still in complete blackout so everything was by feel. "Okay, we have to get the life vests from behind the seats; I'll drop down and try and find them."

"Wait!" Sydney snapped. "Don't leave me! You just came around again; I'll go, you need to keep breathing the air. I've groped around the cockpit in the dark already, I'll find them faster."

Carlos hesitantly agreed and explained where she should find them in mesh pockets on the backs of the seats.

Sydney gathered her wits and with a final long intake of air ducked under the water and Carlos could feel her moving around below him in the pitch black. Everything being upside down was confusing, especially in the cramped cockpit area, and she started feeling her way around the instrument panel and yokes before realising she was facing the wrong way. Turning around she found a seat, felt behind it and quickly discovered the mesh bungee pocket and ran her hands down until she could feel the opening. Fortunately the elasticated mesh pocket had held its contents in place despite being inverted. Finding what she assumed was the life vest she dragged it out and shoved it up towards Carlos. He figured out what she was doing and took it from her as she moved sideways across the roof to retrieve the second one from the other seat. It already felt like she'd been holding her breath forever although she knew it had only been twenty seconds at most. That panicky feeling started creeping in again and she clawed at the mesh behind the seat while telling herself to calm down and be efficient. She finally plucked the vest from the seat back and shot back up to get air, running straight into the yoke with a sharp pain from her already bloody head.

Carlos felt her bashing around below him and grabbed her shirt to guide her back to the air pocket. She gasped for air and desper ately clung to him, relieved to feel the safety of his presence even if she couldn't see him.

"Great job my love, now we need to get out of here." He wheezed as he spoke, the air in the pocket providing much less oxygen than before. Sydney too could feel the difference; she struggled to catch her breath after the effort and had to force herself to settle down and draw long, gentle inhales.

He continued, "Put your vest on and make sure it's secure. We'll inflate them just a bit to help us go up, but not too much. When the water pressure gets less as we go shallower – the air inside will expand and fill out the vest."

They found the valves on the vests and tried putting some air in but, between the effort and the fact they had to dunk their heads under water to do it, they didn't get much accomplished.

Straining for breath and tiring out, they agreed it was time to go, "Once we're out the door opening kick smoothly using your whole leg, don't flap your feet…" Carlos started but Sydney cut him off.

"I grew up on this island, I know how to swim, Carlos!"

They both coughed and spluttered, all the valuable oxygen gone from the small reservoir of air that had kept them alive.

"Okay, let's go," he said softly and with a long, final intake of air they ducked for the doorway, clutching each other's hand.

Bouncing off each other and the door frame they struggled out of the sunken seaplane and pushed off the fuselage in what they hoped was the direction of the surface. After several long sweeping kicks it was clear they were more than twenty feet submerged. Sydney made big steady strokes with her long legs and soon felt the strain on her arm of Carlos falling behind. Hoping she was heading in the right direction, she kept swimming hard and pulled him along but her lungs were screaming for air. She could feel a puzzling pressure all around her chest and midriff and instinctively put her free hand to her chest. The life vest was inflating just as Carlos had explained, which meant they were ascending. A surge of relief ran through her for a moment but the desperate urge to get air soon overcame it. The natural impulse to suck in air was becoming powerful despite her brain telling her that's the reflex that causes people to drown. She kept kicking smoothly but was losing strength and her heart rate was climbing alarmingly from the effort. Carlos felt like a sack of potatoes dragging behind and her hypoxic mind felt angry at him for holding her back. Despite the lessening pressure letting the air expand in her lungs, it was stale, used air depleted of oxygen and her body begged to take a breath. Sydney's mind seemed to fold in on itself and everything became instantly overwhelming where thought was no longer possible and instinctual reaction consumed her. Her mouth opened wide and drew in as hard as her lungs could manage, no longer able to fight off the craving. A salty mix of sea water and air shot down her throat causing her to splutter and cough and gasp for more air, which she got.

Carlos surfaced beside her, was immediately blown into her, and the two were swept away on a wave. The noise was deafening after the silence of submersion and the wind-driven rain and spray felt like a machine gun of water pellets stinging their faces. They fought to stay hold of each other as the seas threw them around like toys. Sydney kept coughing and fighting to catch her breath but Carlos appeared fine.

She shouted to be heard, struggling to speak between breathes, "I almost drowned!"

Clinging to Carlos and wheezing she added, "And I thought you had!"

He managed a smile. "I was conserving my air and trying to stay relaxed and you were dragging me like a galloping horse!"

After the inky blackness of being underwater the dim light of the stormy night was a welcome relief but they still couldn't see any lights. They blew a little more air into the life vests for as much buoyancy as they could manage and looked all around as the choppy waves raised them up. The rain was too heavy to see any distance so even if there were lights close by they'd be out of their sight.

Carlos cursed in Spanish. "The case, I forgot the case!"

In their haste to survive and escape the plane he hadn't given it a thought and now the cargo they'd risked everything for was on the sea floor in a wrecked plane.

Sydney tried to calm him. "We'll retrieve it after the storm clears. There was no way to get it out of the plane with us, we barely made it alive. Our bag of clothes too, our passports are in there."

He shook his head, water flinging from his soaked hair. "They'll be looking for the plane as soon as the weather breaks, we'll never get back to it without being seen."

The noise of the waves and storm seemed to be getting louder and Sydney screamed to be heard, "I think we have bigger problems right now!"

They were picked up and thrown on a huge wave that crashed instead of rolled beneath them, tossing them underwater like rag dolls. They felt like they were inside a washing machine getting turned and tossed around but really moving nowhere until suddenly they launched forward with alarming power. Both their bodies were scraped over something hard and jagged before bursting through the surface and carried up on a swell again.

Sydney gathered up her wits and winced with pain – it felt like her whole body had been raked by a barbed wire fence. Carlos hung on grimly to Sydney's hand, terrified he'd lose her in the chaos. His legs were on fire from whatever they'd hit but the water seemed less tumultuous now and he pulled her back close to him.

"That was the reef!" she shouted excitedly. "We're in the sound, the waves took us over the reef!"

He looked around but still couldn't make out anything in the squall. The storm and the waves were incredibly loud but the crashing of the ocean on the reef was dying away and the size of the swells had dropped in half.

"How far are we from land if we're inside the sound?" he asked.

"About five miles to the south side, but less if we knew which side to head for. Trouble is we'd have to swim as the storm is blowing us south. If we chose the wrong way we could go five miles across the path of the storm."

They rode the waves and thought for a minute. Maybe the best idea was to let the storm carry them towards the south shore, but that was a daunting prospect. Sydney finally broke the silence.

"The lights I saw were on our left as we flew south – they must have been Rum Point. We circled back and crashed outside the reef which we just went back across to get into the sound so my best guess is we flew up and back on the east side of the sound. If we head parallel to the reef and go east, which is right if we turn back around and face the reef, we will come to Rum Point."

He nodded, impressed at her deductions. "What if we're actually on the west side of the sound?"

She shrugged. "Then we'll swim a lot further but still get to Rum Point."

"Okay, we swim east, but we need to keep within earshot of the waves crashing on the reef or we'll not know which direction we're going." He finally let go of her hand to start swimming.

"Yes," she shouted, "and try to keep up this time."

Carlos immediately checked up and reached for Sydney again, clutching her vest straps. "Hear that?"

She strained to hear over the weather. She could definitely make out a new sound. "What is that?"

The boat idled into view, rocking and rolling on the waves, a bright light scanning the waters. Sydney instinctively yelled, "Over here, we're over..." Carlos lunged and covered her mouth, knocking her underwater for a moment. "Be quiet! We have no idea who they are!"

Sydney was stunned but realised he was right. It didn't matter, the search light was on them and the boat eased over carefully as the two bodies and the boat got tossed around in the surf. It deftly rotated around and a ladder swung down between the two outboard motors that shut down so they could safely board. Sydney grabbed the ladder and hauled herself up, assisted by two pairs of hands on the boat.

Carlos followed, figuring friend or foe didn't matter, they had no choice. As he stepped onto the deck in the rolling seas he saw his girlfriend in a fervent embrace with a good-looking, dark-skinned young man. She finally released him and turned to Carlos.

"Carlos, this is my brother Thomas!"

They shook hands and exchanged an enthusiastic smile, Carlos relieved to be out of the water and in safe hands.

Thomas turned to his side where a pretty, young, blonde lady in a rain jacket stood steadying herself in the swells.

"Guys, meet my friend, and my boss, AJ Bailey."

6

———————

Silvio knew a man that ran a bar in town that was open late. The bar owner's wife knew the wife of the man who owned the smaller of the two markets in Jucaro. Jucaro was not a big town; in fact it was a pretty small fishing village with dirt roads. The store keeper was unimpressed to be woken late in the evening when he had to open at 6am the next morning and strongly suggested Silvio come by then. It took threats of Russians and G2 to persuade the man to meet him, but Silvio finally got what he needed and made it back to the boat, loaded with shopping bags and supplies.

He'd rousted his first mate Julio, who reluctantly hurried to the boat and topped up the diesel from the storage tank on the dock while Silvio was gone. Julio had been progressing well on romantic plans with a young girl from a neighbouring village when he got the call. He was in a foul mood but Silvio was pleased he'd thought to start the motors idling so everything was warmed up. Carlos often helped crew on the boat and the three of them made a good team. With only two heading who knows where, it was going to be a challenge. The Russian wasn't keen on getting his hands dirty so Silvio didn't expect any help from him and figured his guests would be equally as reluctant.

He stowed the supplies while Julio released all but two lines to the dock, readying for when the Russians arrived. They met in the wheelhouse and Silvio checked the weather. "Well, let's hope they want to go anywhere but west, that storm looks really bad."

The sound of a helicopter grew louder and the two men peered outside to see a military chopper coming in to land in the car park up front. The rotors blew dust and rubbish around, forcing them to duck back inside.

"Guess that's our passengers showing up," Silvio muttered as he slid the door closed to keep the wind out.

"Bet they'll get to sleep tonight," Julio complained, slumping into the captain's chair. "Doubt we'll be so lucky".

Mikhail led the two men through the building and out the back door to the dock. Both were in their late twenties, dressed in dark grey business suits, hair short and trimmed, and each had a black gear bag slung over their shoulder. One of them also rolled two large hard cases. Silvio looked down from the wheelhouse at the three Russians about to board the boat. If they're not operatives or agents or whatever the hell they call themselves then I'm an American Hollywood star, he thought to himself. He smacked Julio on the arm. "Get down there and help our guests aboard or the boss will be mad before we've even started." Julio reluctantly headed down to assist the new arrivals and show them their staterooms. He chuckled to himself at the term 'stateroom'. Wait until these arseholes see the crappy little cots they get to enjoy, he thought. But then he remembered they would at least get to sleep even if it was a crappy little cot and stopped chuckling.

Mikhail slid the door open to the wheelhouse and studied Silvio. In his usual detached monotone he gave him the destination, "Grand Cayman."

Silvio tried to hide his irritation but knew he had failed.

"Problem, Silvio?"

"Have you seen the storm that's to the west sir? It's over Grand Cayman – we'll be heading straight for it." Silvio nervously pointed to the radar screen showing a large expanse of angry red and yellow.

Mikhail didn't take his eyes off Silvio and let the silence linger uncomfortably for what seemed like forever. To Silvio's relief he finally spoke, "Grand Cayman. As fast as possible. I'll be back once we've cleared the inlet and you can give me your time estimate for the journey." With that Mikhail left the wheelhouse and Silvio breathed again.

He punched George Town harbour, Grand Cayman into the GPS and let it start plotting the route while he stepped out and looked for Julio. The younger man appeared on the deck and Silvio pointed at the remaining two lines and thumbed the air, signalling time to release them. Returning to the console he checked the GPS screen which displayed details of the route to Cayman along with a pop-up box showing 'Warning! Dangerous conditions on this route.'

"No shit," Silvio muttered, shaking his head.

7

———————

The ride across the North Sound was rough to say the least and navigated solely from GPS as the storm raged on, keeping visibility at almost zero. AJ drove the boat while Thomas wrapped their wet guests in towels and tried to get them warmed up. The 'Mermaid Divers' rigid-inflatable-boat had a centre console so getting dry was impossible as the rain continued to douse everyone. Thomas passed around a thermos of tea they'd brought, which was eagerly consumed. It was hard to do much for their scrapes and wounds in the rough waters; they'd have to wait until they could attend to them properly back on shore.

Thomas fussed around his sister as the two relayed the story of their harrowing flight from Cuba and their escape from the submerged plane. They reached the waterways leading to the marina and the waters settled considerably, making conversation possible.

Sydney was shivering but relieved to be out of the water. "How on earth did you find us?!"

Thomas smiled. "The storm hit shortly after you texted me that you were coming tonight, so we were ready at the boat. As the weather worsened, blowing from the north, AJ suggested we move the boat to Rum Point so at least we'd have the storm behind us to pick you up. Once we got out there it closed in really badly when the sun went down, far worse than predicted. Honestly it was pure luck we heard the plane go over and then shortly after come back over. We waited but didn't hear it again so AJ said let's do a quick sweep and see if radar picked up the plane, presuming you'd landed. We heard you yelling in the water."

Carlos couldn't believe it. "That's incredible you found us, thank you so much."

Sydney let out a long sigh, lost to the howling wind. "You've no idea how scary it is to be lost out there, alone in the open ocean!"

AJ smiled and she and Thomas exchanged glances. Thomas started, "AJ knows a thing or two ab—" but AJ cut him off.

"I'm sure it's very unpleasant, it was good fortune we found you."

AJ winked at Thomas – she figured there's no point comparing lost-at-sea stories. He got the hint and left it at that.

Carlos looked puzzled. "How long did it take you to find us?"

Thomas answered, "We only went a few hundred yards – you were really close to Rum Point."

Carlos spoke passionately, "That should make it easier to locate the plane, right? We have to find it and get the evidence I brought. There's some cases inside the plane; we have to get one of them as soon as possible."

AJ glanced over at the bedraggled Cuban. "First thing tomorrow we can get you to the police, you can relay your story and we'll work on getting you asylum. They'll help us locate the wreck."

Carlos jumped up and joined AJ at the helm. "No! No police! The Russians will be after me for sure. As soon as they hear where the plane is they'll come for it and for me." He was beside himself, adamantly pleading, "I'm so sorry to involve all of you but none of us are safe now, these guys are very bad people, very serious, very serious believe me."

AJ tried to calm him. "If you're held by the authorities here you'll be safe – they'll detain you while they look into asylum. Surely they won't be able to reach you?"

Carlos shook his head. "Believe me they can reach me, and besides, once they explain how I stole a Cuban government-owned plane and equipment there's no way I'm getting asylum, they'll hand me over to the G2 and that's the last you'll see of me or the evidence I brought."

Thomas put his hand on Carlos's shoulder, "Surely this can be explained to the Caymanian authorities? They're reasonable people."

Sydney spoke up, "You guys don't understand how powerful the Russians are. Anything they ask for in Cuba, they get. That's not how things normally work in Cuba, everything takes forever and goes through ridiculous red tape, but not with Mikhail – Carlos says he gets whatever he wants as soon as he asks for it."

"It's true," Carlos interjected. "I've never seen anything like it. We were doing the geological studies from the boat last year and Mikhail says 'we need a base' and by midsummer we had a building with a dock and a lab!"

AJ carefully manoeuvred through Governors Creek, still using nothing but GPS to find the yacht club where she had a slip. "Thomas told me you had information that would stop your government doing something they shouldn't but he didn't know much else. What are we talking about here?"

Carlos looked at AJ carefully. He'd just met her but she'd risked a lot to pluck the two of them from the sea and had agreed to pick them up on nothing but Sydney's word via Thomas. That's a lot of trust on her part. At this stage he had little choice but to trust her and Thomas in return.

He looked her straight in the eye. "It's all about oil."

8

They left Jucaro and cleared the small scattered islands outside the bay, heading south west towards Grand Cayman. Their path would take them through the uninhabited archipelago of Jardines de la Reina into the deep water of the Caribbean Sea. They would pass north of Cayman's sister islands, Cayman Brac and Little Cayman, before reaching Grand to complete the 190 nautical mile journey.

Silvio had explained to Mikhail that this would take them around sixteen hours, to the Russian's displeasure. Nothing new, Silvio had thought, he's in a constant state of displeasure. The old boat had seen plenty of hours on the water and 11 knots was what she'd run at in wide open, favourable seas. Since they were heading straight for a storm front he'd also pointed out that sixteen hours was the best they could hope for as they'd be down as low as seven or eight knots in high swells. More displeasure.

They had given the boat a fancy title of 'survey vessel' when it was presented to the Geology Institute eighteen months ago, but the moniker couldn't hide that she was a 1960s trawler that had seen many a better day. They scrubbed off the old name 'Consuela' and painted on her new name 'Explorador de la Reina' as a further attempt at authenticity. She did fine running back and forth between Jucaro and Jardines de la Reina in the relatively calm waters the island chain protected, but runs across the open ocean were not the old girl's forte these days. Still, she was Silvio's old girl and he loved nothing more than being at her helm.

Everyone generally left him alone in the wheelhouse. Carlos would hang out with him sometimes but he didn't mind that. Although Carlos was ten years younger than Silvio they got along well. He was easy to chat with and they shared a love of the water, although Silvio preferred staying above it and Carlos was more interested in being under the surface. Carlos always asked after Silvio's daughter and, unlike most young men, was happy to hear Silvio rattle on about his little girl. At seven years old she was becoming quite the young lady. Silvio saw her so infrequently he could tell how much she'd grown each time. It shouldn't be that way for a father, he thought, she should grow such a small amount each day you see her that it happens unnoticed in front of you. But he lived in a crappy little apartment in Jucaro and his wife and daughter lived in another man's house in Havana. Once a month he took the seven-hour bus ride to the city to spend a few precious hours with his baby, take more grief from his ex-wife, and make the seven-hour journey back.

9

———————

AJ stepped from the shower and wrapped herself in a towel. She finally felt warmed up after a long evening of being doused by rain and sea water. It was still seventy-two degrees outside despite the storm but the wind and rain soon chilled the body down and made it seem much colder. Drying off she threw on a tee shirt and shorts and joined her guests in the living room of her small apartment. She'd let them clean up first and now they tended to each other's scrapes and cuts wearing clothes they'd borrowed from her and Thomas, the meagre belongings they'd brought left in the sunken plane.

Thomas had dropped a change of clothes off for Carlos and headed back to his house to clean himself up and get some sleep. They figured it was better to hide their two fugitives at AJ's little apartment in the grounds of a nice house, tucked away and private on Seven Mile Beach. The best she could offer was a sofa bed but she assumed correctly it would be welcomed after the ordeal they'd been through.

AJ grabbed some white wine from the fridge and three glasses from the cupboard before dropping into a chair and pouring a drink for each of them. She'd already handed out the thin food supplies on hand, which were reduced to crumbs in short order. She noticed Carlos curiously eyeing her full-sleeve tattooed arms. Her left had a colourful reef scene, the right a black and grey wreck with a deep-sea diver. She smiled to herself; she was used to people staring at her artwork.

Sydney paused from cleaning up the abrasion on Carlos's cheek. "We can't thank you enough for all your help AJ, you've been too kind. Not many would do this for a couple of strangers."

AJ shrugged. "Well, you're Thomas's sister so although we've only met a couple of times, we're like family by default. And Carlos is part of the package you came with, so here we are." She sipped her wine and carried on thoughtfully, "We need a plan though. What exactly are you hoping to do in Cayman? If you're seeking asylum we have to go to the authorities and start that process."

Carlos urgently brushed Sydney's hand away from his cheek. "I tell you we cannot go to the police or anyone else until we get this story to the press." Sydney rested her hand on his shoulder to try and calm him back down but he carried on, still animated, "I don't care what happens to me…" He stopped himself and looked at Sydney, apologies in his eyes. "I do care, I'm sorry, I care, but this is bigger than me, more important than me. Too much depends on this. I cannot be selfish about it – if I go to jail then so be it but this story must be told, the people must know."

AJ was surprised by the passion in his voice and even more curious now. "You said it's about oil? Why don't you tell me what's going on and then, maybe, we can figure out what to do next?"

Carlos settled back into the sofa and allowed himself a sip of wine before beginning his story.

"Okay, I'll give you the whole story so this will take a minute and please forgive my poor English."

AJ chuckled. "It's a lot better than my Spanish believe me; you're doing great."

He allowed a smile and began, "After university they sent me to work at the Instituto de Estudios Geológicos in Jucaro, which at the time was just an office in town and a boat. They built a proper building for it this summer. I had studied geology at school and they taught me to fly in my military service so they wanted me there as they were getting a seaplane to be able to take people and gear up and down the coast. I had no idea what they were up to when I got there and I was surprised to find the studies were being run by a Russian man named Mikhail Gurov." Sydney cringed at the mention of the man's name.

Carlos continued, "All the offshore oil fields in Cuba are to the north where there's a triangular area Cuba owns and three rigs that supply most of our oil. But the rights are owned by a mixture of other countries and in the past we've received subsidised supplies from Russia, which is one of the world's largest oil producers. The biggest problem with the oil from the north is the quantity isn't enough to supply the whole country, especially after they sold the rights away for too much of it. Now Cuba has been hunting for other reserves around the country.

With Russia's help they found a seam on the south side and from the surveys we did it appears to be a large reserve and is suspected to be higher quality. Most of our surveys showed it to be in deep water outside the island chain but two months ago we found a seam that runs towards the mainland right under Jardines de la Reina. They figured they can put rigs on the islands or in the shallow waters around them and tap the reserves through the seam that extends there without having the expense of deep-water rigs offshore.

You have heard of Jardines de la Reina? It is Gardens of the Queen in English?" Carlos queried.

AJ nodded. "Absolutely, seen it in the dive magazines, looks amazing. Dive it from live-aboard boats, right? Nobody lives on the islands?"

"That is correct, so the number of divers is very limited and the reefs are in pristine condition. It is a marine sanctuary and has a reef system running most of its length. Beyond the reef system the bottom drops away to the deep ocean water, much like here in

Cayman, so we get many sharks and deep-water fish; it is truly a special place."

"And that's where they want to drill for oil?" AJ asked, amazed.

"Unbelievable isn't it?" Sydney replied.

"So why are the Russians involved in this?" AJ was now on the edge of her seat, consumed by Carlos's story.

"Russia is a huge oil producer – there are massive reserves across Siberia, they rival the US and Saudi as the top producers in the world but it's low-quality oil like our oil in the north. The Russians need high-quality oil and Cuba needs more oil so they're both strongly motivated to find it anywhere they can. Russia holds the notes on all the major government loans Cuba has accumulated over the years, which adds up to large amount of debt. The Russians are using the loans as bargaining to get the Cuban oil; they forgive some or all of the loans in exchange for high quality oil. Compare that to the income from a few hundred divers visiting the islands and the government won't think twice about 'adjusting' this marine sanctuary."

AJ shook her head, lost for words for a moment. Sydney added a little wine to all their glasses. Thoughts raced through AJ's mind about what she'd just heard and her blood boiled at the thought of thousands of years of reef growth being destroyed over a non-sustainable fuel that was destroying our own atmosphere.

Carlos sipped his wine and put a hand on Sydney's knee. "I had to do something. As soon as they found how accessible the ribbon that stretches to the islands is they've been rushing to get started." He looked at AJ with pain in his eyes. "We have very little time, the barges and crews to start construction are on their way from the north. On Monday they will begin blasting the reef in preparation for the footings for the rigs and the pipeline. In a week the Jardines de la Reina will be torn apart."

AJ had to think about what day it was. With the crazy hours she had lost track of time. It was 1am on Thursday; he was right, they didn't have much time.

"So what's the evidence you have? It's going to take something pretty conclusive to make any difference; even then I don't know that bad press would deter them," AJ wondered.

Carlos managed a smile. "What I have will, I believe. I have two sets of plans. Both sets have official government stamps on them. The first shows how the oil rigs, terminals, pipelines and tankers will not affect the marine sanctuary." He leaned forward. "The second shows what will actually happen."

10

Mikhail settled into the smelly, cramped bunk of the nicest stateroom on the boat, which differed from the others simply by having one cot instead of bunks. Most men would be wondering about their career choices, stuffed into the belly of a sweaty, fish and diesel infested, rotten trawler, traipsing across foreign seas into a raging storm, chasing an idealistic pain-in-the-arse Cuban kid. But not Mikhail. He didn't know why these things didn't bother him but they didn't. He'd always been this way since he could remember. His father was the same which was probably the main reason, now he thought about it. His father was KGB during the cold war days. That was when this line of work really meant something, those guys were truly front line, risking everything when it wasn't all computer tracking and databases at your fingertips. It was almost too easy these days. Everyone's on the Internet, everyone has a mobile phone. It was so simple to find people. Although Carlos hadn't made it easy.

Mikhail had immediately checked all flight records and unidentified traffic picked up by radar; nothing, as expected. Carlos had clearly flown low, under radar, which meant he'd stayed over water as inland meant mountains to cross and he'd have been picked up at some point. Next clue was range – the seaplane could manage about 500 nautical miles which ruled out looping around Cuba to Florida or south to Venezuela and made Mexico or Honduras a stretch. Especially as anything west or southwest had to go around the storm. That left Jamaica, Haiti or the Dominican Republic, none of which Carlos had any connection to so their only appeal was a place to land which didn't add up in Mikhail's mind.

He then checked on the girl. The Cuban government had been keeping an eye on Sydney Bodden since she and Carlos started dating while Carlos attended the University of Miami for a semester two years ago. Carlos had returned, finished his education and been placed in the geological study program with Mikhail without complaint or apparent issues, so the interest in Bodden had remained low priority. As a Caymanian she could come and go to Cuba as a visitor without a problem, which she appeared to do every three months or so. A quick search revealed Sydney had flown into Havana two days ago and taken the bus to Jucaro the next morning.

The Russian was going on a hunch but logical deduction told him the seaplane had headed for Grand Cayman, despite the storm. He wasn't sure what Carlos's plans were once he reached Cayman, but he knew they wouldn't align with his own. Which aligned with Mother Russia's. He would stop Carlos and return him to Cuba, or not, using whatever means necessary.

Unperturbed by his paltry quarters he laid his head down and slept while he had the chance.

11

Sydney lay sound asleep next to him, but Carlos, as exhausted as he was, couldn't get his eyes to close and his mind to rest. Maybe the adrenaline, he thought. Maybe it was the weight of what his actions had caused. Lying on a sofa bed in a stranger's apartment felt like a different planet from the life he'd thrown away this night, and for what? Did he really think that he, Carlos Miguel Rojas, could dissuade the combined force of the Cuban and Russian governments from destroying a stretch of reef that most Cubans didn't even know exists? He felt like a pebble at the foot of a mountain. More than that he'd dragged the girl he loved, her brother and the owner of the sofa bed he rested upon into this mess with him.

He was now a wanted criminal in his homeland. His poor parents, they'd done so much for him. He pictured the police banging on the front door of his mother and father's house in the middle of the night, telling them their son was a traitor to the Republic, a thief, a conspirator. He feared his father, a respected professor at the University of Havana, would be stripped of his position and dishonoured. Unless he denounced his son. Maybe they'd go easy on him if he disowned me, he pondered, praying his father would. For the sake of his mother and his little sister he prayed his father would know how much his son loved him and have the confidence to disown his only boy and believe their love would not change.

Carlos pictured the proud look on his father's face the day he graduated from Ciudad Universitaria Jose Antonio Echeverria in Havana. The same look he had when Carlos completed his two years of national service, leaving home as a seventeen-year-old boy and returning a young man with a pilot's licence and a confident stride. He would do anything to speak to the man he loved deeply, the man he'd respected and looked up to his whole life, the man he was desperately praying would denounce him and yet not be disappointed in him. Carlos couldn't bear the idea of his father not understanding what he had done, or why he had to do it. He had to have faith his father would know his son would never do anything frivolous or without compelling reason. He'd give anything to hear his voice and explain it all. But his mobile phone was at the bottom of the inlet in Jucaro where he'd thrown it last night, and any contact would only make things harder for his family.

Faith, he had to have faith. Not religious faith, but faith in the bond between father and son, a love that had never been in question. Until now? He felt in his heart, no, deeper than that, with every fibre of his being he knew his father had to believe his son was doing the right thing. Regardless, he'd come too far and brought too many people with him to turn back or give up now.

He closed his eyes and imagined he was back on the reef. The bubbles exhaled from his regulator were the steady, rhythmic soundtrack to the movie playing from his many memories of dives at Jardines de la Reine. Giant sea fans danced back and forth in the gentle surge as a pair of butterfly fish chased each other round a coral head. The crusty antennae of a hidden lobster probed the waters as a silky shark glided effortlessly across the reef, curiously eyeing the divers. Beautiful trumpets of orange sponges protruded towards the sunlight and a tiny blennie poked its head from one of the pores while a juvenile angelfish flittered away to hide amongst swaying fingers of soft coral.

He looked to deeper water and there, stretching as far as he could see through the cut-glass water was a bright orange line. Running along the reef and secured every twenty metres by a skewer in the coral was the marker for the concrete oil pipeline. Each skewer marked the spot for the concrete support to hold the pipeline. Two metres square of gouged-out reef replaced with marine-grade concrete to hold up the pipe to pump the crude oil from the platforms to shore. Further up were larger squares marked off with more orange line. These were ten metres long each side and marked the feet of the oil platforms, four per rig. Large boats flooded the ocean with thrashing sounds of propellers and diesel engines. An industrial hammer drill smashed the coral to pieces, the water dampening the sound to reverberating thuds. Pieces of broken and shattered coral floated about in the water as the ocean clouded over with debris, silt and dead fish.

Carlos shuddered awake and blinked back to consciousness, slowly recognising where he was lying, on a stranger's sofa bed. Damn it, he thought, dreaming may be worse than thinking.

12

____

The seas had picked up overnight and now the rain joined in to make it a gloomy morning, destined to decline further as they headed towards the storm cell. The forecast showed the front clearing through the region in the next eighteen hours but as they were halfway through their outbound, that wouldn't help them. Julio had taken a four-hour stint at the helm now Silvio had just relieved him and planned to take them the rest of the way. His four-hour nap went by quickly so Silvio had some strong Cuban roast in a big mug and a couple of thick slices of bread toasted and buttered to start his day. The Russians had been in the dining area off the galley when Silvio had grabbed his breakfast but he was happy to avoid conversing with them; they all made him nervous.

Mikhail hadn't slept well, but adequately to his mind. Now he sipped coffee and took the opportunity to assess the two men he'd been given. They were both young, special forces-trained operatives that functioned as 'problem solvers' for the SVR, the Foreign Intelligence Service of the Russian Federation formed in 1991 after the demise of the Soviet Union and along with it the KGB. Seemed overkill to him to send two of these guys on what should be a relatively simple retrieval exercise. The plan was to do this quietly and diplomatically, not start World War Three. Apparently someone in Moscow was looking at this a little differently, or perhaps they were just planning for any scenario. Either way Mikhail didn't need these guys going full commando mode on a tiny island they were yet to confirm Carlos had landed on. He sat at the opposite end of the dining table and kept to himself; the two agents drank coffee and told stories. The more they told stories the more they forgot Mikhail was there and the more Mikhail listened and sized them up.

Mikhail hadn't planned on being a geologist. Trained as an agent in the GU, the Russian Foreign Military Intelligence Agency, he was keen to serve his country in the field, as close to the action as he could get. His problem was his scores on strategy and management tests; he performed too well and the agency wanted him overseeing projects and coordinating efforts from headquarters. Directing his group in a joint mission with another KGB department in London he made the mistake of ignoring a senior official's command to abort the mission when one of their men was identified by MI5. Mikhail pulled the operative, stepped in himself and completed the mission.

His next, and possibly his final, assignment was running security around the oil fields in Siberia, penance for crossing his boss's wishes. Desperate for something to challenge his sharp mind and figuring oil fields were now his existence, Mikhail took a geology course and gained his university degree. His luck turned when someone recognised his oil field experience combined with his management skills made him a good fit for a project they planned in Cuba. Things continued to move quickly from there when the southern oil deposits were identified and interest in getting oil flowing as soon as possible ramped up. Carlos was causing an unwanted glitch in those interests. Perhaps these goons will be useful, he thought to himself. One of them seemed a little sharper than the other, maybe he could be trusted to go ashore without causing an international incident.

Mikhail surprised the men by speaking, "What identification papers did they send you with?"

The man Mikhail had noted spoke up, "There was no time to generate papers for the oil industry, the best we already had was for marine biologists, sir."

Mikhail looked indifferently from one man to the other, then surprised them again by asking in English, "And what are three marine biologists from Russia doing in Grand Cayman?"

The other man glanced at Anatoly, clearly not understanding the question but Anatoly didn't hesitate and replied in English, "We could be conducting a study comparing the health of the reefs in Cayman to that in Cuba, sir?"

Mikhail nodded and returned to Russian to address his colleague, Pavlo Yeltsin. "You are to remain on ship at all times and monitor the computer, I'll let you know if you'll be needed on shore." Turning back to Anatoly, he added, "What's the name you're using?"

"Anatoly Karin, sir."

"That's the name on your papers?"

"Yes, sir."

"Okay, you'll be with me, we'll go onto the island once immigration has cleared us."

Mikhail took his time topping off his coffee before continuing, "Here's what will happen, once we arrive we'll inform the Port Authority by radio that we are here and they will either request we dock and see them or they'll send a boat out to meet us. I assume you gentlemen are armed?"

They both nodded.

"Cayman has strict gun laws so we'll need to carefully hide the firearms in case they decide to search the ship. If this goes correctly you won't need them for this operation. We'll hide your additional identification papers as well."

The boat was rolling more and more as the seas worsened the

closer they got to the storm and things were starting to slide around. Mikhail let the men scramble to catch cups and plates and continued calmly, "Our first priority is to locate the seaplane if he indeed came to Cayman. If he landed legally we'll find record of it, if he landed illegally the plane must be on the water somewhere as there's nowhere to land on the island besides the main airport."

Pavlo was starting to look a little green but Mikhail paused even longer until each of them was uncomfortable whether they felt ill or not. Finally he finished his brief. "Our objective is to return with Carlos Rojas and all the information he brought with him – recovering the plane itself will be secondary. The girl, Sydney Bodden, we'll handle as necessary; she's a Caymanian citizen so her disappearance will cause more problems than an illegal Cuban thief."

Pavlo timidly raised his hand and Mikhail nodded his consent to speak.

"What's our timeline, sir?"

Mikhail glanced at his watch to verify the date, the last twelve hours of unexpected action blurring his internal clock. "Today is Thursday, on Monday work is scheduled to begin on the new oil field. We must resolve the situation in the next twenty-four to forty-eight hours."

Anatoly raised his hand more confidently. "Are we taking Rojas alive, sir?"

Mikhail didn't flinch, "From the island, preferably yes. Reaching Cuba, unlikely."

13

———————

The sound of a coffee maker gurgling gently eased Sydney awake. She blinked a few times and slowly recalled where she was in the dimly lit living room of AJ's apartment. The sofa bed creaked as she sat up rubbing her eyes. The sound of rain pelting the windows and roof told her the storm had yet to pass.

AJ whispered quietly from the kitchen, "Sorry to wake you but I figured we should get going."

Sydney carefully stepped out of bed leaving Carlos mumbling but still asleep and walked the few steps to the tiny kitchen that was open to the living area. Her body ached and the scrapes stung, reminding her of yesterday's ordeal.

"Coffee smells good."

AJ poured her a cup. "The storm will clear out overnight tonight so the airport will probably reopen in the morning. I'm guessing anyone looking for you would fly in then?"

Sydney nodded, "I think that's a fair assumption – don't know how they'd get here before then."

Carlos's voice came from the living room, "We must find the plane before then – once they're here I cannot say what they'll do but it'll be harder to move around knowing they're looking for us."

He joined the two girls and AJ poured more coffee. "We're going to need some help finding the plane. My RIB only has a simple pinging depth finder, we need a CHIRP Digital Sonar that paints a picture of the sea floor or we're shooting in the dark. It's going to be rough as hell on the north side and the water is badly stirred up, so visibility above and below won't be much better than it was last night."

Sydney smirked. "Well, I can tell you I couldn't see a thing last night and I'm in no hurry to go anywhere near that plane again. Diving is Thomas's thing not mine. I'm a normal Caymanian, we prefer to stay on top of the water."

Carlos rubbed her arm affectionately. "No problem, I'm happy to do the diving part."

AJ found a half loaf of sliced bread and popped some in her toaster, grabbing marmalade from the fridge. "Breakfast is thin pickings I'm afraid."

Carlos asked, "I know the sonar you mean, they are wired into the boat with the transducer underneath aren't they?"

"Correct, so it's not the sonar we need it's a boat with the sonar, but luckily I know a man."

Carlos was unsure. "We must be careful involving anyone else. I already feel awful we dragged you into this and the more people the more chance someone says something or leaves a trail the Russians can pick up."

The toaster sprang and AJ retrieved the toast, offering it to her guests. "Are you certain they know you flew here? You mentioned last night you stayed under radar – how can they know it was Cayman you flew to? You could have gone anywhere."

Carlos eagerly took the toast. "Mikhail Gurov is a smart man, I know he and his people watch everyone involved in the project so by now they will have seen Sydney entered Cuba a few days ago. When we first started dating in Miami we didn't have a reason to hide our relationship so there's enough evidence we're connected and since then she's visited every few months. I didn't tell anyone at work but he asked me how my girlfriend was when she visited the last time. It was his way of telling me we're always being watched. He will have narrowed it down to Cayman."

AJ put the last few slices in the toaster. "Why wouldn't they just report you to the authorities here? That way the Caymanian police, port authority and Department of Environment would be looking for you and the plane; they could just fly in and pick you up from their custody."

Carlos shook his head. "No way, they'll want this to go away quietly, no story about a Cuban trying to escape or anything about oil. They'll try and cover the whole thing up like it didn't happen."

AJ thought a moment. "Okay, if we wait one day the storm will have passed and the north will still be rough but a ton better than today. Why don't we try early tomorrow morning? It would still be before any flights arrive here."

"I know it's crazy," Carlos countered, "but we must go today. I tell you these men are very resourceful, if there's any way to get here sooner they will do it."

"Well then," AJ relented, "we need sonar if we're going to find this plane of yours and especially if we're going to be crazy and dive in this storm. To have sonar we need a boat that has it so I have to involve someone else, but don't worry, he's a great friend and you can trust him completely."

Sydney agreed, "If you trust him then we must also."

Carlos nervously nodded.

AJ dialled a number on her mobile and waited for the person to pick up. "Hey, morning. Feel like diving north today?" She paused and chuckled – the response was clearly not positive. "Well Reg, you don't have to dive. It's not you I want, it's your fancy sonar."

14

The wind and rain was indeed as intense as it had been the night before as AJ led the rain-jacketed group down the dock at the yacht club. It had taken forty-five minutes on the phone for AJ to convince Reg Moore, that although it wasn't a good idea to dive the wreck of a recently deceased seaplane in the middle of a storm, it was indeed a necessity. She'd given him the whole back story on the Russians and the oil discovery but what finally convinced him was telling him she was going with or without him, and he knew she wasn't kidding.

AJ guided them aboard a thirty-six-foot Newton dive boat and a large man in a yellow rain slicker greeted them under the open cabin. AJ introduced him. "This is my good friend Reg." He extended a meaty hand. "Reg, meet Carlos, and this is Thomas's sister Sydney."

They exchanged greetings as AJ and Thomas set their dive gear bags under the bench along the side of the stern section. The wind was still loud enough that they had to raise their voices to converse.

"Are you guys sure you have to do this now?" Reg queried in his heavy London accent. "It's gonna be mean outside the reef. If there's any option to wait for calmer seas I'd suggest we take it."

Carlos stepped closer to the big Englishman. "I wish there was, sir, we appreciate you doing this; unfortunately time is not on our side, we need to retrieve some items from the plane as soon as possible."

Reg nodded. "There's life vests in the cabin, put them on." And without further discussion he waved to Thomas to release the lines to the dock.

AJ and Thomas set their gear up on tanks and donned their wetsuits as Reg manoeuvred them out of the marina. They knew once they hit the sound things would get too lumpy to move about the boat. They could barely see fifty feet around them, the downpour obscuring anything farther away, so Reg navigated from GPS as AJ had the night before.

They idled slowly up Governors Creek and the swell picked up noticeably as they approached North Sound.

Reg yelled down from the fly bridge, "Hang on to something, it's gonna get lively."

He wasn't kidding. Sydney was the only one who hadn't experienced rough seas before; the night before she'd been in a daze and they'd headed with the swell instead of into it. She was wide eyed and white knuckled as the Newton rode the four foot swells rolling at them across the sound from the north. They were coming from the Yacht club on the west side of the sound so they crossed the waves at a forty-five degree angle, making the boat yaw and roll madly as it slid down the back of the waves, occasionally crashing down in the troughs. As she wondered what it would be like outside the protection of the reef she reminded herself she'd already been out there... without a boat! Somehow it didn't feel reassuring.

After fifteen minutes of running, using the GPS, Reg lined the boat up to run through the cut in the reef to leave the sound. The cut was marked on either side by two buoys on approach and lights on marker poles at the cut itself, none of which they could see through the weather. AJ hung onto the roof frame next to Reg and tried to spot for him in case they got close to the markers.

He looked at her. "Of all the hare-brained crazy ideas you have, this has to make it pretty close to the top, my girl."

She grinned and Reg pushed the throttle lever forward and the powerful diesel engine surged the boat forward to face the first eight-foot roller ploughing through the deep cut ahead.

The Newton rose up the front of the wave like it was climbing a building before nosing over and plummeting down the backside as Reg accelerated harder to regain speed ready for the next wave. The rise and fall over these waves that could swamp the thirty-six-foot boat was terrifying and a miscue that turned them sideways would be instantly catastrophic. As they crested the fourth wave AJ shouted as loud as she could over the thundering crash of the waves on the reef and the storm raging around them, "Green light! I see the light on our right! Need to go left, Reg!"

He knew he couldn't cut much to the left without the next wave turning them sideways but he veered as much as he dared and kept the props driving them as hard as he could. They rose up the front of the next wave at a slight angle and he tried to square them up over the crest. They dropped off the back in a weird twisting motion and crashed into the trough, knocking all the forward speed from the boat. The motor strained and groaned as it tried mightily to turn the props faster and pick their speed back up; they were sitting ducks without forward motion. The three on the deck below had the shelter of the fly bridge overhead but were being thrown around like rag dolls. Hanging on to the overhead hand rails they tried their best to anticipate the rises and falls but the last hit left them on the floor and they scrambled to get a hand-hold before the next wave.

Reg had the throttle pegged and painfully slowly the Newton picked up speed as the biggest wave yet was bearing down on them. He glanced at the GPS and then at AJ who yelled, "The light's off our stern, this should get us through!"

He made sure she was running straight up the face and kept the motor singing but they'd lost a lot of momentum and the boat struggled up the bigger wave. Just as he thought they might stall out the Newton crested the peak and rode down the backside picking up speed as she went; they were clear of the cut. Into the open ocean.

15

———

From the main channel through the reef they needed to head several miles east toward Rum Point. The cut had concentrated the swell through a narrow, relatively shallow section which forced the water into a taller wave so once they cleared the cut, the waves were back to five or six feet. They ran along the incoming rollers so although the heavy winds made the surf choppy and rough, Reg charged down the troughs, easing over each crest to the next trough to keep them heading east.

As they made progress they starting discussing the best plan of attack. AJ began, "Based on where we picked them out of the water and how we heard the plane from the pier at Rum Point my best guess is it's outside the reef where it arcs out off the point. That's the closest the reef gets to the north wall, which helps lessen our search area a bit."

Reg turned on his fish-finder CHIRP sonar and the bright screen lit up their faces in the grey, stormy day. He dimmed the screen setting a little and pointed to the screen that was attempting to map the sea floor below them. "The sonar is having a hard time in these swells as the boat is rolling and moving up and down so much, we keep moving relative to the bottom. We're not going to see a perfect image of a plane down there like we would on a calm day – we'll have to really pay attention to catch a glimpse."

AJ hung on to the railing and leaned over the back, shouting down, "Carlos, come up here please."

Carlos gingerly climbed the ladder as the boat swayed and rolled and the rain continued to pelt them. He huddled next to AJ as he adjusted to the bigger swings from being higher above the sea on the fly bridge.

AJ tried to narrow down their location. "How deep do you think it is, Carlos? How long was the swim to the surface? The wall drops off around a hundred feet and the shallows before the reef are about fifteen feet so it must have been something in between?"

Carlos thought carefully. "I have done some free diving so I think I have a reasonable idea but everything was kind of crazy in the dark and we didn't have good air to start. For sure it was more than ten metres but it was not more than twenty." They both did the quick conversion and agreed they should look between thirty and sixty feet.

Reg moved the boat slightly deeper until the depth, which was varying by six to eight feet at times, averaged around fifty five. Checking the GPS map they were now straight north from Rum Point. "Okay, this is our north-east corner and we'll work back and forth parallel to the reef and make our way shallower each time." AJ and Carlos nodded and Reg continued, "I'll concentrate on keeping us on course, you two watch the sonar. You're looking for anything that appears unnatural. That means straight lines usually – nature doesn't do things in straight lines but planes have straight lines, wings, fuselage and what have you."

AJ smiled. "Wish we had this a few years back, Reg!"

He nodded. "Yup, that's why I bought it! Told Pearl it was for fishing but she knew better."

The search began, tediously trolling back and forth in the broiling seas, staring at a fifteen-inch screen looking for the prover-bial needle. A plane is a large object until you drop it in an ocean where it becomes a speck in the vastness. Carlos and AJ kept thinking they saw something and would optimistically point at the screen until the screen refreshed and whatever it was would blend with the coral heads and growth below them.

After three painfully slow runs they were now at about fifty feet depth when they both pointed and yelled at the sonar. A distinct square profile appeared and went away again as they continued forward. "Turn around, Reg!" AJ shouted excitedly. "That was a wing tip!"

Reg carefully turned the boat, timing it as the swells rolled in so he didn't get caught sideways. It was treacherous trying to manoeuvre at low speeds as the seas tossed them around and made it almost impossible to find the same spot again. It took four more attempts to stumble back over the same piece of water and this time the image of the plane was clear to see, even with the sonar giving a confused image as the boat rose and fell on the surface.

AJ raced to the ladder and Reg yelled after her, "There's no way an anchor will hold and I don't want to drag the reef. I have to stay live so I'll keep crossing the wreck and I'll throw you a line when you come up!"

She gave him the okay sign and hurried down to don her dive gear; Thomas was already putting his on. The wind and rain continued to pummel them and she leaned in close to his ear to be heard.

"Thomas, we're in fifty feet so bottom time won't be an issue but Reg is going to get beaten to hell up here trying to stay around this spot so we'll be as quick as we can. Carlos said there's a bunch of hard cases in the back but the one we need is smaller than the rest and there's also a tube we need to find, the kind you'd put maps or building plans in. The plane is upside down and access is through one front door that's missing."

Thomas grinned. "If it's where and how they left it."

AJ shrugged and grinned back. "Yeah, let's be ready for anything down there."

With the heavy tanks strapped in their buoyancy compensator devices – the jacket-like piece of equipment that held the tank, ballast weight and air pockets, known simply as a BCD – they were even more unstable. The boat kicked and bucked around as they carefully made their way to the stern and the swim step where they wriggled their fins on. Carlos tried his best to hold them stable but they were all in danger of being thrown over at any time. The swim step was disappearing under the water as the stern dipped down and then rising violently back up four feet clear the next moment.

AJ shouted final instructions, "When Reg tells us to go, be ready for the next down swell. When the swim step starts going down take one step on it and keep going into the water, striding well clear of it. If you don't it'll wipe you out on the way back up! Go straight down, don't wait on the surface."

Thomas looked nervous. He'd logged a lot of dives in the past few years since he became a divemaster and handled some rough conditions, but this was by far the most extreme.

Reg bellowed from the fly bridge, "Go!"

AJ pulled her mask in place and stood watching the platform rise. She stepped on it as soon as it started down and used it as a stepping stone to launch into the water beyond. With a violent splash she went straight under and with her BCD fully deflated she stayed under, inverting quickly to head down, kicking until she was sure she was well below the boat. Once clear she turned to locate her dive buddy. Thomas timed it almost as well but he'd ridden the platform down a moment too far so his fin dragged the step as he tried to stride into the water. Instead of taking a giant stride he took a stumbling trip and fell into the surf. Fortunately the swim step only hooked his finned feet on its way back up and flipped him head down so he kicked a few times and found himself next to AJ before he really knew what had happened.

They hurried straight down before the pull of the swells could move them off the wreck site. Visibility was twenty feet, AJ surmised, which was terrible for Cayman but not bad considering the conditions. With the storm clouds darkening the skies and robbing the light, it almost felt like the beginning of a night dive, going in at dusk when the light was fading. The ferocious seas were stirring up the bottom and swirling around any loose particulate and debris. At least they were over coral; if they'd been in a sandy area it would be zero vis.

Reaching the coral at fifty feet AJ couldn't see the plane and the surge was dragging them back and forth an alarming amount. She headed straight north, figuring if they'd been pulled in any direction it would have been towards the sound. Thomas stuck close by and they picked up a rhythm of being pulled back in the surge and then kicking hard as it released them to shoot forward and make some ground.

Thomas grabbed AJ's arm and pointed to his left; at the edge of visibility was something large and whiter than any of the natural coral and growth. They finned over and surveyed the wreck of the seaplane, arriving at the tail first. It was wedged against a coral head, upside down as Carlos had said, with the right side wing tilted awkwardly up. From the tail they couldn't quite see the nose in the poor visibility but they made their way down the fuselage to the opening from the missing door. They quickly noticed it wasn't just the two of them moving in the surge, it was powerful enough to move the plane as well. The Cessna was being dragged back about a foot and then slammed against the coral head it was butted against. AJ could see it was the wing that was holding the plane in place and it appeared the aluminium was starting to buckle. Pretty soon, if the heavy seas kept up, the wing would fold and the steady destruction of the wreck would begin. Carlos's urgency to get out here was probably well placed, she thought, as she could see the overwing flexing and bending under the force of the ocean.

AJ took out her torch and signalled for Thomas to stay outside the fuselage. She shone the beam inside the cramped cockpit and for a moment imagined being trapped inside that space, in the dark, while the plane flooded as it descended to the bottom. She shivered at the thought. She shone the light beyond the front seats to the mess of cases and equipment piled up in the narrowing rear of the cabin. With everything inverted the gap between the seats and the roof was filled so there was no way to get back there, not that there was room for a diver to move around back there to start with. She would have to pull everything out through the space between the seats and the roof.

She moved her torso inside the cabin and reached back for the first case she could get to and found a handle. Pulling hard it didn't budge at all but the whole plane eerily rocked in the surge and strange groaning sounds emanated from the complaining sheet metal. She wiggled further inside until her tank banged against something above her and halted her progress. She flicked the light around again and spotted a black tube about six inches in diameter sticking forward of the stack of cases on the far side. Reaching as far as she could she was able to grab it and to her surprise it wasn't pinned down. With a solid tug the tube slid forward and she twisted it free and shoved it towards the door opening. It then disappeared from her view so she knew Thomas, vigilant as usual, had taken it.

Turning back to the cases she got as close to the roof as she could and searched the back with her torch. She spotted a smaller black case wedged against the roof at the bottom of the pile. She had no idea what was in all these hard plastic waterproof cases but they seemed quite heavy and she puzzled over how to move them. The plane rocked and shifted again with a horrible creaking but seemed to wedge itself more firmly this time. She pulled her feet into the tiny cockpit space and tried turning herself around to make room by the doorway, when the plane suddenly rolled with an ear-splitting crack as the wing broke in two.

Debris, pieces of coral and sand whirled around her, reducing visibility to nothing, and her fin pushed against something firm where she thought the opening had been. Fighting back panic she knew she had to wait for the mess to settle down again before she'd be able to see what happened. She could hear an annoying thud and wondered what was banging against the fuselage until it dawned on her it was her dive buddy. She answered Thomas's signal on the metal side with a few knocks, relieved to know he was still with her. The water settled and visibility slowly returned so she was able to assess her situation. The plane had rolled almost onto its side, the collapsed wing the only thing stopping it going all the way over. The door opening was now facing down, the metal of the wing folded flush across it blocking it completely. She was trapped inside.

AJ gave herself a minute to gather her thoughts and she checked her dive computer to verify she was fine on air and had twenty minutes usable bottom time remaining. She shook her head and slumped against the upside-down pilot's seat. How on earth do I do this to myself? she thought. Along with the attention and praise she'd received for discovering the wreck of the World War Two U-boat a few years back she'd also taken a lot of grief and criticism from parts of the diving community. There was no doubt she'd taken a lot of risk then and apparently she hadn't learnt her lesson as she was now sealed inside a seaplane wreck, fifty feet down in the midst of a violent storm.

More thuds from the outside brought her back to reality and she noticed they came from a different direction. Thomas was now above her and knocking on the window of the opposite door. The plane continued to strain and moan as the surge kept shoving it harder against the coral head, reminding her the ocean wasn't done dismantling the wreck. She twisted to look up at Thomas through the window and could hear him yanking on the door handle from the outside to no avail. She searched for some kind of lock on the inside, finally finding the handle and releasing it. The door started opening and Thomas heaved it against the water until it ground to a stop. The high wing of the Cessna had folded on the other side but had also twisted its roof mount so the other side pointing towards the surface had bent over a bit and now the door was stuck partially open against it.

Thomas reached in and patted AJ on the arm. The contact made them both feel a little relief and helped them stay calm. AJ estimated the opening was just enough for her to fit through so she turned her attention back to the cases. Again she shone her torch around and looked for options. Everything had shifted yet again with the roll so it was all stacked against the left side and roof of the fuselage. She could reach the small case and with a good pull it came free this time. Until it hit the seat. It wouldn't fit through the gap between the top of the seats and the roof and she sat back, confused. Shining her torch she confirmed there was no back door of any kind. She was wondering how they loaded all this stuff when it occurred to her. Fumbling beside the seat she found the handle she was looking for and once she had squeezed herself out of the way, the seat back folded forward, opening access to the back of the cabin.

She wriggled around to grab the case, shook it free of the others and stuffed it through the narrow door opening. It didn't want to fit but Thomas pulled mightily from the outside and managed to flex the door enough to get it through. The plane creaked and complained some more, persuading AJ it was a good time to get out while she could. Using a trick she'd employed before, she quickly unbuckled her BCD and shoved it, with her tank attached, through the opening to Thomas who held it just outside so her regulator hose still hung inside for her to breath. She squeezed into the opening and pushed on anything she could find inside to shove herself through, her teeth clenched on her regulator as it was trying to tug free with Thomas and her rig thrown around in the surge still rampant outside the plane. Once clear she slid back into her BCD and Thomas squeezed a hand on each shoulder, his eyes wide with concern inside his mask. She patted his arm and winked back, grateful to have him with her. She took the small case while Thomas held the unwieldy tube and the two started back towards the surface. She hoped with all her heart they had the right cases. Her pulse was still racing and she certainly had no intention of going back down today.

16

Topside was no fun for Reg, Carlos and Sydney. The wind and rain had not let up and riding around with the choppy ocean swells hammering in left them hanging on for dear life while still trying to keep the wreck located. Reg had put Sydney to work on deck preparing lines for when the guys surfaced and Carlos was invaluable helping with GPS and sonar to help Reg navigate back to the right spot.

Carlos had begged AJ to let him dive with her but she'd insisted she and Thomas be the ones. Her reasoning had been that the two dived together almost every day and knew each other and the terrain so well they made a safer team. Carlos argued that he knew the plane and what they were looking for which would be invaluable, but he had to admit once they were out here he was secretly glad he didn't have to dive in this mess. Now, with time moving like molasses and every passing minute multiplying their concern, he wished it was him in the water. They frantically scanned the surface thinking they'd missed them come up somewhere and been swept to the shallow reef guarding the sound, but there was no sign of them.

Then Sydney screamed as loud as she could from the deck, "There, over there!"

Reg and Carlos saw where she was pointing and picked up one of the divers waving from the surface, twenty yards off their starboard side and slightly behind them. Reg let the next wave roll under the boat before swinging the Newton hard around to port and chasing the back of the wave as fast as he could to get south of the divers. Once there he veered around again to run straight into the oncoming waves.

Yelling to Sydney, "Throw out the starboard line," he rode the next wave and steered as close to the first diver as possible, shutting the throttles down just past them. Thomas grabbed the trailing line and as soon as Reg saw he had the line he opened up the throttle again so he maintained control and could stay bow first into the swells. Carlos leapt down the ladder to help Sydney and they hauled on the line to drag Thomas to the boat, which took incredible effort as the boat was still moving. Reg shut the drive down in each trough to let them haul him closer and then had to gas it up again over the waves. Finally they had him at the back and timing it between dips of the stern and swim platform Thomas handed up the big plastic tube. He wrestled his fins off and threw them onto the boat while still clinging to the line but now came the hardest manoeuvre. The steps were connected to the swim platform and hinged to be lifted out of the water while the boat was moving. In the rough seas they were like a large metal hand slapping up and down in the surf as the platform rose and fell. Thomas waited for the next downswing which dragged the ladder under water with the platform but swung it outward as the water resisted it, hinging it backwards. He quickly pulled himself across to the ladder and hung on as the stern rose swiftly back up, bringing the ladder and Thomas with it. At the top of its rise Thomas scrambled up the few steps and lurched into the back of the boat, landing sprawled across the starboard bench.

Reg didn't miss a beat; he swung around in the next trough and went after AJ. She had disappeared in the squall. They'd dragged

Thomas north while she was being taken south by the seas so now the race was on to find her before she was taken to the shallow reef where the boat would founder. Carlos climbed back up to the fly bridge to help Reg spot as Thomas shed his gear and readied to help AJ aboard. Reg slowed as they got closer to where he guessed she'd been carried to, concerned he'd miss her, or worse still run her over. Visibility had not improved and trying to spot someone bobbing between all the crests and valleys of the churning surf was a challenging task.

Reg kept an eye on their depth; they were already at twenty-five feet and with the way the swells rose and fell along with the coral heads he knew extended towards the surface, he couldn't risk going shallower than fifteen. Carlos grabbed Reg's arm and pointed excitedly but Reg couldn't see anyone. Carlos yelled, "I saw her, right there, twenty metres ahead to the left!"

But there was nothing there in the water. The boat rose up as the next wave rolled in from behind them and sure enough there was AJ in next trough ahead, getting precariously close to the North Sound reef. Reg thrust the throttle lever and the Newton chased the wave toward shallower water where the swell was rising rapidly and crashing violently over the reef that was just in view now. AJ was kicking against the seas as hard as she could but had nothing against the power of the ocean and was being drawn to the reef at an alarming rate. Reg stopped looking at the depth; he was making a run for her whether it said sixty or six. He came up level with her as another wave swept under them from behind and carried them both shallower still. As soon as it passed under he cut hard to port and throttled up to put the boat within ten feet of AJ as Thomas threw the line to her. He pulled back the throttle while she wrapped her free arm around the line, her other hand grimly hanging on to the black case. The next swell approached and the water drew down under them as the wave loomed large. The bottom of the boat crashed against the reef just as Reg pushed the lever forward and asked everything from the diesel motor. The awful scraping sound made him cringe and pray the props weren't being ripped off but they surged forward, so they must be still attached, to his relief.

Once they reached deeper water they repeated the boarding exercise with AJ taking the ladder ride onto the boat and being unceremoniously dumped upon the deck. Once all the gear was safely stowed they began the uncomfortable ride back to the yacht club with the boat noticeably shuddering under power. AJ peeled out of her wetsuit and threw on a sweatshirt and rain jacket before joining Reg on the fly bridge.

"Thanks Reg," she said, leaning on his shoulder, "I think that went quite well all considering."

Reg chuckled. "Girl, you owe me a bloody prop."

17

Julio lay in his bunk and absentmindedly flicked through the pages of an American motorcycle magazine. A friend who worked on one of the dive boats had snapped up the colourful magazine left behind by a client and Julio was about the fourth person to borrow the rare glimpse into the ostentatious life outside Cuba. Silvio was on his own in the wheelhouse where Julio had learnt he liked to be left alone. One of the Russians was on deck puking and the other two were in the galley drinking coffee and smoking cigarettes.

He was surprised more of them weren't seasick as the swells had picked up and the weather deteriorated considerably as they closed in on Cayman. The boat was rocking and rolling as it trudged along at the best pace the old diesel could muster. Julio was born and raised in Jucaro which, as a coastal fishing village, meant career opportunities were thin and what there was almost all involved the water. Julio wasn't bothered by the rough seas; he'd been out in a skiff with his father in worse conditions than this. Of course his father was a drunk and repeatedly made poor decisions about many things beyond weather predictions. It was clearly a bad choice to drive himself home from the bar a year ago in the state he'd been in. His rusted-out 1989 Russian-built Moskvitch-2141 four-door hatchback was no match for the bus whose lane he had wandered into. The bus would have attempted to avoid him but as his father neglected to turn his lights on the driver never saw him coming. They told Julio and his mother that they'd extracted the body so he could be buried but he was pretty sure they just shoved some parts into the coffin and called it good. The Moskvitch had flattened like a pancake.

Once rid of her deadbeat husband his mother took Julio's younger sister and moved back in with her family in the larger town of Ciego De Avila, further inland. Julio was happy to be rid of his father, who'd been prone to beating his son in his intoxicated rages, and Ciego De Avila wasn't too far away to see his mother every so often. He'd been lucky to pick up the job with the geology studies people when they set up in town. It started with some basic repairs and upkeep on their boat but eventually grew to full time for maintenance on anything they needed worked on. He kept himself to himself. Silvio and Carlos treated him okay; he hated the Russian, but apart from talking to him like he was an idiot, generally the man left him alone. Julio was used to being talked to like an idiot, his father had done plenty of that. At least he wasn't being beaten with a broom handle now.

He considered checking the engine room again, but he'd already done that three times this morning and it was hotter than hell down there and stank really badly. He could join Silvio in the wheelhouse but Silvio would probably just think up something for him to do and put him to work. Julio was happy taking the path of least resistance. Chasing girls around Jucaro and the neighbouring towns was about the only thing that piqued his interest; not much else did. He let his mind wander to the young lady he'd been so rudely pulled away from last night, a night he thought was going to end pretty well for him. But instead, here he was bouncing around in this old tub, chasing that damn fool Carlos who didn't know a good thing when he had it. He'd been trained to fly, sent to university and given a cushy job flying around in a beautiful part of the country and now he'd thrown it all away and would probably end up rotting in a cell somewhere.

He liked Carlos, Carlos didn't treat him like an idiot. In fact on a couple of trips to Jardines de la Reina he'd shown him how to use his dive gear and they'd spent some time on the reef together. That was something else he liked, now he thought about it: diving. But that didn't matter, Carlos was going to be dragged to jail and he was Julio's only hope of diving again. You didn't get to be a dive-master in Cuba unless they picked you from a university to study marine biology and that wasn't happening for Julio.

He half-heartedly shrugged his shoulders and went back to thumbing through the magazine, lingering on a scantily clad young brown-haired girl sprawled across a fancy motorcycle with more chrome than a fifties Chevy. He sighed and thought, there's two more things not happening for Julio.

18

Carlos tipped the black plastic tube up and poured the salt water out. A clump of sodden papers followed and splattered on the ground in the backyard of Reg's house. Carlos swore in Spanish and knelt down to gather up the pulpy mess with the rain still coming down, albeit lighter than earlier.

It had taken a while to get back to the yacht club. Reg had been nervous about surfing the incoming waves through the cut with the damaged prop, but it had gone without incident. They gathered back at Reg and Pearl's house where everyone could dry off and warm up in a more spacious setting than AJ's tiny apartment.

Carlos went back inside and joined everyone eagerly tucking into the spread of food Reg's wife Pearl had conjured up.

"No good, I could feel the weight of the water and hear it sloshing inside." He held up the remains and Pearl guided him to a rubbish bin in the kitchen. "It has ruined all the charts," he announced despondently.

Sydney stood over the travel case they'd retrieved, with the lid open. "Well everything here is bone dry, so all is not lost!"

Carlos looked relieved and rushed over to examine the contents. Inside the case was a hard drive from the desktop computer in the

Instituto de Estudios Geológicos laboratory. He held it up and examined it before handing it to Sydney.

AJ asked curiously, "Is it not password protected or secured in some way?"

"That's where I come in," Sydney answered. "I'm the computer hacker. Well, I'm actually a programmer, that's what I studied in Miami, but I'm going to attempt to be a hacker and get into this."

Carlos grabbed a sandwich and spoke between bites, "That's why I was hoping to use just the charts, they had most of the information we needed to show on them. The hard drive was a backup plan. I was hoping it might cause some delays with the operation as well." He chewed voraciously. "Now we have to get access into it and I don't know the password, they kept that secret and changed it regularly. I think Mikhail is the only one who knows the latest password; we all used other computers and sent him our reports and notes to save on the server. I don't know what's on there exactly but it's the main server computer so hopefully it's got all we need."

Sydney grinned at him, "And maybe the password is something easy like Mikhail's favourite pet?"

Carlos laughed, waving his hands in the air, "Mikhail doesn't have pets, he has people as his pets! Besides, how lucky have we been this far?!"

Reg walked in, fresh from a shower and a dry set of clothes. "I'd say you were bloody lucky – not often you survive a plane crash."

Carlos mocked being offended. "We did not crash the plane Señor Moore, I landed the plane! The storm and the ocean then took the plane."

Sydney slapped his arm. "We pretty much crashed, Carlos."

Pearl brought out some more sandwiches for the hungry group and joined the conversation. "Wouldn't they have this stuff stored in backup systems somewhere, on a cloud or something?"

Carlos finished chewing another bite and eyed the new batch Pearl had set out. "Thank you so much for the food, we were really hungry! And yes, it is all backed up to a cloud-based government server so we didn't take the information from them, we just took a copy of it stored locally. Believe me their plans will continue uninterrupted if we don't cause enough international concern to stop it. The missing hard drive will just be an inconvenience to them."

AJ curled up in a comfy chair with a plate of food. "How do we do that? How were you thinking of releasing this information?"

Carlos looked a little sheepish. "I probably didn't give that part enough thought or planning... I always had it in mind we'd go to 'The Press'... but honestly I've never even spoken to a reporter or a newspaper before; I've no idea how to do that."

Reg glanced over at AJ as Thomas came in from the spare bathroom where he'd been cleaning up. AJ caught Reg's look but before she could say anything Thomas blurted enthusiastically, "AJ knows lots of reporters from all the stories on U-1026, don't you AJ?"

AJ had never been comfortable as the centre of attention surrounding the discovery of the U-boat location but her mother had parleyed it into an income stream for a while, for which she was grateful. It all happened two years ago so she had no idea if the people she met were still reachable. She played it down, shy to offer something she couldn't deliver. "I did meet a few people I can try and contact but I've no idea if they'll even respond now; it was a while back all that happened."

Carlos was excited by the prospect of help with the part he hadn't planned out very well. "Perfect. One of your contacts must be interested in this, surely? We're talking about a government covering up a major impact on the environment! People must care about that, don't they?"

AJ cautiously replied as no one else seemed willing to burst Carlos's bubble, "Well... many people are concerned but only a few truly do much about it, and governments, especially the American government, are very slow to do anything meaningful. Usually it takes a catastrophic event to get the ball rolling."

Frustrated, Carlos threw his arms up. "Believe me, this will be catastrophic!"

"I get that," AJ sympathised, "but getting enough worldwide

attention to make a difference won't be easy and it needs to be in the American press to create any real pressure."

Reg sipped a beer, leaning against the wall. "What you need is someone who knows all the press and is used to working with them, rather than you lot trying to figure out who to go to at every paper in every country. Needs to go out on the AP wire to get picked up."

Pearl smiled at AJ. "What about your young fella, AJ?"

AJ shifted uncomfortably in her seat. "First of all, he's not 'my' fella." She thought a moment. "But I could ask him if they'd get involved – they're certainly not afraid to take on governments for a worthy cause."

"Your boyfriend could help us?" Carlos asked enthusiastically, "Who is he?"

AJ rolled her eyes, "He's not my boyfriend. I happen to know a guy that works for Sea Sentry, they're an ocean environmental group that take on issues all over the world, and they're aggressive about it. They've been fighting governments for years to stop the mass slaughter of sharks for their fins. Jackson works on one of their boats but maybe he can put us in touch with their PR people."

"That's exactly who we need!" Carlos eagerly exclaimed. "I've seen what these guys do on the Internet, they're always being shot at or rammed when they put their boats in the way to stop these bastards taking the shark fins and illegal fishing. If your friend Jackson can help us, that would be incredible."

Thomas chuckled. "Pretty sure Jackson thinks he's your boyfriend…"

Reg and Pearl both laughed and AJ just hung her head, hiding behind her purple-streaked blonde hair that fell around her face.

19

———

The storm was moving south faster than the old trawler was chasing it from the north-east and it appeared to Silvio that the winds and rain were lessening. The rough seas were still hammering them but he could tell they were starting to abate, although the seasick Russian probably didn't agree. Silvio was dog tired. He had been worn out before the phone call yesterday evening and now, on four hours of restless sleep, he was exhausted mentally and physically. He took another swig of coffee but the caffeine had lost its effect hours ago and the liquid tasted bitter. It also made his tongue feel like it was covered in a weird velvet but the action of sipping kept his eyes from closing, so he kept sipping. The door slid open and he tensed as Mikhail entered.

"How much farther?" The Russian demanded.

Silvio glanced at the GPS. "We'll approach the east end of Grand Cayman in less than an hour and then another forty-five minutes to an hour around the island to George Town harbour. I was planning to go around the south side as the storm came from the north – not sure it'll make much difference but hoping it'll be a bit smoother."

Mikhail eyed Silvio while he hung on to the console as the boat still rolled and heaved in the swells.

"Do you have a radio frequency for the Port?"

Silvio slid from his captain's chair and rifled through a drawer of maps and books. Selecting one he settled back in the chair that at least made it easier to ride out the waves. He flicked through the pages until he found what he was looking for and reached to the VHF radio and tuned it to 156.7, the frequency for George Town's port security.

Mikhail removed the microphone and pressed the transmit button on the side. "George Town port security, George Town port security, this is Explorador de la Reina, over."

A short time later a crackly reply came, "Explorador de la Reina, six eight?"

Mikhail reached over and turned the radio to channel sixty-eight, the general chat frequency and after waiting a moment to make sure the channel was clear Mikhail keyed up again. "George Town port security, George Town port security, this is Explorador de la Reina on six eight, over."

The same crackly voice came back, "Explorador de la Reina this is George Town port security, how can we help you this fine day? Over."

Silvio glanced around at the rain still lashing the windows and raised an eyebrow at the man's optimism. Mikhail made no reaction or expression, he simply pressed the button.

"George Town port security this is Explorador de la Reina under the Cuban flag requesting customs and immigration clearance upon arrival, we're ninety minutes from you, over."

The pause was a little longer this time and the voice less jovial, "Explorador de la Reina, may I ask the purpose of your visit... And... Has any paperwork been filed prior to arrival? Over."

Mikhail replied without hesitation, "George Town port security this is Explorador de la Reina, we are marine biologists under Cuban and Russian government papers, no paperwork has been filed prior to our departure, we apologise for the clerical error on our end."

There was silence for a long time before a different voice was heard, "Explorador de la Reina this is George Town port security, please radio back on 156.7, channel sixteen, when you are approaching George Town, and we request you fly the Q flag per procedure. The harbour is closed from the storm but we can send a boat out to meet you, please have all your paperwork in order when we board, over."

"George Town port security this is Explorador de la Reina, roger and over." Mikhail hung up the microphone on the VHF radio and turned to Silvio, "I'll be back in an hour, alert me if they attempt to contact us before then. Do we have a Q flag on board?"

Silvio thought a moment, trying to recall if they had the plain yellow flag that signifies you're a foreign vessel requesting inspection to enter the country. "I believe we do, I'll have Julio find it."

He presumed Mikhail was satisfied by his answer as he left without another word.

20

AJ stared at her laptop computer screen as she sat on her sofa in her apartment. She'd left Carlos and Sydney at Reg's place where they had a spare room, a bit more comfortable than AJ's fold-out sofa. They'd decided it was best to keep them both out of sight until they figured out what to do and how to do it. Besides, Sydney needed some space to work on the hard drive. As AJ left she'd been connecting to Reg's computer to try and figure out how to access the data.

Now AJ sat conflicted about hitting send on the email she'd typed to Jackson.

As a crew member on one of Sea Sentry's ships, the Sword of the Sentry, Jackson had stopped over in Cayman for a week about six months earlier on their way to South America. Early in the week members of the crew had given a presentation about their work at a restaurant in George Town, which AJ along with most of the diving community attended. Jackson Floyd was a tall, slender, twenty-eight-year-old with a close-shaved beard and straggly long dark brown hair, tied up in a ponytail. An American from northern California, he had a soft-spoken voice which emanated passion and commitment when he addressed the crowd. After the talk the crew mingled late into the evening and Jackson appeared popular with the young girls, who swarmed around him and his shipmates.

AJ, despite her bold appearance, was generally shy and not at all into the singles scene and dating as a sport. Once the girls flocked around the crew guys she stayed back and was happy to hang out chatting with friends. When she heard a voice say her name she turned and was surprised to find it was the good-looking guy from the crew she'd really enjoyed listening to.

"Hi, sorry to bug you but I really wanted to say hello. I read all about the U-boat discovery you made. I was blown away when someone said you were here tonight, so had to meet you and at least shake your hand. I'm Jackson, Jackson Floyd."

He extended his hand which AJ shook firmly while unable to find any words.

"Do you still get out there and dive the submarine? It's a ways offshore right?"

She managed to regain some composure and conjure an answer. "Hey, yeah, we go out usually once a month when the weather allows – we get a restricted number of permits each year to dive it. Kind of a deal we worked out with the Cayman DOE."

He spoke with enthusiasm without being boisterous. "Man, that's gotta be a thrilling dive, crazy to think the interior is still dry and everything is as it was left in, what? 1945?"

AJ relaxed; talking about diving was much easier for her than talking about herself. "We're working on a project to penetrate the inside before the hull breaches, which it will eventually do. The only reason it hasn't so far is because it was completely undamaged when it went down; they sat it down there rather than it being sunk. Once the decay thins the pressure hull enough the water pressure will be too much and it'll flood. Hopefully we can safely rescue a lot of the artifacts before then."

Jackson was fascinated and wanted to know all the details and the two talked until the restaurant kicked everyone out at midnight. They made plans to meet up the next day after AJ got back from morning dives, and she took him shore diving from cemetery beach. He'd learnt to dive in the cold waters off northern California and hadn't done a lot of warm-water diving, so he soaked up the abundant sea life, the beautiful coral and crystal clear water. She couldn't believe he was interested in spending time with her when there were lots of pretty and racier catches, keen to show him a good time on the island. Her diffidence and cautious nature wouldn't let her see he was thoroughly besotted with her and had no interest in the others. She began to believe when they finally kissed after the third day of spending all their free time together, and he graciously said goodnight without pressing for more. She found him easy to be around, relaxing, amusing and conversation came naturally between them. They shared common interests in the ocean and the preservation of the reefs and natural balance. He had believed in Sea Sentry enough to give up his job at the Monterey Bay Aquarium research department to work for food and lodging which was supplied aboard a ship spending most of its time in perilous waters and situations.

The week went by swiftly and on the final evening after a dinner party thrown for the crew by the Cayman Islands Department of Environment they walked along Seven Mile Beach in the moonlight with the gentle sea lapping up the white sand over their bare feet. He told her he was having a seriously hard time getting back on the boat and leaving her. She told him she couldn't be responsible for depriving the cause of such a committed team member, but tears rolled down her face and gave away how her heart felt about him leaving. They spent that last night together, sleeping, making love but never leaving each other's embrace. He quietly slipped out early the next morning and the Sword of the Sentry left Cayman at sunrise. She woke to find a note where he'd lain in her bed. AJ, a girl who rarely cried and had always taken her time to get emotionally involved, found tears on her cheeks for the second time that night.

'I cannot describe how you make me feel. But know that it is unique and profound. This won't be easy but I'm all in if you'll have me, JF.'

He'd been away at sea since. When they docked somewhere in South America it was only for a few days and there'd been no time to meet up, even if she could take time away to fly down to him. They kept in touch by online video chat and email when they had Internet service on the ship, but the time and distance was murderous. He never seemed to waiver in his interest or desire in AJ but her own self-doubt slowly ate away at her confidence that he'd return – or, when he did, would it be the same? It had been nearly a month since they last spoke.

She finally hit send, set the laptop aside and went to the kitchen to grab a Strongbow cider from the fridge. No sooner had she closed the fridge door than her computer dinged, indicating a video chat request. She rushed back to the screen and froze with her finger hovering over the enter key to accept. There it was again. That doubt her stupid brain had conjured up, especially over the last four weeks when she hadn't heard a word from him. Had he given up on her? Or forgotten her? He probably had an AJ Bailey in every country they stopped in, a girl waiting on his email or call thinking they were the one.

With trepidation she hit enter and a video window opened; the fuzzy, pixellated image slowly cleared and there sat Jackson with a big smile.

"Hi there beautiful! Man I've missed seeing your face, it's been a mess down here, we've been at sea since we spoke last. Our Internet on the boat has been down, we've been sending all our reports over the radio. We're finally in port at Limón in Costa Rica. It's so good to see you!"

AJ sat there staring at the screen. What an idiot I am, she thought. He's fighting shark finning in the open ocean for four weeks and I'm dreaming up scenarios to destroy the best thing that ever happened to me. Being cautious was one thing but being self-destructive was another and she kicked herself for being such a fool.

"Are you okay AJ?" He leaned in as though that would bring

him closer across the web. "What's the matter? Something happen?"

She realised she hadn't uttered a word and pulling herself together she broke into a big smile. "Everything is fine, I've just missed talking to you. Well, there's some stuff going on but I'll tell you about that in a bit, I want to hear all about your voyage first."

21

From the roof of the small police and customs boat the officers were able to scramble aboard the old Cuban trawler. Port security had guided the Explorador de la Reina to an area outside the tiny harbour in George Town where the bottom was sandy and directed them to anchor there. The rain had finally died down to a steady drizzle as both boats rolled around, tied together in the lumpy seas. Mikhail had everyone on deck and they clung to the railing in the stern as the three officers carefully negotiated the precarious boarding.

The Russian greeted each official with a handshake and offered for them all to go below deck out of the weather. Two of them were in government department coats and hats while the third was an armed policeman in a bulletproof vest complete with Velcro-affixed accessories and an intimidating presence. Errol Watson, a burly brown-skinned Caymanian, introduced himself as an officer of the Department of Immigration and eyed Mikhail suspiciously.

"Do you have any firearms aboard the vessel or on your persons, sir?"

Silvio nervously shuffled and was glad they weren't asking him but Mikhail was ice cold as usual. "No sir, we're marine biologists, no weapons aboard; I have our papers below if you'd care to get out of the rain?"

Watson glanced at the other official, who'd introduced himself as Jaden Porter, Customs Department of the Cayman Islands, and with a nod from Porter they followed Mikhail and crew below deck.

The galley and dining area was the largest room in the trawler but was cramped for nine dripping-wet men in jackets and coats. The armed policeman shuffled about trying to get a spot where he could keep an eye on everyone and the three Russians instinctively noted his every move.

Mikhail offered the ship's papers, laying them on the table along with each man's passport and their Cuban-issued ID cards showing their government approved profession. Two of them were real, two of them had been created for this trip and one was chosen from Mikhail's collection of identification papers he used for various situations.

Watson examined each passport and ID, using the pictures to associate the person while Porter looked at the registration paperwork.

Watson looked up at Silvio and addressed him in Spanish, "Boat captain, huh? It says here you work for the Institute of Geological Surveys; that's not marine biology now is it?"

The man had a friendly smile which said trust me but his question was clearly weighted and Silvio felt a lump in his throat and his voice came out shaky, "We do... We do a lot of work on the reefs."

Struggling to find the words and knowing Mikhail understood Spanish he stole a quick look at the Russian. Mikhail blinked. The man never normally seemed to blink – he just held that blank, piercing stare. Buoyed by a touch of confidence that the blink was an affirmation, Silvio managed to continue, "The reefs off our coast, often I take these biologists on the boat to the reefs for their studies."

Watson grinned, noting the subtle exchange between the two

men. He turned to Mikhail and continued in Spanish, "May I ask why Russian nationals are leading Cuban geology expeditions, sir?"

Mikhail knew it would be more suspicious if he didn't speak Spanish as he worked with the Cubans and replied in kind, "Marine biology, sir, we're working with them in marine biology." Mikhail was too sharp to be caught out by this wily official but he was slightly impressed the man was good at his job. "We have many cooperative projects with Cuba – both states benefit from our combined knowledge."

Watson nodded slowly, switching back to English. "I see, and why, pray, would you choose to travel through this storm to get here unannounced? Surely it would have made more sense to wait a day? What's the big hurry – our beautiful reefs have been here a long time, I don't think a day would make a difference?"

Mikhail remained unflinching but he did pause before replying, buying time to straighten out the story in his mind. "We Russians are keen on our schedules, sir, besides, we are used to the Bering Sea, this crossing was not rough for us." Mikhail managed to curl the edge of his mouth in what appeared to be an attempt at a smile.

Watson chuckled for a moment and then turned to look at the seasick Russian. Pavlo looked bedraggled with a pasty complexion and sagging eyelids he could barely keep open.

"You don't look so good there, mister marine biologist?"

Pavlo started to attempt a response but he clearly didn't understand the question and decided to shut his mouth. Mikhail laughed to everyone's surprise but it broke the tension, "Every group has a new guy, right? He's ours."

Watson relented. "Okay, let's take a look around the boat if you don't mind. Mr. Gurov, perhaps you can give us a tour?"

Mikhail didn't hesitate. "This way, gentlemen."

22

———————

Chief Pilot Kemar Robinson pointed the police Airbus EC135 helicopter north-west following the West Bay coastline at an altitude of 1000 feet. His co-pilot, Line Pilot Joseph Connell, scanned the water's edge and beach for signs of storm damage. So far it was limited to palm fronds, washed-up seaweed and small debris. They idly chatted over the intercom about this weekend's football game as Kemar cleared the north-west corner by Villas Pappagallo and left the island's beaches to trace the outer reef across the North Sound, spanning to Rum Point. Barker's National Park, the mangrove reserve, stretched away to their right as they flew over the shallow reef heading east. The seas remained rough but had settled down considerably from the prior two days' storms, and visibility had returned, revealing the beautiful reef and sandy bottom of the sound.

Both men leaned forward in their seats at the same time. Joseph mumbled, "What in God's name is that?"

What appeared to be a large, white, metallic-looking board stuck up from the ocean side of the reef at a strange angle as they neared Rum Point.

"That a piece of a boat?" Kemar asked, nosing the helicopter down closer to the water.

"Looks more like a billboard, or maybe something fallen off a freighter?" Joseph noted as they began circling at 200 feet over the mysterious object.

"Oh shit!" Kemar swung the helicopter around and dipped the nose so they could both see from the front window. The wreckage of a small aircraft could be plainly seen in the clear water forty yards outside the reef, the fuselage easily identifiable.

"That's the wing of the plane stuck against the reef over there! I didn't hear any reports of missing planes, did you?" Kemar asked.

Joseph was already hitting the radio button. "AOU this is Victor Papa Charlie Papa Sierra, we have a downed aircraft outside the North Sound reef in shallow water, maybe… Half a click from Rum Point, over."

After a short delay the radio crackled back, "Joseph, did you say a downed aircraft? Over."

"Yes, Jacob, that's what I said, now get Whittaker on the horn, he's gonna want to know about this!"

Detective Roy Whittaker was enjoying a cup of coffee, sitting outside the Greenhouse Café at the edge of George Town. The humorous owner, Jen, brought him a large pastry, placing it on his table with a grin. "Yesterday you told me to deny you if you ordered anything fattening."

Roy looked up from his newspaper with a smirk. "Looks like you may have ignored me?"

Jen explained, "Nope, I made this special with low-fat butter, locally sourced skimmed milk cheese and lean meat."

Roy looked surprised. "Really?"

Jen put her hands on her hips and shook her head at him. "No, not really, I make a living selling food not denying people food, I ain't your diet police. Enjoy." With that she left him with a smile on her face.

Roy laughed as he reached for his mobile phone buzzing on the table. "Detective Whittaker."

He listened for a few moments to the excited voice on the line. "You don't say?"

More excited babbling before Roy could interrupt them. "Calm down a step Jacob. Listen, did the fellas see any signs of life or any bodies?"

The reply appeared to be negative. "All right then, I'll organise a boat and some divers. Tell Kemar to stay close until we get out there, we don't need a bunch of fuss before we have a chance to take a look."

Whittaker picked up his coffee and pastry, waved in Jen's direction inside the café and headed for his car.

Reg stood in the car park out the back of the yacht club and watched as his boat was pulled up the ramp on a large trailer towed by a rusty old tractor. His boats were his babies and all three of his Newtons were regularly serviced and any issues were taken care of swiftly. This one was to receive a new propeller.

His phone rang in his pocket and checking the caller ID he was only mildly surprised to see Roy Whittaker was calling him. Curiously he answered, "Good morning Roy."

"Morning Reg, how's that lovely wife of yours? She playing tonight?"

Pearl had a regular gig on Friday nights at the Fox and Hare pub in West Bay where she played guitar and sang. Roy Whittaker and his wife would often stop by and enjoy the show.

"She's keeping me in line as usual so I reckon she's alright – hasn't kicked me out yet so I'm still the luckiest man alive. She'll be there, starts at seven."

Roy allowed himself a chuckle. "You might be at that Reg, she's a good one." His tone shifted as he switched to business, the part Reg was waiting for. "What do you have going this morning, Reg?"

"Got two boats out on west side now it's laid down and I'm at the yacht club pulling the third to fix the prop. Why, need some help with something Roy?"

Reg had often helped the Royal Cayman Islands Police Service – the RCIPS – over the years with search and rescue, recoveries and diving. The service had a whole marine division and several capable divers but no one with Reg's experience, especially when it came to technical or difficult conditions.

"Not sure quite yet, just heading out there myself, but we've got the wreckage of a small plane on North Sound reef. No sign of bodies and no reports on the plane going down so I'll probably need some divers in the water to do a search and identify the plane. Guessing it's still pretty rough out north so wouldn't mind having you there, if you're not too busy?"

Reg was surprised the plane had been found so soon – it had only been daylight for an hour, but figured the best way to keep tabs on what was happening was to be there.

"Let me grab my gear and some tanks off the boat before they pull it into the maintenance yard here. You got someone that can pick me up?"

"I do, I'll be at the yacht club in ten minutes. I have a marine unit picking me up, I'll see you there in a bit."

Reg shouted to the tractor driver to hold up; he had ten minutes to get his dive gear together and figure out what he should find and not find at the plane. He was okay not telling his friend Roy a few details but he wasn't prepared to lie to him so he needed to get his story straight before he arrived at the wreck of the Cuban seaplane for the second time.

AJ had a scuba tank in each hand, heading from her van to her dive boat tied up alongside the dock she shared with Reg at the north end of Seven Mile Beach. She and Thomas were just about done loading the boat for the morning trip and customers were starting to arrive, ready to get some diving in now the weather had cleared. She enjoyed the physical work that came with running a dive business and her lean, muscular physique was proof of the effort.

She felt her mobile phone vibrate in her pocket and hustled as best she could with a forty-pound tank in each hand to reach the boat. As she set them down the phone stopped ringing and she looked at the caller ID to see who she'd missed. It was Reg.

Thomas joined her with the last two tanks and they loaded them into the racks in the stern of the boat. The dock was busy with two of Reg's boats as well as AJ's getting outfitted and customers milling around eager to get out on the water now the weather was back to the usual beautiful sun-filled day on Cayman.

"Can you start getting everyone on board and signed in, Thomas? I need to call Reg back."

Thomas gave her the okay sign and began shepherding guests aboard and helping them organise their gear or get fitted for rental equipment. AJ stepped off the boat and found a quieter spot to talk on the phone. Noticing she had a voicemail she listened. 'Hey, it's Reg, they found the bloody thing already, Detective Whittaker has asked me to dive it for him, he's picking me up in a few minutes. Not sure there's much I can do but tell him what I find down there. Don't want to make more trouble for 'your lad' but I'm not going to lie to the police either, we'd be in deep shit if he knew we'd already been out there and didn't say anything. Friend or no friend you know Roy is by the book. Anyway, he's pulling up so text me if you think of anything."

"Bugger." AJ couldn't help but swear out loud. She was hoping it would be a day or two before the north calmed down enough for dive boats to head back out there and someone stumble across the plane. It was one thing having the possibility of the Cubans and Russians hunting for Carlos and the seaplane, if indeed they were looking in Cayman, but a whole other problem if the police were also trying to find a Cuban pilot. Of course once the news broke a Cuban plane had crashed in Cayman, they'd know for sure.

She tried to think it through. What would be the least intrusive in getting Carlos's story out to the press? They needed time. Jackson was working on it from his end but who knew if or when they'd be ready to run with the story. Before that could happen Sydney had to get into the hard drive or there was no story. The other thing they didn't know was how the Cuban government would react when asked about their missing plane. Didn't seem like they'd reported it missing, which tied in with Carlos's theory they'd send the Russians to clean up the mess quietly.

They definitely needed time. Best thing would be for the police to stay tied up looking for a body on the north side; that would keep them busy, especially as she knew there wasn't a body to be found.

She texted Reg, 'Best thing is a body search, keep them busy.'

As AJ strode back down the pier towards her boat she smiled at Reg's text back, 'You're in deep shit if I miss Pearl playing tonight.'

23

———

The North Sound was a whole lot calmer than yesterday afternoon, Reg noted to himself, as the Royal Cayman Islands Police Service Marine Unit boat completed the run across and coasted up to a sister boat anchored short of the shallow reef. The wing of the seaplane could be seen pointing to the sky, trapped against the reef on the ocean side.

They tied alongside and two men approached the railing of the other boat to meet them. Reg knew the first man, George Grayson. He was a Marine Unit officer and diver and the two of them had dived together both on official business and recreational. He was a good man and a capable, dependable diver in Reg's opinion. The second man introduced himself as a representative of the Cayman Islands Airports Authority. Cayman rarely had need of an aviation accident investigation team so when something did happen someone from the CIAA would be present to oversee the crash site before an expert could be brought in from the UK.

After brief pleasantries Reg got things moving, "Alright George, let's gear up here where it's calmer then they can zip us around through the small cut and drop us on the site." He turned to the boat captain, "You'll have to pull off the site until we come back up and then come grab us. If we're not marking a particular spot for any reason we'll head away from the reef underwater so expect us to surface in deeper water, safer for everyone."

George threw his gear bag over and joined Reg and the two began getting prepared. Roy chatted to the CIAA inspector for a few minutes before briefing the two divers.

"First thing will be to identify the plane, tail number should be enough, and then see if there's a victim on site. Next would be a quick look to see if there's identifiable cargo, illicit or otherwise and whether there's any contaminant risks beyond the usual fuel leakage. If you suspect anything dangerous on board then abort and we'll tackle the scene differently. If there are no victims on site and you have time to begin an area search please do what you can."

The two men nodded and waved to the captain to take them around to the ocean side.

Reg and George splashed in right over the wreck site and descended quickly to get away from the choppy surface. The waters were quickly settling after the storm, visibility was coming back and although the surge worsened the closer they got to the shallow reef it was workable near the plane itself. The fuselage had clearly rolled shallower than where it had been last night; the high wing must have finally separated completely allowing it to tumble until wedging itself hard against a large coral head, where it now resided. Both doors were gone, both pontoons detached and the tail wings were badly twisted and mangled, but it lay upright with the right side against the coral head.

Reg signalled to George to take a sweep around then let him know he would take a look in the plane itself. He then noted the tail number from the rear of the fuselage, writing the numbers on a slate he had clipped to his BCD. Finning between surges of current he eased closer and poked his head inside the door opening. A lot had gone on inside this little space in the past twenty-four hours, he mused to himself, picturing firstly Carlos and Sydney fighting their way out and then AJ getting herself trapped inside before rescuing some of the cargo. Sea life was already taking an interest in the new arrival: a few squirrelfish lurked in the back and a handful of tangs flitted out the other door. The seat was still folded down and the larger cases scattered about, one now all the way forward against the console.

Reg scanned the console, noting the broken radar screen and one intercom headset up against the windshield, still tethered by its cord. The second headset was nowhere to be seen, probably thrown clear at some point he surmised. For no particular reason he slid the headset aside and something shiny caught his eye, wedged between the windshield and the top of the console. He reached forward and carefully picked up the metallic object, a wristwatch. Reg turned it over in his hand and examined it. It was clearly a woman's watch with a smaller face and decorative strap. On the back he could just make out an inscription, 'Todo mi amor, Carlos.' Shit, Reg thought, this must be Sydney's, a gift from Carlos. He slid the watch into a BCD pocket and zipped it tightly closed, looking around to make sure George wasn't close by and thankful it was him who had found it. If there was any way to keep Sydney out of this mess the better it would be if it all went sideways... And Reg was pretty certain this was all going sideways before they were done.

Of course Reg knew there were no bodies to find but he went about his work as though there could be and carefully examined the interior for signs of distress or in case they'd left any other evidence he needed to clear. George returned and by hand signal communicated he'd found the pontoons but no sign of victims. With plenty of air and bottom time remaining they began an area search using an expanding square pattern and other than debris from the plane coming apart they found nothing of interest. As he passed by a coral head that reached almost to the surface he noticed a fresh-looking gouge in the top and realised it was probably from his prop the day before. He felt awful killing coral, knowing how long it took to grow and how vital it was to the ecosystem of the oceans – but coral could at least grow again, AJ couldn't.

After an hour they headed due north staying at a depth of

fifteen feet to give themselves a good safety stop, allowing the nitrogen in their tissues to comfortably dissipate before surfacing and signalling the boat captain to retrieve them.

Back on board the two divers gave Roy and the CIAA man a thorough debrief on the condition of the plane, the cases inside and the layout of the wreck site. Reg referenced his slate, "Tail number is CU-FDRY and it's a Cessna, I saw badges on a few…"

"CU prefix you say?" interrupted the inspector.

Reg confirmed, "Correct, Charlie, Uniform, dash, Foxtrot, Delta, Romeo, Yankee."

"Hmmm." The inspector looked concerned. "That's a Cuban prefix, this plane came from Cuba."

"Someone seeking exile possibly? Doesn't really explain the cases," Roy suggested.

Reg needed to keep this on track, "Well, whatever poor sod was in that plane is surely floating in the sound or washed up on the shore somewhere, so we better start looking before the critters get them."

"True enough." Roy nodded. "I'll call in what we know, they can ask the Cubans if they have a plane missing, might help us know who we're looking for. But until we get some idea what's in those cases we'd best stay out of the water."

The sound of a helicopter drowned out any further speech and they all looked to the skies.

"Damn it," Roy exclaimed in a rare show of anger, "it's the news guys."

24

Sydney growled under her breath. After crashing out from exhaustion the night before, she'd awoken early and hadn't moved from the computer since 5.30am. She was now on the Internet searching for help articles on accessing a hard drive and finding mainly sketchy ads for software that was 'the only software you need to crack any hard drive'. Pearl brought her another cup of coffee and traded out mugs, giving her a supportive squeeze on the shoulder.

"Thank you Pearl, you're an angel," Sydney mumbled.

"I'll fix some breakfast, I think I heard Carlos stirring back there," Pearl replied over her shoulder as she headed back to the kitchen.

Sydney sighed and stared at the screen. She could build you a beautiful website, set up a mean Sharepoint site or program in Java, C++ and Matlab. But finding a way around the protection on this hard drive was stumping her. She thought about the classes she was currently missing in Miami, the school her parents were spending all the money they didn't have to send her to. She won a scholarship in high school towards college tuition, she had student loans and still her parents had to scrape together what they could to make it work. Even her little brother Thomas was helping when he could. Her amazing little brother who had saved their lives based on a brief phone call for help two nights ago. Yet here she sat, back on Cayman, unbeknown to her loving family, missing classes. A wave of guilt raced through her and she felt a lump rising in her throat. Sydney believed wholeheartedly in what they were trying to achieve but what if she did end up in trouble? She could lose her scholarship or get kicked out of school. She could be arrested for being party to stealing a plane. If Carlos was right, the Russians could go to any lengths to hide their plans and recover the evidence. What did that mean, any lengths? Stuff from the movies with bad guys and guns and secret agents making people disappear? She was letting her imagination get away from her; none of that stuff really happens and especially on their sleepy little island in the middle of the Caribbean sea. The sound of the television coming on in the living room brought her back to the moment and she heard Pearl call her.

"Sydney, Carlos, you better come and see this!"

Carlos stumbled sleepy eyed from the guest bedroom as Sydney joined Pearl in the living room.

"What's up?" she asked and Pearl just pointed at the television.

The video was from a news helicopter looking down on the water where several police marine unit boats could be seen. An excited reporter was describing the scene, "Police are on site where the as yet unidentified plane can be seen on the sea floor in the shallow water just outside North Sound reef. Police and the Airport Authority have declined to comment at this early stage so many questions remain unanswered, such as where did the plane originate from? Was it a victim of the storm and who was aboard? It is still undetermined whether the pilot survived this frightening crash or if it now becomes a search and recovery."

"We didn't crash, we landed," Carlos muttered defensively as Pearl turned the volume down on the reporter as he babbled on repetitively with no new information.

"Reg texted me and told me to check the news – he said

Cayman 27's news helicopter was out there. He got a call to help investigate the wreck this morning," Pearl explained.

Sydney was surprised, "Reg is out there with the police?" She and Carlos both looked at Pearl, confused.

Pearl smiled. "Don't worry, they ask him to help any time there's tricky diving involved, but he won't give anything away."

Relieved about Reg, Carlos still rubbed his temples anxiously. "I can't believe the water is so clear already, I thought we'd have days before anyone would find the plane."

Sydney shook her head. "Look how it's smashed up against the reef; the wing's sticking out of the water so even if they didn't see the plane they would have found the wing and started looking. I still can't believe we were inside that at the bottom of the sea."

"This is bad," Carlos groaned.

"What does this change?" Pearl asked as the news station continued to loop their one minute of footage.

Carlos looked at her with tired and worried eyes. "They know we're on Cayman."

Pearl agreed. "Sure, but there's no way anyone seeing this will believe someone could have survived."

Carlos slowly shook his head. "With no bodies? Mikhail will figure it out."

25

———————

Mikhail stood by the window of his third-floor hotel room overlooking a stylish pool and Seven Mile Beach beyond. He dialled a number on his mobile phone and waited for an answer. Speaking in Russian, he glanced back at the television screen showing the news coverage of the crash scene. "They're here in Cayman, they crashed in the storm. Or more likely they made it look like they crashed in the storm; no bodies recovered so far."

The man on the other end of the crackly connection sounded older and spoke with an authoritative tone, "Then your decision to go straight there was fortuitous."

Mikhail ignored the dig. "We won't have much time; the authorities were suspicious when we arrived, now they have a Cuban plane mysteriously crash at the same time we showed up. They'll want to talk to us again."

"You'd better get started then, this business needs to be successfully concluded right away. You have two days maximum," the man asserted.

Mikhail paced about the room while he listened to his superior but remained calm in his response, "I understand. Make sure the Cubans tell them it was Rojas alone in the plane," he instructed. "If the local authorities think the Caymanian girl was aboard we'll have a lot more trouble."

The man replied in an annoyed tone, "They have been instructed, do not concern yourself with the details this end, you need to focus on finding Rojas."

"Still no trace of Bodden in Cuba, correct?" Mikhail probed.

Even more irritated that his operative continued to question, "Of course not, we'd have informed you."

"She was on the plane as well, I'm sure of it," Mikhail said more to himself than the Russian official.

The man continued in his gruff tone, "Monday, construction begins Monday, Gurov, it's in your hands to make sure none of this nonsense interferes with that. I got you out of Siberia, I can send you back there, understand?"

Mikhail smirked ever so slightly. "I understand."

"Good, I've given you two good, capable men now you need to find that boy."

Mikhail stopped pacing as he replied, "He won't show himself. It's the girl I'll find, she'll lead me to him."

26

———

One day it was storming and the next it was clear blue skies with a few wispy white clouds and a gentle breeze knocking the edge off the balmy heat. Such was the tropics. AJ motored up to one of the government-placed dive-site buoys and Thomas used a long gaff to grab the line and tied in the boat. The west side hadn't lain down perfectly flat like normal yet, but was settling quickly and the boat gently rolled back and forth. She shut the motors down and glanced at her phone sitting on the console, noticing she had a text from Pearl.

'Story's out, call me when you have a chance.'

"Shit," she muttered to herself; she too had hoped for a couple of days of anonymity for Carlos.

Thomas scrambled back from the bow and started helping the guests get their gear ready for the dive. They had a full boat of eight divers, the maximum they'd take at any time, which left plenty of room to set up gear and move about on her thirty-six foot Newton, a sister boat to Reg's fleet.

AJ slid down the ladder from the fly bridge and joined Thomas in helping folks and chatting with the clients. She nudged Thomas when she got the chance. "Can you take first dive?"

"Of course." He saw the concern on her face. "Everything okay Boss?"

She forced a smile. "I think so, just need to make a call or two, I'll fill you in between dives, I'll take the second one."

Thomas nodded, wondering what may have happened now. He considered himself adventurous, being one of the only Caymanian divemasters and instructors on the island he felt proved that, but somehow all the adventure seemed to happen at one time which he found a little overwhelming. When his sister had called him a few nights before, she'd said she and Carlos were in Cuba and she was helping him leave and seek asylum. Thomas had never met Carlos but he knew his sister had been dating him for a while and was very serious about their relationship, so that was good enough for him. He'd asked AJ if she could help and she agreed right away, because she trusted him. Now, with Russians and Cubans and crashed seaplanes and stories of oil deposits and cover-ups, it was getting much bigger than a humble island lad's world was used to and he felt incredibly responsible dragging AJ and subsequently Reg and Pearl into all this.

Thomas realised people were looking at him expectantly and confused he turned to AJ who chuckled. "Briefing?"

"Yes! A briefing," Thomas recovered quickly. "We're at Eagle's Nest here on the west side wall…"

AJ left it to Thomas to finish his briefing and checked her phone again: another text, this time from Jackson. Her heart skipped a beat and she smiled at her own reaction. As the past four weeks had worn on she'd progressively tried to disconnect herself from her feelings for him, preparing herself for the loss she convinced herself was coming. It felt enlivening to brush all that aside and be warmed by thoughts of him again.

She read the text: 'Boss is fired up over this, needs to see the proof. Apparently I'm much nicer to be around since I spoke to you yesterday, shipmates say thank you.'

AJ laughed like a schoolgirl and now it was her turn to have a boat full of people stare at her. Blushing, she set her phone aside and threw her hands in the air. "What? Why are you looking at me, the water's that way! Anybody want to go diving today?!"

She beamed as she and Thomas helped the customers into the clear blue water and Thomas slipped into his BCD and followed them in. Once everyone had safely descended AJ grabbed her phone and called Pearl.

"Hey Pearl, what's going on?"

Pearl sounded concerned. "The police spotted the wreck first thing this morning; Roy Whittaker got hold of Reg and had him go out there – I presume he's diving it now. The news channel already picked it up though – didn't take them long. Now they're trying to make it into a big story."

"Boy I'm surprised they found it so quickly but if north is anything like the west side the waters have really lain down fast after the storm, vis even looks really good." AJ thought for a second and then asked, "How's Sydney doing with the hard drive?"

Pearl spoke quietly, obviously keeping out of earshot of Sydney, "She's having no luck, I don't know a thing about computers but it seems this is harder than they thought to get into. She was swearing at it earlier but I haven't heard any profanity in a while so fingers crossed she's got something figured out. She's a smart one so I'm sure she will."

AJ agreed, "She will. Tell them Jackson says the Sea Sentry guys are interested, so that's hopeful."

Pearl promised to let her know of any updates and AJ switched to returning Jackson's text. She smiled all over again as she reread his note. She typed a reply, 'Pleased to assist in making you more friendly! Working hard on evidence this end, locked on a hard drive we're trying to access. Hopefully today.'

27

Reg took his time getting his gear ready to dive again, besides, Roy had them on hold until he knew more about the cases. In the detective's mind they might need a Hazmat team out here and Reg was fine letting him worry about that for now. George didn't hurry him along either; Reg figured he was thinking the next thing they would probably find would be a body, and he was fine delaying dealing with that. Even if the pilot had only been down there for twelve hours the ecosystem of the ocean would have started its work and human corpses picked apart by crabs, shrimps and fish were an ugly sight. A few more police boats had joined them and could be heard trolling the reef's edge and shoreline, otherwise the day was finally sunny, peaceful with the soft waves of the North Sound lapping against the hull, and George seemed content chatting with his old friend.

Detective Whittaker broke the tranquillity stepping over from the boat they were tied to.

"Okay gentlemen, we know a little more. The Cubans have suddenly noticed they have an aeroplane missing now we've told them we have it."

Roy rested a foot on the bench next to the divers and studied his notebook. "According to them a young man named Carlos Rojas took the plane from his place of work, along with some equipment and information, hence the shipping cases you discovered Reg. They seem rather keen on recovering those cases which they say contain nothing hazardous, just geology gear."

Reg offered, "We can bring those up but will need some lift bags. Still a bit rough out there to use a boat winch, don't you think, George?"

George nodded in agreement. "We could wait till tomorrow when it lays down some more and winch 'em, or we can float 'em if you need 'em out today."

Roy thought for a moment. "I'd say bring them up as soon as we can." He tapped his notepad on his knee and pondered a little more. "Strange coincidence, if you entertain such lines of thinking, which in the police force we tend not to… There's a boat, from the same Geological Studies Institute the plane was stolen from, here in George Town harbour. Showed up last night apparently. Cubans are saying we should hand over everything we recover to the man in charge, a Russian guy. Bit odd, never seen or heard from any Cuban exploration or geology groups before and in one night a boat shows up and a plane crashes all from the same place."

"What about the pilot, this Rojas guy? They want him too I presume?" George asked.

"Oh yes, they want him. Asked us to arrest him if we find him alive and they'll have him picked up immediately. Facing some serious charges back home."

Reg scoffed, "Doubt they'll have to worry about him, the way the doors were ripped off the plane and coming down in that storm I'm sure we'll find their man floating somewhere in the sound."

"Dare say you're right, Reg. Well, the Port Authority were going to hail the Cuban boat and track down this Russian fellow but no point waiting on him. What do you need to lift that gear out?"

"Have to run back to my lock-up," Reg answered. "Grab some lift bags, lines and some spare tanks. Take me an hour or two to round everything up but we should have them up this afternoon."

Reg figured that would stretch this project out a bit longer at least and hoped the girls were making progress on their end. He'd need to get clear of Roy and George before he could call and find out.

"I'll come and help," George volunteered.

Damn, Reg thought, but he couldn't come up with a good reason to have him stay. "Alright George, thanks."

This whole situation was accelerating at an alarming rate and Reg was getting more and more uncomfortable not being straight with Roy. It was one thing hiding the kid for a night or two but now with Russian government officials from Cuba showing up, that escalated this thing out of all of their leagues. He felt like he'd been dropped in the middle of a James Bond movie. All this based on the word of one Cuban kid. What if he was just a thief? Wouldn't be the first time a nice girl like Sydney had the wool pulled over her eyes by a smooth-talking fella. He thought about Carlos and the little time he'd spent with him so far; didn't seem like a bad bloke and he's not really the smooth talking type… more of an excitable, good-looking nerd… Reg stowed his gear for the ride back across the sound and decided to play along a little longer. What could he say to Roy at this point anyway? "Hey Roy, forgot to mention, I happened to be out here yesterday in the storm diving the plane and your Rojas boy is currently in my living room eating everything we put in front of him." No. Best roll with it for now.

28

Jeremiah and Wilma Bodden had lived in the same single-storey home in West Bay since they married twenty-six years ago. The house flooded during hurricane Ivan in 2004, had a new roof after Paloma thanks to an errant tree branch, but they'd happily raised their two children there and had no need or plans to move. The back yard was a good size, and seemed a little bigger once they had trimmed the rest of that tree down some and fit the whole family whenever they had an excuse for a gathering. Wilma enjoyed her mornings to herself. Jeremiah would leave early to get his fishing boat on the water at dawn, Thomas was gone before sunrise to prepare the dive boat for the day and of course Sydney was in Miami in school. She missed having her little girl in the house but was proud of what both her children were achieving.

She and Jeremiah had worked long and hard to pay off their house which was how they could manage a little help putting Sydney through university. Once the kids were both old enough for school, Wilma took a job cleaning rooms at one of the hotels on Seven Mile Beach, but Jeremiah finally talked her into quitting a few years back and now she ran a sewing business from the house. Curtains, clothes, covers, Wilma could sew just about anything and kept a steady stream of work running through her machine. Didn't pay quite as well as cleaning hotel rooms but she could get her day's work done by early afternoon when her husband returned and they enjoyed spending their afternoons together pottering about the house and running errands.

Wilma was folding up some tablecloths she had finished sewing for a local café when she heard a knock at the door. Wearing sweatpants and a faded old Mermaid Divers tee shirt she didn't feel very presentable for company but if it was her friend who mentioned she may stop by this morning it'd be fine. It wasn't her friend. When she opened the door a stern-looking man in his forties with square shoulders and close-cropped hair, wearing business slacks and a jacket with a button-down shirt, stood before her. He sported aviator sunglasses which he didn't remove. She'd never seen this man before.

"Can I help you?" Wilma asked in her thick Caymanian accent.

The man flashed some kind of ID card at her and replied in English with an accent she didn't recognise, "Are you Mrs. Wilma Bodden?"

"Well… yes, I am, how can I help you?" she repeated, more than a little suspicious.

He continued without changing expression, "May I come inside? I'd like to discuss your daughter."

Wilma didn't step aside and continued to hold the door half open, "What about my girl? Who did you say you were now? Why you asking about Sydney?"

"I represent the Cuban government Mrs. Bodden. We have reason to believe that your daughter may have got herself mixed up with an unsavoury gentleman. Ma'am, it would be better if we could step inside and discuss this."

The man leaned to the side a little to see past her but she couldn't tell exactly as his eyes were hidden behind the dark glasses. He was really making her nervous by his words, but more by his manner.

"My Sydney wouldn't be mixing with the wrong crowd mister,

besides she's in Florida, she's in the university there. My boy Thomas talked to her just the other night and he didn't say nothing about her being in Cuba. She been there a few times I know but that's to visit a nice boy she met at school."

"Is Thomas home?" the man persisted, "Maybe he knows where his sister is, kids don't always tell their parents everything."

"I'm telling you she's in Florida, you must have her mixed up with someone else," Wilma continued, getting flustered, "And no, Thomas is at work like he is every day, he'd just tell you the same thing I'm telling you, my boy don't lie to his mama."

The man softened his tone slightly. "I'm sure that's the case ma'am but perhaps he may remember something he forgot to mention. He has a regular job then, Thomas?"

"Of course he has a regular job," she retorted indignantly, "He's never missed a day of work for going on three years now since he started."

"And where is that ma'am? Where does he work?" he asked as politely as he could muster.

"On the water I guess, that's where dive boats go don't they?"

His politeness vanished. "A dive boat? Well which dive boat Mrs. Bodden, which dive boat does your son work on?"

"You really don't know nothing around here do you mister?" She glared back. "I ain't telling you where he works same as I ain't letting you in my house!"

The man finally removed his sunglasses and stared menacingly at Wilma. "We have reason to believe your daughter has been party to stealing government property and illegally transporting it out of the country. It would be better for you and much better for your daughter if you'd tell me where I can find her." He leaned in closer and rested a hand on the door so she had to strain to hold it. "You understand harbouring a fugitive is aiding and abetting and is a federal crime? I assume you don't want me inside as I may find your daughter is here?"

Wilma was terrified and confused by this brash stranger making all these wild claims about her baby girl, but beyond that she was getting mad.

"Listen here fella, I don't know who you are or what this nonsense is you're talking about, but my girl is in Florida at school. There ain't nobody but me in this house but I'll be damned if I'll let you in without a policeman I know saying you're supposed to be knocking on my door! Hear me?"

She shoved the door but he effortlessly resisted and glared at her for what felt like forever. Finally he eased back, glancing down at her shirt before she fell forward slamming the door closed.

Learning all he thought he could, Mikhail stepped away and considered his next move.

29

———————

AJ's thoughts had left Carlos and the oil fields behind as she chatted with her customers on their surface interval between dives. They'd moved the boat further south and closer to shore for the second dive, which would be shallower. Her clientele tended to be return customers or referrals from her regulars and she enjoyed building relationships over time with her divers as they visited the island time and again. Word of mouth was her best marketing and she and Reg worked together on handling each other's overflow to make sure they never turned their folks away. AJ kept the RIB on the north side throughout the summer, running from the yacht club and the Newton west from Reg's dock in West Bay. On days she had both boats running she and Thomas would split and she'd borrow a couple of divemasters from Reg to double up. Often she or Thomas would help Reg's crew out in afternoons or night dives when Mermaid's wasn't going out. After a few years of running they had a pretty good system that worked for everyone.

Thomas was on the fly bridge chatting with a young couple from Finland. They were marvelling at the starkly different climate from their home country where often diving meant cutting holes in ice. Thomas checked his dive watch and leaned down from the railing. "Been up nearly an hour if you want to get ready for the second dive, folks."

That triggered a flurry of activity as the divers pulled their wetsuits back up and turned their tanks on in preparation. After making sure the group was about ready, AJ gave them a quick briefing.

"We're tied on La Mesa for the second dive; it's a beautiful flat topped coral head which is how it earned its name 'The Table' in Spanish. The really cool part about this site is the overhang that forms a channel around part of the coral head. We'll be able to swim through that channel and it's teeming with juvenile fish and critters. We'll approach carefully and quietly as there's sometimes a nurse shark hanging out or very often a cleaning station in action. You'll see a larger fish like a grouper with mouth wide open hanging there. If you look carefully you'll see tiny wrasses, gobies and shrimps inside the grouper's mouth and gills, giving him a good cleaning. Free dentist trip for the grouper and free meal for the cleaners. Top of the coral head is around thirty-five feet and the base around it is maximum fifty so we'll get a nice long dive of an hour at that depth. As usual, keep an eye on your air and let me know if you're getting low. To finish the dive we'll do a three-minute safety stop at fifteen feet before we surface. Any questions?"

With no hands in the air, just smiling, eager faces, AJ continued, "Pool's open, start getting in and I'll meet you at the bottom by the mooring."

If AJ had any lingering thoughts and tensions from the mayhem topside over the past few days it evaporated entirely as she glided down through her undersea world. Everyone appeared to be excited about the storm passing, not just the divers. The fish hurried about the coral head refamiliarising themselves with their territories after hiding out from the rough seas. A large school of young horse-eyed jacks circled mid-water over the reef, calmly making laps en masse.

AJ gathered her group and started a slow, easy lap around the large coral head. Picking up a hawksbill turtle off to her right she pointed him out to the group and they waited and watched while he pulled himself their way with his prehistoric-looking front flippers. The lens effect underwater made him seem five feet long as he approached and nearing he appeared to shrink rather than grow, closer to his actual size of maybe two feet. Ignoring the divers, who held no interest for him, he continued over the coral head and out of sight on the other side. AJ returned to the tour and finding the entrance to the channel, she carefully floated down below the overhang and leisurely finned her way forward. Sure enough, as she'd hoped, there was a big fat grouper with his mouth gaping open, getting a good cleaning from his little friends. The grouper eyed AJ suspiciously but she halted right away and stealthily ushered the diver behind her to come alongside and take a look. Carefully rotating the group through got them all a glimpse into the daily life of the reef before the grouper decided he was clean enough and with a quick flare of his gills the little cleaners scattered and the big fellow moved on about his day.

No luck with a nurse shark but plenty of other sights made the hour pass swiftly. Reluctantly they headed up and, after performing their safety stop, climbed back aboard the boat. AJ and Thomas hustled around helping people get out of their gear and stowing tanks away, but AJ could tell right away Thomas was not his usual chipper self. When they ended up next to each other hauling up the ladder she whispered, "What's up? You seem agitated."

Thomas nodded his head towards George Town, about a mile to their south. "I'll show you through the binoculars up top."

Anxiously curious, AJ finished getting everyone squared away before dashing up to the fly bridge, where Thomas handed her the glasses. "Look just outside the port, not as far out as the cruise ships."

AJ trained the binoculars on the crane in the port and then tracked them across the water until a large trawler came into view. Her first thought was how strange to have a trawler here at all, there was restricted fishing all around Cayman and nothing a trawler would catch in the deep waters. Then she noticed the flag flapping lazily in the breeze.

"Holy shit! That's under the Cuban flag." She dropped the glasses down and looked at Thomas, stunned. "Carlos wasn't kidding about these guys."

30

Mikhail and Anatoly sat in their rented mid-size with the windows up and the air conditioning cranking. They'd both been in Cuba for more than a year but still couldn't get used to the heat and humidity of the tropics. They were positioned in the diminutive car park by West Bay dock facing Reg's dock next door. They'd ditched the jackets but were still cooking in their slacks and button-down shirts as they sipped on jumbo-sized sodas they'd picked up from the petrol station. Such decadent extravagances were hard to come by in Russia or Cuba. They'd been waiting for about forty-five minutes and so far one of Pearl Divers boats had returned to Reg's dock and a couple of other outfits were unloading customers and tanks on the main West Bay dock.

Anatoly jumped when someone knocked on his passenger window. Smiling at them was a young divemaster in shorts and a tee shirt. Anatoly powered down his window and the guy leaned in and talked with an Australian accent, "Hey fellas, would you mind moving your car so we can pull our truck in to load these tanks?"

Anatoly glanced over at Mikhail who turned his head slowly towards the guy until he got a reflection of himself in the Russian's aviator sunglasses. "This is a public dock, yes?"

"Yeah mate, but we go in and out of here every day, if you could just move over there it'd be a big help." The Aussie pointed to the other side of the car park.

"So this is the public car park that goes with the public dock, yes?" Mikhail's voice was as monotone as usual.

"Well yeah, but mate, just asking a favour here to help us out, gotta bunch of tanks to move." Normally the tourists are happy to oblige so the guy couldn't understand why these two were being so difficult.

Mikhail held the button and the window started back up, sending the kid back in surprise. "Not my problem," Mikhail replied and turned back to concentrate on the other dock.

"Jeez, what a dick," could be faintly heard from outside as the window closed and the young man left to figure out another place to put his truck.

Mikhail's mobile rang and he hit receive on the car's screen in the centre console to play the call through the Bluetooth system, answering in Russian, "Hello?"

The voice on the other end was the man he spoke to earlier, not sounding any happier, "The Cayman police are retrieving the cargo from the plane this afternoon; we have told them you are acting as a representative for the Republic of Cuba. You should go to the crash site now. Your contact will be a policeman, Detective Whittaker. I will text you his mobile number when we hang up."

"Okay," Mikhail replied flatly.

"The Caymanians suspect the pilot is dead, they are searching for the body which they have yet to find."

Mikhail was tiring of the conversation. "We are proceeding on the presumption the pilot survived."

Anatoly nudged Mikhail and pointed across the water as a boat approached looking similar to the first one that pulled up to Reg's dock. Except this one had 'Mermaid Divers' on the side.

"I don't need to tell you how important it is to verify the hard drive and maps are part of the recovered cargo," the man on the phone continued sternly.

"Then why are you?" Mikhail retorted, becoming more irritated.

"Why am I what?" the official asked, confused. Anatoly stifled a laugh.

"I will go there now." Mikhail hit end on the screen. "Idiot," he muttered under his breath.

AJ brought the Newton alongside the dock and Thomas hopped off the boat and tied into the cleats. The two Russians watched every move.

"The girl with the tattoos and purple in her hair is the Bailey girl, she runs the boat. The dark-skinned guy tying up the boat must be Thomas Bodden. Follow him – if his sister's alive he may take us to her," Mikhail directed Anatoly, who looked around confused.

"Are you taking the car?" Anatoly asked.

"Of course," Mikhail replied.

Anatoly shifted uncomfortably in his seat, "Sir, how do I follow him without a car?"

Mikhail turned and stared at Anatoly. "I chose you over the other moron because you appeared to be more intelligent. You're a trained Russian agent, figure it out. Without trying, I see ten cars and six bicycles around me, now get out."

Anatoly blinked a few times while he processed this, before realising he should be moving and scrambled out of the car.

"Anatoly," Mikhail spoke before the agent closed the door, "be inconspicuous."

With that he backed out of the parking spot and drove off.

Anatoly stood in the middle of the car park. Be inconspicuous, he thought, standing here in slacks and a shirt on a stinking hot day by the beach about to steal a vehicle of some sort to chase this local kid all over town. At best he was about to look like a partnerless Mormon roaming the island streets for new converts. He looked around. The Australian guy was stacking dive tanks in the back of the truck and paused to look over at Anatoly standing alone. Anatoly smiled, figuring he needed to fit in. The Australian flipped him the bird and carried on stacking tanks.

"Bloody great," Anatoly mumbled.

31

Reg and George had two large bags of gear they'd retrieved from the storage locker at Reg's dock in West Bay. They lugged them down the pier at the yacht club and loaded them on the police boat, readying to head back to the wreck site. According to the police officer driving the boat, Roy had told him they had another passenger coming. Reg looked up and saw a tall, athletic man in slacks and nice white shirt approaching. He looked and carried himself like a military man, short cropped hair, neatly shaved, polished shoes and a confident stride without appearing hurried. He wore aviator sunglasses and remained expressionless, even when he introduced himself.

"Mikhail Gurov, I represent the Republic of Cuba, I believe you are expecting me?"

The policeman acknowledged and waved him aboard. Reg extended a hand. "Reg, and George here, we're the divers." Reg smiled but eyed the man carefully, "That accent nor that name sound very Cuban."

"Russian," was all Mikhail offered as they found a seat and the policeman moved the boat off the dock.

"Are you an accident investigator?" Reg persisted, hoping to get something from this guy.

"No." Mikhail retorted, uninterested in talking with a police diver. Thinking about it some more, he decided maybe this diver could have some information on the plane, after all he'd apparently dived the site that morning.

"You have dived the plane wreck already today?"

Reg looked at him squarely. "Yes."

George chuckled as Reg moved seats away from the Russian and the boat picked up speed, leaving the no-wake zone of the marina. Mikhail watched the Englishman walk away and sit next to his fellow diver. He may have grinned slightly, but it was hard to tell with Mikhail.

32

———

Anatoly was sweating profusely as he pedalled hard to keep Thomas in view up ahead. The bike he'd grabbed was a cheap mountain bike and he hadn't had time to adjust the seat which was clearly set for a much shorter person than the Russian's large frame. It did have an Australian flag sticker on it and another claiming 'Aussie Rules' so he was content he'd stolen the right bike. They'd started up Town Hall Road, then turned left on the ominously named Hell Road and since then they'd made several turns on small streets that if they'd had signs he missed them. He was becoming convinced he'd never find his way out of this warren and his agent training sparked alarms ringing that he was being led on a goose chase. But Thomas had never even glanced behind him and now his beach cruiser turned right into the driveway of a nice-looking bungalow with small trees and shrubs surrounding it. Anatoly stopped a hundred yards short and pulled over to the side.

He shoved the bike between some bushes and carefully walked along the edge of the road under a scattering of Pimento and Iron-wood trees. The bungalow was the only home on this part of the narrow street so Anatoly felt concealed staying close to the trees and bushes lining the road. He reached the corner of the front garden and could see a Jeep in the driveway and Thomas's beach cruiser leaned against the wall just inside the open door of the garage. The Jeep had decals on the doors and a spare tyre cover with Pearl Divers logos on them. He paused a moment to check for sounds and movement but picked up nothing, so moved closer to the building, staying hidden by the flora. He was about to move closer to the house when he heard a vehicle approaching on the road. Anatoly crouched down a little lower and waited for it to pass. It didn't pass. The van slowed to a stop right in front of the house and peeking around the bush he saw the tattooed girl from the boat hop out and walk towards the house. The front door opened and Thomas came out to meet her; now Anatoly had two people not more than twenty feet in front of him with only the shrub between them.

The blonde girl and Thomas greeted each other and she handed him a mobile phone.

"Thanks, sorry for leaving it, appreciate you bringing it over," he heard Thomas say.

The girl began her reply, "No worries, how's Sy..." when something moved under the bush and startled Anatoly, rustling the shrub loud enough for the conversation to stop. Anatoly stumbled backwards, dropping to his backside on the ground as a large blue iguana scuttled out from under the bush, high-stepping towards refuge in the next tree. AJ and Thomas turned to look and saw the iguana fleeing. Anatoly held his breath. He couldn't see the two of them and prayed they couldn't see him.

"Alright, I gotta go fill tanks, I'll see you later." The girl's voice started to fade as she must have been walking back towards her van. "Let me know any updates, okay?"

"Will do. If not I'll see you at the Fox and Hare tonight," came Thomas's reply, followed by the sound of the front door closing.

The van drove off and Anatoly finally breathed again. He got to his knees and surveyed the front of the house. Realising he needed to get closer to see inside, he scrambled to the next shrub and from that to the corner of the bungalow itself. Between him and the front door was a wide window but to get to it would leave him exposed in the front yard. He looked down the side of the home where there were two windows. That part of the house was in shadow and there were shrubs in a flower bed all down the side. He chose the shade and edged along to the first window where he fought the prickly shrub to get a peek inside.

The window lit a living room with a couple of sofas and an open-plan layout to a dining room and the kitchen. Leaning against an island in the kitchen was a slender, dark-skinned girl in her early twenties. He brought up a photograph on his phone and compared it to the girl he could see across the room. Trained to make identifications he ran through a series of checks, looking at individual features rather than the overall appearance. Hairline more than hairstyle, width apart of the eyes, shape of the nose, jawline. Anatoly was confident he'd found Sydney Bodden.

Another woman stepped into view. She was good looking, curvy figured, late forties or early fifties, he estimated. Probably quite the stunner in her earlier years, the younger man thought. Pearl would be flattered by Anatoly's assessment, but oblivious to the Russian's surveillance she continued making lunch. The two women appeared to be in conversation but the hurricane-resistant windows blocked all sound efficiently. He noticed Sydney turn and address someone out of his sight, which he assumed must be Thomas. Anatoly looked down at his phone and began typing a text message.

"Come and grab a sandwich you two," Pearl called across the room and Carlos didn't hesitate. Thomas followed Carlos to the kitchen, away from the computer, and the cable leading down to the hard drive on the floor. Thomas glanced out the front window as he crossed the living room, noting the usual afternoon scattered clouds were staying away today. Carlos smiled broadly at Pearl, thanked her while he grabbed two sandwiches and wandered back over to the computer.

. . .

Anatoly hit send on his phone and peeked back through the window. There was Thomas. He'd joined the two women in the kitchen. Anatoly backed away and scurried through the edge of the garden and back down the road to retrieve the stolen bicycle. Bringing up maps on his phone he dropped a pin to find this location again and studied how to extricate himself from West Bay and return to their hotel. Finally he had something that would make Gurov happy. He'd found the Bodden girl. Now maybe they could use her to locate Rojas and the computer files.

33

———————

The police boat pulled up alongside its sister on the far side of the North Sound short of the reef, and again they were lashed together. Mikhail looked at his phone and read a text that appeared.

'Found the girl. House belongs to Pearl Divers owner I believe, have coordinates. No sign of Rojas.'

Mikhail looked at the logos on the bags now being opened on the deck of the boat and the tee shirt Reg was wearing. They all had Pearl Divers logos. He wished he'd engaged in conversation with the man now, he could have learnt something. It also registered with a degree of concern that the guy diving the wreck well may be hiding the fugitive they're looking for. If his theory was correct and Sydney Bodden had been aboard this plane and survived just fine, then Carlos Rojas must be alive too.

"You must be Gurov?"

Mikhail looked up and a light, brown-skinned Caymanian man was extending a hand in his direction.

Shaking Roy's hand, Mikhail replied, "I am Gurov – Detective Whittaker, I assume?"

"Yes sir," Roy responded, "good to meet you."

Roy scratched his temple and carried on in a friendly tone, "So being a simple policeman on a tiny island I guess I'm a bit confused…"

Mikhail had been studying Reg now that he knew who he was, but he turned his attention back to Roy.

"How is it that a Russian officer represents the Cuban authorities?" Roy finished and smiled, putting on a credible perplexed look.

"Our governments have many common interests, so we assist in different ways, this is an example," Mikhail offered politely.

"I see, sounds like a friendly arrangement, probably good for everyone," Roy continued with the dumb local routine, Reg catching every word.

"But you're with a geological study group are you not? So you're not actually with any law enforcement agency, correct? You study rocks and the like?"

Mikhail straightened a little taller and his cheeks flinched ever so slightly, annoyed at the interrogation. "I'm actually a marine biologist but I assure you I have the authority to represent the Republic of Cuba, Mr. Whittaker."

Roy smiled again. "I have no doubt sir, that's what I was told. I'm just trying to get an understanding of how things work in other places, you know, broaden my awareness of foreign cultures."

Mikhail nodded, relieved this local paper pusher was done with his questions and moved towards Reg, hoping to start over with him. But Roy wasn't quite finished.

"Hell of a coincidence you guys rolling in here last night in your boat, probably less than twenty-four hours after this plane here crashed into our island, huh? Strange time to be on the water, or especially in the air, when a storm is going on like that."

Mikhail turned back and sighed impatiently. "We must presume the thief stole the plane once he knew we'd left port for our voyage here."

Roy kept digging. "Why would a man stealing an aeroplane fly it to the location he knew the company he stole it from was heading?"

Mikhail turned away with clenched teeth. "When we drag his body from your bay here maybe we can ask him. Until then how about your men get on with their job of returning our cargo to us?"

Reg had his wetsuit pulled up around his waist and his shirt off. At sixty-four he was still in great shape and he stood the same height as the Russian. Stepping in front of Gurov with his broad chest puffed out a little he spoke in a calm but firm voice, "If you'd like to step to the other boat right now you're the only thing in the way of us doing our job."

Mikhail fumed inside but simply stared through his aviators eye to eye with Reg. This wasn't the time. Deciding to let it go for now, Mikhail walked around Reg and his gear and stepped over to the other boat. He caught Roy giving Reg a wink.

The Russian was frustrated simply due to the time restraints he was under, but he actually appreciated both men. The policeman was doing his job and his suspicions were accurate, albeit inconvenient. Reg, he could tell, was a military man like himself and his first impression was of someone quite capable physically and mentally. Mikhail enjoyed a good adversary and these two would keep him on his toes he was sure. He watched them carefully from the other boat.

The swells had lain down a step further and visibility had improved again as the two men made their second dive of the day on the seaplane wreck. The surge was easing so the fuselage was no longer being rocked and bashed against the coral head. The cases were unwieldy but actually quite buoyant as they were sealed full of air. The professional waterproof containers were holding up well and as Reg suspected they didn't really need lift bags to float them as they hadn't flooded. He dragged the first one out across the folded seat through the door opening and George helped him rest it on the side of the plane which was facing the surface. George tied the deflated lift bag around the handle then Reg took the regulator from his mouth and, using the purge valve, blew air inside the lift bag. The bag filled out like a bright yellow balloon and rose up immediately, tugging on the handle of the case. From thirty feet down it only took a few seconds for it to pop to the surface and the men heard the swooshing of a prop in the water and the drone of an outboard engine as the police boat promptly swept in and retrieved the case.

The two divers repeated the process for the other three cases, which were all a similar size, and had fortunately remained watertight. With the interior now cleared Reg was able to wriggle inside and cram himself into the back of the cabin to search for anything else pertinent or useful. He was barely able to turn around in the restricted space that tapered even tighter towards the tail. He thought again about flying this small plane through the violent storm and then being trapped inside it as it went down in the pitch-black night. Reg had been in some terrifying situations as a navy and then commercial diver, crazy depths, zero visibility, deep inside wrecks, aggressive creatures, you name it, but imagining the two kids' perilous trip still gave him the willies. Finding nothing of consequence, Reg was happy to extricate himself from the plane so he and George could surface.

Motoring back through the cut to the North Sound, Reg could see at least five or six boats making search patterns. Several were police craft but they only had a handful of marine units so they'd called in some reserve boats, owned by people like Reg who helped when needed. Of course a pang of guilt shot through Reg as he realised again how he wasn't actually helping but deliberately stalling the operation. With George along the whole time, he still hadn't spoken to AJ or Pearl but he knew they'd text or call if anything major happened.

They tied up once again and as soon as he could step aboard the Russian sprang over and beelined for the cases.

"Hold up a minute there fella!" Roy shouted. "Those are evidence and need to be processed appropriately."

The officer from the CIAA stood next to Roy nodding knowingly.

Mikhail wheeled around. "These belong to the Republic of Cuba and contain important information, I need to check them immediately."

Roy stood firm. "What you think you need and what we're going to do here may not be aligned Mr. Gurov." For reinforcement both the police boat captains made their presence felt and Mikhail noticed they were both armed, which they hadn't been earlier.

Roy continued, "Once we've logged the evidence in, photographed it and CIAA have cleared us, we'll hand them over. Should be by sometime in the morning I'd say." Roy stood with his hands on his hips staring at the Russian with a polite smile.

Mikhail weighed his options, which didn't take long. He was in no position to do much. He had no idea how many cases Carlos took or exactly what was in them. He was sure at least some of these had been in the plane before it was stolen but now they could contain the charts and hard drive. Did they crash the plane or abandon it? He had to see inside the cases to know if they contained the evidence or not.

"As you wish, Mr. Whittaker." Mikhail relented and turned to Reg, "This was everything in the plane, you searched completely?"

Reg grinned and replied offhandedly, "Sure."

That hardly felt like reassurance but it did reinforce Mikhail's theory Reg was part of whatever help Rojas was getting on the island; he was certainly not helping expedite the return of the evidence. Mikhail wanted to stare Reg down but the Englishman went about sorting his gear and ignored him so he was forced to address Roy again. "Perhaps you'd be so kind as to return me to the dock then as I can accomplish nothing here."

"Be happy to," Roy replied cheerfully, "No problem at all."

34

Pearl beetled about the house getting her gear ready for her gig later in the evening. She liked to be organised and have everything ready as Reg had a habit of being late, causing them to be in a panic to make it to the pub and be ready for her first set at seven. As much as he adored hearing her play he was always helping somebody with something that couldn't wait and he'd wind up in a rush. Pearl was more the get ready early and relax type. She was half expecting things to run late with Roy on the North Sound as they were looking for a body after all, not the kind of thing you knocked off early and call it a night for, so she assumed they'd keep searching until dark. That was around seven o'clock this time of year hence the expectation that she'd be getting herself over to the Fox and Hare. Half six she decided, if he's not home by then I'm leaving and he can meet me there. As she finished that thought a piercing squeal came from the living room. Pearl rushed in to find Sydney and Carlos huddled around the computer babbling excitedly.

"What's going on?" Pearl asked.

Sydney leapt up from the chair and threw her arms in the air. "I'm in, I cracked it!"

She scurried over to Pearl and gave her a big hug. "The trick was hacking in to become administrator, that was the hard part; once I got that it was simple to reset all the security protocols and I was in!"

"Sweetie, I've no idea what you're saying but I knew you could do it." Pearl gave her a big squeeze and her ample bosom just about pushed all the air out of Sydney's lungs. "So let's see what you've been telling us about on these files." Pearl released her bear hug and they joined Carlos.

"Here are the maps and charts they are going to show the world; they have it in this PowerPoint presentation," Carlos explained eagerly, bringing a map of the south-east part of Cuba up on screen. "See, it shows the oil deposits here, the drilling platforms they will place here," he pointed to an area along an archipelago labelled Jardines de la Reina. "And here in orange are the reef areas impacted by the construction of the platforms, the running of the pipelines and the boat traffic supporting all this. See how it's small areas of orange surrounding the platforms and a narrow strip where the pipeline cuts through the islands towards the mainland. Now, I'll open the map they don't want anyone to see."

Carlos selected a different file and a new map of the same area opened with vastly different colouring. The orange sections were ten times the size and he pointed to a wide strip that didn't appear on the first map running along the island chain. "This is the pipeline that runs between all the platforms right on top of the reef. Why?"

He turned and looked at the girls, his eyes alive with anger. "Because it's cheaper, that's why! They run the pipes in the shallows here or they have to run them in open ocean much deeper which costs more money so they choose to destroy the reef!"

Sydney rested a soothing hand on her boyfriend's shoulder. "This is what the world needs to see."

"Also," Carlos carried on, "there are emails I have copies of…" He paused while he clicked until he opened what he was looking for. "Here…" An email opened, written in Spanish, and Carlos looked at Pearl before he realised she probably didn't read Spanish. "Sorry, I'll tell you what it says."

Pearl surprised him. "I can read it, it's from a Russian fella that's saying see the attached spreadsheet, it shows the cost breakdowns between options…" She points to a word she's not sure about.

"It means 'strongly recommend', which is this guy's way of saying do it the way I say or Russia won't pay for it," Carlos translated for her.

The door from the garage into the kitchen opened and AJ's voice echoed through the house, "It's just me."

Pearl called back, "Good timing. Sydney did it, we're looking at the files now."

AJ joined them all huddled around Reg's little fifteen-inch monitor. "Nice going Sydney! Where's your brother?"

"He went home to clean up," Sydney replied.

"Well, let's see what you have," AJ asked keenly.

Carlos went back over the maps and email, explaining everything they showed to AJ while Pearl sent Reg a text to let him know they'd made progress.

"Reg says they're continuing the body search along the reef," Pearl read from her phone. They all looked at Carlos.

"Pretty weird, there's probably a hundred people looking for your dead body right now!" AJ said with an amused smile.

Carlos didn't smile. "And a Russian that wants to make sure I end up that way."

Pearl ruffled his hair, "Don't worry, we won't let anything happen to you."

AJ remembered, "We saw your trawler slash research boat today, they're moored off the harbour, does that mean your Russian guy is here?"

"He's here," Pearl added. "I told Carlos earlier Reg had the pleasure of spending some time with him today, he could only text but he said he's all over getting the cases from the plane."

AJ continued, "We have the evidence now, why don't we contact Whittaker and tell him everything? No reason to keep hiding from the authorities, he's not just going to hand you over..."

Carlos cut AJ off, "No way, not yet! I can't talk to the press from a jail cell, we have to see this through. Can you contact your boyfriend?"

AJ shook her head, more at the not telling Whittaker part than the boyfriend comment. Since their call she was feeling more like she did have her boyfriend back and was still annoyed at herself for doubting, especially as apparently he hadn't been.

"Yes, yes I can try and reach him." AJ dialled a number in the Internet video chat app on her mobile and they waited while it took forever to make a connection and start ringing.

After some dinging and fuzziness Jackson's face finally appeared on the screen and his voice was clear, "Hey there beautiful," he said in his mellow tone with a big smile.

Instantly blushing, AJ quickly halted him. "Gotcha on speaker phone with a room full of people so keep it PG, okay!"

Jackson laughed and Sydney tipped the phone around so she could see him. "Oooh, he's dishy! Hi Jackson!"

"Alright, alright, enough playing about." AJ pulled the phone, back turning even redder. "Jackson, this is Sydney, Carlos, and Pearl who you met when you were here." She rotated the screen around while everyone said hello.

"So AJ told me about your guy's ordeal, that sounds crazy, glad you made it through okay, not many people can say they survived a plane crash," Jackson began.

"Technically we didn't crash," Carlos quickly corrected, "I landed the plane, then we crashed. But no matter, let me show you what we have."

AJ held the phone's camera facing the computer screen and Carlos went through it all again with Jackson asking a few questions along the way. At the end, Jackson took a moment to think before asking, "Who actually owns these files? Meaning, who legally owns that hard drive containing them and I'm sure the maps all have some kind of disclaimer and legalese on them? Property of or something?"

Carlos despondently admitted, "Sure, of course, it all belongs to the Republic of Cuba, but we have to tell the world about this, show the people – surely if enough people see this we can stop it?"

"Hopefully," Jackson responded, "but we have to be careful how we handle this. You've broken the law and are illegally in possession of all this, we can't take these files from you or we'll be accessories and if we get caught up in a legality issue then nothing will happen until that's resolved, and by resolved I'm guessing Cuba would get their property back."

Carlos was desperate. "So there's nothing you can do?"

"I didn't say that, but you can't send me those files. I need you to take a screenshot of the key maps and that one email and send me those. AJ has my personal email. I'll show the screenshots to my folks here and we'll see what we can do, okay?"

Carlos was clearly hoping for something more. "Sure, we'll send you the pictures right away. Please understand, it doesn't matter what happens to me, if I go to prison then so be it, but the world has to know why if we have a chance of saving Jardines de la Reina. Jackson, you have to see these reefs, they are the most beautiful sight in the world, so much life, so healthy, when the world is losing coral so quickly. I don't think most people know how the reefs influence life in the oceans and are a big part of filtering the air we breathe; saving the coral plays a big part in saving our planet."

"Believe me, I hear you Carlos and agree completely, but if we get stopped by a court before we can ever tell people then all your efforts will be wasted. Let me get with my bosses here and see what we can do, okay? What I hope is that we can facilitate some kind of press release or conference for you to present what you have. But I think it's important for you to know we can't shelter you from the law – you stole a plane and government data, at some point that will be addressed and if we put on a press conference at a physical location you'll likely be arrested."

Carlos nodded sternly. "I understand. As long as I have told this story then what will be will be, but please, just give me the chance to show this to the world."

35

The two Cubans sat in the wheelhouse of the anchored trawler and chuckled at the Russian agent sunning himself on the forward deck. Clearly he hadn't packed shorts so he was down to his underwear and the exposed parts of his milky white body were turning a crispy red in short order.

Julio dragged on a cigarette and smoke puffed from his nostrils in waves as he continued to snicker to himself. His skin, like Silvio's, was deeply tanned from their Hispanic heritage and a life outdoors on the water. They spent their efforts sheltering and covering up from the sun rather than exposing themselves to it. The man frying himself to a painful few days ahead was nothing but comical to them.

"This will be fun watching that idiot tomorrow when it hurts to move," Julio managed between laughs.

"Probably take it out on us is what he'll do. They're all a big enough pain in the arse as it is. When he can't sit down to take a shit 'cos his arse is burnt he'll be mean as hell." Silvio offered and the two laughed again.

"Damn Russians, bad enough we have to deal with our own

authorities, let alone these bastards," Julio mumbled after a few minutes.

Silvio shook his head. "True, but at least Russia puts some money into our economy, we'll take all the help they want to give. They want some oil and they're willing to pay, I say we give them oil."

"Carlos must be crazy, stealing that plane and everything, don't you think?" Julio asked, looking over at the older man.

"I think his carcass is at the bottom of the sea, that's what this crazy shit did for him. Probably better off if he is dead, I don't want to think what they'll do to him if he's still alive," Silvio snapped back.

"You think he could have survived crashing the plane?" Julio took another long drag on his cigarette.

"If he did I guarantee the Russian will find him. He's not one I would mess with, he's mean, but more than that he's really smart. I wouldn't get on the wrong side of him." Silvio crossed himself for emphasis. "Don't get me wrong," Silvio continued, "I like Carlos, he's a good kid and I hope somehow he's okay but if they find him he'll wish he died in that plane. And then his family…" Silvio looked over at Julio with dread. "They'll go after his family too, even when they know nothing of what he's done."

Julio nodded in agreement. "Scary shit." He thought a moment and took another long drag and exhaled slowly. "Well, you know me, I like Carlos and I like that reef and the fishes and all that, but what I like more is a simple, easy life, with no problems. Cold beer and a few nice girls, that's good enough for me."

Silvio finished the conversation, "Anyway, there ain't nothing we can do for our boy Carlos, he's either dead or as good as dead."

36

Jackson sat at a table next to the captain of the Sword of the Sentry with all eyes on a monitor on the wall in front of them. The man on the screen was in his sixties with white hair and goatee. He spoke energetically in a bold and confident tone.

"It's all well and good this kid's got some files but if we touch them we're in deep shit."

Jackson nodded and replied in his easy, unflustered voice, "I explained that, which is why we're looking at screenshots only. I tell you, this guy's all in, all we have to do is set up a time and place and have the right ears listening, he'll deliver the message and show the world the files. He told me if that means he gets jailed in Cuba afterwards, then he'll accept that."

The captain spoke, "The evidence he has, if it's correct, is pretty damning. Clearly they'll destroy a good part of that whole reef structure, we're talking the majority of a 150-kilometre reef system will be affected, a lot of it lost for good."

"How sure are we that the info is legit?" came back the man on the screen.

Jackson was careful and precise in his reply. "We know the kid worked for the geology group which is a shell for oil exploration over there. Everything he showed me had government stamps and warnings on it. We know the Cubans are hopping mad and desperate to find him, along with the Russians. I have personally spoken with him and have seen him looking through a hard drive full of these files. The whole project is Russian backed and funded. The guy they've sent after him is Russian. They certainly appear very concerned about what he can reveal."

"But can we trust him? He's not just looking for his fifteen minutes, or seeking asylum and making a show of it is he?" The man was still cautious.

Jackson thought for a moment, "I've only spoken to him the one time, just a while ago, but he doesn't strike me as a 'limelighter'. The people that are helping him on Cayman, I know them a little better and I don't believe they'd get involved in a sham, they're as straight as they come and strong environmental advocates. I'd also add the clock is ticking pretty fast on this. Once the Russians find him he'll disappear and we'll never hear from him again."

"How long from Limon to Cayman?" The white-haired man asked.

"Thirty hours give or take, a little under if we push it," the captain replied.

The man on the screen contemplated a moment. "Alright, next stop was Florida anyway, guess you'll take a detour. Get there as soon as you can, I'll get the press conference organised from here. I'll look at flying down tomorrow. We'll shoot for the day after tomorrow, early morning so we capture America and Europe. To be clear, we'll facilitate this and stand by him but the boy is on his own to present; we can't even set up the computer for him, understand?"

Both men nodded.

"And Jackson?"

He looked up at the man on the screen. "Sir?"

"Make sure your friends keep that kid and his evidence safe until we get there. I've dived Gardens of the Queen, it's spectacular, the planet can't afford to lose this reef."

37

AJ glanced at her watch as she hopped in her van outside Reg's house. Five o'clock. She had an hour and a half before she needed to leave for the pub and help Pearl set up. Plenty of time to clean up, she thought, maybe I can actually catch up on customer emails and bookings. She swung the van around in the narrow lane and sped off towards her apartment. She didn't notice the mid-sized rental car backed into a dirt access road a hundred yards from the house.

Mikhail and Anatoly watched AJ's van zip by and disappear around the corner. By their count this left the woman they presumed was Reg's wife and Sydney in the house. They'd watched Sydney's brother leave earlier, now the girl from the dive boat. Mikhail figured Reg was still out on the North Sound with the police. If there were other players in the equation they hadn't come across them yet. Then, of course, there was Carlos. As the search continued with no sign of a body and the fact that Sydney seemed to be staying here rather than her own parents' home suggested to Mikhail that Rojas was here too. He was sure Sydney had flown with Carlos so if she was unscathed then surely he was too. Time to find out.

Anatoly led his boss to the window at the side of the bungalow through which he'd seen Sydney. Anatoly warned him to watch for lizards. They carefully squeezed around the prickly bushes and peered through the same window. Across the living room sitting in an armchair making notes in a journal was Carlos Rojas. Apart from scratches on his cheek and legs, he appeared in perfect health. It dawned on Mikhail that Reg Moore was doing a pretty good job leading the Cayman police and the Cuban government around in circles looking for a ghost on the North Sound. Here, in the man's own living room, sat the fugitive. Why on earth would he be harbouring and covering up for an international criminal? Helping out the local girl he understood but why would he, and the Bailey girl, get involved so deeply? Ultimately he didn't care why but as a man that insisted on being in control of himself and all around him it bothered him to not know the answers.

They waited a few minutes to see who else was in the house; they could see Rojas was talking to someone although they couldn't hear him. Finally Sydney came into view and sat on the arm of the chair, running her fingers through Carlos's hair. Pearl walked over to the kitchen which completed the head count.

"I don't think the door from the garage is locked, we can enter through there," Anatoly whispered.

"No," Mikhail halted him. "We are not in a position to take them."

Anatoly pulled a handgun from under his shirt and showed Mikhail. "Sure we are."

"You fool, I told you no guns." Mikhail broke his deadpan demeanour for the first time, "We don't need a gun to take two women and a boy."

Anatoly tucked the gun away quickly. "Sorry sir, I am trained to always have my sidearm, didn't feel right to leave it behind."

"We are not in a position to take them because we don't know for sure where the hard drive is." Mikhail recovered his calm, condescending tone. "If it's in the cases and we grab them we have three hostages we have to deal with until tomorrow. Someone will be looking for them before then. Carlos can't go anywhere, he's a fugitive. The police are looking for him, his picture has gone out now on the television this afternoon, and he must know we're on the island. He's stuck in that house. If it's not in the cases we'll come and grab him tomorrow and we'll know the hard drive must be with him."

"If the Reg guy is in on all this and helping Carlos, he will surely take the hard drive before the police get it?" Anatoly surmised.

"Correct, in which case they still end up here by tomorrow." With that Mikhail took one more peek at Carlos Rojas through the window before leading Anatoly away and back to the car.

There were still too many loose ends bothering the Russian and he kept rolling them around in his mind. The longer this dragged on the more chance there was for things to escalate and become more complicated. Tomorrow, he told himself, tomorrow we wrap this job up and head home. Carlos may have miraculously survived a plane crash but tomorrow his run of luck would end.

38

Reg pulled his van into the gravel car park of the Fox and Hare pub, taking a minute to find an open spot, a good indication it was a busy night. Striding across the car park he checked his watch and berated himself for being late. It was 7.10pm. He opened the door to a wave of sound in stark contrast to the quiet of twilight he had just left. The bar was bustling with customers chatting and laughing but the sweet sound he had come to hear was the strong, smoky voice of his beloved wife. Pearl caught his eye right away and smiled warmly at him as she strummed her guitar on the small stage, covering 'I'm the Only One' by Melissa Etheridge. The big man's heart melted every time.

He found Thomas and AJ at the bar where they'd saved a stool for him. He gave AJ a quick hug and Thomas a slap on the back before taking a seat.

"How much did I miss?"

AJ shook her head. "Just a couple of songs. She's brilliant as usual. How did it go up north?"

The barkeeper leaned over, greeted Reg and asked if he wanted his usual.

"Please," Reg nodded.

He paused until the man had turned to fix his drink before answering in a hushed tone all of them huddled to hear, "We brought everything up this afternoon, went fine, it's laid down quite a bit so it wasn't bad. Met this Russian bloke our lad's been talking about, a real dickhead, says he's a marine biologist representing the Cubans but he's military, or at least ex-military. Maybe from the KGB or whatever they call themselves these days; he ain't no biologist, though. He was mad as hell when Whittaker wouldn't let him look in the cases."

"He didn't open them?" AJ asked, surprised.

"Nope, Whittaker played him like a violin, made me feel really bad not being straight with him. We dived twice more this afternoon along the outside of the reef, looking for the body. Surprisingly we didn't find anything," Reg grinned. "Roy sent the Russian packing, told him he'd have the cases ready to hand over tomorrow; no one's opened them yet to my knowledge."

Thomas nudged Reg. "I think that Russian guy went by my house this morning, scared the crap out of Ma, asking all kind of questions about Sydney. Ma said he told her he was from the Cuban government but she said no way was he Cuban. Had a weird accent she said." Thomas was clearly concerned. "Think he'll go back and bother Ma again? She was pretty upset."

Reg mulled it over, "I doubt it unless he really thinks Sydney is there."

"But it means they must think Sydney was with…" AJ stopped herself saying his name, "our lad… And if they're looking for her they've figured out or guessed they survived the plane crash," AJ reasoned.

"The Russky wasn't too bothered about finding bodies it appeared to me, all he cared about was looking in those cases," Reg added, pausing again as the barman handed him his bourbon. "Cheers mate." He took a quick sip as the barkeeper moved on to the next customer. "My guess is you're right and they've figured out they're both alive and well and somewhere on the island. The way he's getting itchy around the cases has to mean he knows they took the hard drive and maybe other stuff they're worried about. Once he finds out it's not in there tomorrow he'll turn up the search a notch I reckon."

"Sure hope he doesn't go scaring my Ma again. It's a good job Ma doesn't know Sydney is here or she'd really be in a panic. As it is she made me text her and I had to pretend she was answering from Florida and everything was okay. It ain't right me lying to her." Thomas shook his head despondently.

They sat and listened to Pearl who'd moved on to a Janis Joplin tune, each lost in their own thoughts for a minute. Reg finally spoke up, "We sure about all this? I mean, it feels like we're in way over our heads this time. You know me, I'm not stepping away from a fight worth fighting, but we're leading Whittaker astray, hiding a kid wanted by a foreign government and being chased by Russian agents? This is James Bond shit. We're risking our livelihoods and maybe our lives here."

Reg was never one to be dramatic and it was usually hard to get two sentences out of him so both Thomas and AJ could see he was really troubled.

Thomas was first to comment, "You're right. About all of it, we're out of our depth... well I am at least. The idea we have Russian agents on our little island is crazy." The young Caymanian shook his head in disbelief. "Man, crazy. But I have to do right by my sister. If she's sure about this kid then I have to be as well. Sydney has always been the smart one that makes good decisions; she's never dated the wrong crowd or been in trouble, she's always been focused on what was important. Like her sports, when she was running track, she worked hard at it but wouldn't let it take away from her schooling, you know? And I like Car... I mean 'our lad', as well. He doesn't seem foolish to me, he seems like a passionate guy on a mission to do something good. I gotta stick with this to the end."

Reg gave the young man a respectful nod before turning to AJ. "What do you think?"

AJ chewed it over a moment. "We've come this far, Reg, what do we say to Roy at this point? Jackson is working on Sea Sentry to get involved on a press release. I think we should give him some time to work that out. If they don't buy in I think we'll have a hard time making a splash in the press – I mean, who are we? Can't see the worldwide press will run with it 'cos you, me and some Cuban kid with a story and some maps anyone could have made in Photoshop says it's true. You'll see Roy tomorrow right?"

"Yup," Reg acknowledged, "heading out again to search some more at seven thirty."

AJ continued, "Why don't you see how things go tomorrow? Hopefully I'll hear something from Jackson and we can decide then. Our lad is convinced he'll disappear if he goes to the police; they'll hand him over to the Russians on behalf of the Cubans and game over."

"Alright," Reg agreed, "we'll play out tomorrow morning and see what shakes. But by the afternoon things better be firmed up and sorted or we gotta come clean with Whittaker."

AJ clinked glasses with Reg and Thomas. "Sounds good, we're going out tomorrow morning anyway. Promised we'd make up a day for some of the customers that missed out this week when we couldn't run in the storms, so let's regroup after that."

Reg remembered something and dug in his pocket. "Here," he showed the watch he'd found to Thomas, "Tell your sister to quit leaving stuff lying around in seaplanes at the bottom of the ocean."

Thomas took the watch and flipped it over to see the inscription. "That's hers alright."

AJ looked as well. "Anything else down there that ties her to the plane?"

Reg shook his head. "Not that I saw and I had a pretty good rummage through it. Mind you it's moved a bunch and stuff has been scattered so there's no telling." He took the watch back. "I'll give this back to her at the house."

Thomas added thoughtfully, "They talked about a small bag with some clothes and other stuff right? We're all loaning them things to wear."

Reg nodded. "I didn't see anything like that but I'll keep an eye out tomorrow – likely that's all long gone in the storm. Probably out to sea by now."

39

The alarm on AJ's phone slowly ramped up with a Metallica song. By the first chorus she was wide awake and fumbling for her mobile to calm the thrashing guitars. Saturday was usually a day for no alarms and sleeping in until eight o'clock, which was the latest her active mind would allow her to rest. But this Saturday she'd promised her clients she'd make up a day of diving lost with the week's bad weather. Normally she wouldn't mind, she loved what she did for a living, but on this day with all the chaos around Carlos and the Cuban oil fields on her mind she would have preferred to have the day free.

She rolled out of bed and took the handful of steps to the kitchen and turned the coffee maker on. Four years she'd been in this tiny one-bedroom apartment. After the whole U-1026 discovery and subsequent media attention she'd put herself in a financial position to buy a place, which she did. Her two-bedroom condo was now rented to a couple of guys that worked for Reg; AJ had never slept a night in it. Not that it wasn't a nice place, in fact it was a gorgeous condo in a small complex on the inland side of West Bay Road at the back of Seven Mile Beach. With real estate prices being Monopoly money on the island it had cost a bundle but she'd rather have someone else make the mortgage payment for her and live simply herself in her comfortable little place. The apartment was actually a guest cottage in the garden of a palatial home overlooking Seven Mile Beach. The American couple that owned it flew down when they could spend time there but were more than happy for AJ to keep an eye on the place in their absence. She paid them a few dollars rent and took them diving; they had never raised the rent and begged her to stay when she bought her condo so it worked well for everyone.

She put on a tee shirt in case anyone was walking along the beach and pulled the curtains back on the sliding doors facing the ocean. The shirt was a men's large with a Sea Sentry logo and hung down to her thighs. It had smelled like the person who gave it to her but she'd worn it so much in the past few weeks now it just smelled like her. At six o'clock in the morning the sun had yet to rise but a bright moon made glittery silver reflections on the calm water and the palms separating the beach from the garden cast long, faint shadows over the lawn to her window. Live simply, she thought, not hard when this is your view each morning, how could I wish for more? Yet she did wish for more.

AJ had been through a handful of serious relationships but they had all been carefully entered into and none devastating to leave. She felt she'd certainly been in love or at least in deep caring before but she was confident she hadn't passed up her soulmate. For many years it had never bothered her she hadn't found the right one and she enjoyed her existence on the island so much she felt her life was fulfilling and fulfilled. Until Jackson. She had never fallen for anyone so quickly before. Her nature, instilled by her mother, was slow and steady, make sure everything's right, or more importantly make sure he's worth it and worthy of you. This had steered her away from frivolous and brief encounters, which she was thankful for, and then she found herself in bed with Jackson after knowing him less than a week. There was something completely different with him. She felt more confident in herself around him, more willing to share, to open up. He was so sincere, he looked at life in such an uncomplicated way. If something was hurtful or harmful to a living thing or a natural place he wanted no part of it. He didn't care about owning anything, although he wasn't against having possessions, he just believed your objects shouldn't own you. Having witnessed people fill their income with lifestyle only to become trapped by their debt, AJ found his clear and uncluttered perspective refreshing.

By being nothing but himself, Jackson had helped her see her life in a different way. He hadn't changed her or tried to change her. Being with him had simply reorganised the pieces of her life and laid them out into a transparent understanding like a map before her. And right there, slap bang in the middle of the map was a gaping hole, a large void she always knew was there but refused to face. The person that completed her. The morning he left she was certain he was her soulmate. In the weeks that passed with no word, her old nemesis, self-doubt, burrowed back in and started working on her, breaking her down. Had she conjured all this up in her mind and he was just a guy, like so many others, who played games with the girls and notched up another score? AJ couldn't imagine being so wrong about someone she felt so right about. The doubt chipped and scratched and clawed away day after day until two days ago on that brief call. And now, as she stared at the email he had sent her yesterday evening saying he was on his way, her heart glowed and her map felt complete.

40

"Who wants to get wrecked this morning?" AJ called out to her eight customers organising their gear on the boat. The response was a loud cheer and waving of hands.

"The Kittiwake it is then," she turned and yelled up to Thomas on the fly bridge. "You heard the good people, Thomas, let's step on it and beat the crowd."

AJ hopped off the boat to the pier and released the lines, giving the stern a shove away from the dock with her foot before stepping back on board. Thomas engaged reverse and the props churned the pale blue water behind the Newton and eased away from the dock. Once it was in motion backwards, he dropped it back into neutral and spun the wheel and the thirty-six-foot boat lazily swung the bow around to face to ocean.

A voice shouting from West Bay dock direction attracted everyone's attention and AJ looked up from stowing lines to see what the commotion was about. The Australian kid, Billy, that she knew worked for one of the other dive operations was standing next to a grey mid-size car yelling at the occupants.

"Come out of the car and tell me what you did with it!" Billy was barking in his thick Aussie accent.

Whoever the occupants were seemed reluctant to roll down a window, never mind get out of the car. Thomas had the boat turned around but was too interested in the scene in the car park next door to pull away.

Billy slammed his fist on the roof of the car. "Listen wanker, I saw you take off on it so either give it back or I'm calling the coppers!"

AJ couldn't tell who was in the car with the morning sun glaring off the windshield but finally the passenger door opened and a large man stepped out dressed in slacks and a white shirt, hardly beach attire. Billy took a step back when he saw the size of the bloke he was now facing but kept at him like a terrier nipping the heels of a Rottweiler. "Why the hell did you steal my bike, mate?"

The man's reply was too quiet to hear from the water but Billy opened the back door, hesitated a moment, then got in the car. The large man turned and looked directly at the group on AJ's boat, all staring in his direction, before sliding back in the car himself and closing the door.

Thomas dropped the boat in drive and steadily motored away from the dock. AJ watched suspiciously as the car backed up and drove out of the car park, presumably for Billy to be reunited with his bicycle.

Anatoly turned to the kid who now looked a little terrified trapped in the car with these two strange men.

"I didn't know it was your bike when I borrowed it, okay? We can sort this out, just calm down and we'll take you to the bike."

"Alright, but we gotta be quick about it, my boat's waiting on me now," Billy replied agitatedly, looking around out the window and wondering where they were going.

Anatoly turned back to the front and switched to Russian. "I've got no idea where I ditched the thing, all these mangroves lining the roads look the same to me."

Mikhail kept driving. "What part of the 'don't draw attention' order did you not understand?"

Anatoly stammered back. "The Bodden kid was taking off, I needed something quick and the bike was right there, I didn't have a choice."

Mikhail looked at him this time. "You always have choices. You made a bad one and now we have a distraction."

Mikhail turned down a narrow road with no homes around and pulled over in a small clearing between some bushes.

"It's here," he said to Billy in English, "I'll show you."

All three got out although Anatoly had no idea what was about to happen, this certainly wasn't where he had dumped the bicycle.

Mikhail met Billy around the back of the car and strode up intimidatingly close to him. "How much did your bicycle cost?"

"What?" Billy struggled to reply, realising his bike probably wasn't here after all.

"Simple question, how much did you pay for your bike my associate borrowed?" Mikhail stared him down.

"Uhhh… couple of hundred CI from a mate who was leaving the island, and I gave him some fins too," Billy managed.

"The fins, how much were they worth?" the Russian continued in his flat tone.

Billy was looking around, trying to figure out a place to run, getting more nervous by the second. "Shit, I don't know, twenty bucks?"

Mikhail reached into his back pocket and Billy cringed, convinced this weird eastern European guy was about to shoot him. Mikhail pulled three hundred Cayman Island dollars from the wallet he took from his back pocket and handed them to Billy.

"That covers your bicycle and some inconvenience."

Billy relaxed and took the cash, happy he was not being shot and pleased with himself for lying about what he'd paid for the old bike.

"Do you plan on telling anyone about this?" Mikhail asked in the same tone.

Billy paused, nervous again. He had figured this was over and he was getting a ride back to the dock. "Uh, no, I guess not?"

He sensed the man move but it happened so fast he had no idea what was going on except he had a pain in his midriff and he couldn't breathe at all. Billy's knees buckled instantly and he dropped like a dead weight to the ground wheezing and gasping for air, the man leaning over him.

"Still guessing about telling people or are you sure now?"

Billy couldn't make words but he shook his head and waved his hand, his other clutching his stomach where Mikhail had punched him with pinpoint accuracy right below his ribcage.

With that the two Russians got back in the car, leaving Billy rolling on the ground trying not to throw up.

Anatoly was nearly as surprised as Billy by the turn of events and while he was still trying to process things his boss turned to him and spoke slowly and clearly. "No more mistakes Mr. Karin."

41

———————

As promised, they reached the wreck site ahead of the crowd and had their choice of mooring buoys. AJ directed Thomas to pull up to the mooring on Sand Chute, the reef buoy next to the wreck, and she tied them in. Gathering the group she gave them the briefing.

"We're on the world famous former USS Kittiwake, a US Navy submarine rescue ship originally commissioned in 1945 at the end of the war. She had a long career in support of sub fleets and travelled many times between the eastern United States and Europe. One of her claims to fame was recovering the black box from the Challenger Space Shuttle disaster in 1986 off the coast of Cape Canaveral, Florida. Decommissioned in 1994 she was purchased by the Caymanian government in 2008 and, finally, after a lot of work and delays, she was sunk here on January 5th, 2011.

"I think a couple of you have been on the wreck before but if it's been a few years you'll find it's moved. Yup, a 251-foot wreck moved in tropical storm Nate, late in 2017. The storm was not a particularly bad one but because of the angle it hit the island the waves and surge here on the west side were worse than most hurricanes we've had. So the wreck broke the chains they had holding her upright, tipped over on the port side and slid down the sand to the huge coral head we're currently moored to.

"It's made the wreck even more interesting to dive as you travel through hallways and rooms tilted over but it also makes it very easy to get disorientated. Anyone prefer not to go inside the wreck?"

AJ looked around the crowd. One couple raised their hands. "Okay, no problem, we'll run from bow to stern inside so you guys do the same along the outside on the port side and you'll meet us when we come out on the stern deck. Just stay together in your buddy team and watch for the group. Alright, sand is at sixty feet and most of the time in the wreck we'll be about forty to fifty so figure on a forty-five-minute dive. Let me know when you get to a thousand psi, stay in line behind me through the narrow stuff and remember gentle fin strokes so we don't silt it up. We moored on the coral head as it's nice to do our safety stop over the reef." AJ glanced over at Thomas, who had the ladders down out the back ready to go. "If there are no questions let's splash in and I'll meet you at the bottom of the mooring... Oh, and bring a light if you have one, it'll get dark in a few spots."

As the divers dropped in the flat, calm water AJ began donning her gear and nodded for Thomas to come over, off to the side. She spoke quietly, "Was that the strangest thing on the dock, with Billy, the Aussie kid? Been bothering me riding out here."

Thomas nodded his head. "Didn't seem right, that guy was a big fella, looked like a businessman but what would he be doing stealing a man's bicycle?"

AJ wriggled into her BCD. "Maybe I'm just being paranoid, but after seeing the Cubans' boat and knowing the Russian bloke is on the island I feel like they could be watching us. They knew to go to your mum's house so they must know who you are. The Russian met Reg. We just have to hope they don't piece all that together and start looking at Reg's house."

Thomas handed AJ her fins, looking concerned. "Should I call and have them leave the house, just in case?"

The last of the customers stepped off the swim step and AJ moved to the stern, ready to follow them in. "Reg is out at the North Sound, Pearl is at the dock covering for Reg and we told Sydney and Carlos not to answer the phone at the house and they both ditched their cells so they couldn't be tracked. I don't think you can reach them."

Talking it out made AJ feel even more anxious and she could see Thomas's mind was racing. "Don't worry Thomas, I'm sure it's nothing, I'm just getting paranoid like I said. We'll check on them as soon as we're back to the dock."

Thomas nodded. "Yeah, it's probably fine."

AJ stepped into the clear blue water knowing full well Thomas didn't think it was fine, and neither did she.

The calm of the muted sound below the surface helped AJ refocus and release some stress. The large coral head spire rose around sixty feet from the sandy slope with a broad flat top littered with healthy fans, brain corals, sponges and smaller fish. Turning to the east, the wreck of the USS Kittiwake spread out before the divers like a surreal alien movie set, the hulk of the vessel looming from the limits of visibility.

AJ led the group from the coral head towards the bow of the ship, ominously keeled over towards the reef. Entering the ship through a doorway on the main deck, she threaded through a couple of rooms amply lit from the openings. Her divers followed, adjusting their buoyancy and trying to adapt to travelling through rooms tilted over at thirty degrees. It made them want to tilt over as well but the air in their BCDs would try and pull them back square to the world again. A stairway with a thin metal railing appeared against the far wall of the next room and AJ turned and glided down them to the deck below and into the darkness. She always felt like Peter Pan floating through rooms, hallways and stairwells that had been built for people to walk through.

Light beams from the group flashed around blackened lower compartments, illuminating startled fish that scurried away to safer corners. Shining her torch below, AJ revealed the big diesel motors that once powered the ship and she dropped down the narrow space around the hunks of steel and circled the power plants. A couple of her group followed but the others decided the confined space deep in the heart of the ship was a little too claustrophobic, and settled for observing from above. Moving forward, AJ smoothly eased up through an opening in the decking returning to the main deck. Turning back towards the bow she led them into the mess hall and then a bathroom where the mirrors allowed the divers to see their reflections in clear areas between the corrosion and growth on the glass. Out through a doorway she turned to look back inside another opening that revealed the hyperbaric chamber the ship carried for use in diver and submariner rescues. The opening into the steel barrel was no more than three feet across but allowed enough room for them to carefully enter one at a time. An eerie blackness filled the chamber and any knocks against the walls made a deep reverberation. A small air pocket from exhausted gas from divers' regulators had formed in the upper corner and shining light on the underside of the water's surface gave a bizarre expectation of dry land beyond. Peeking a masked face above revealed a rusty steel surface and a deafening echo through the gas undampened by the water.

After each diver had sampled the chamber, AJ finished the tour, backtracking again to meet the other two divers at the stern. A big boom extended the length of the stern and schools of jacks cruised just above in the open water, circling the wreck like a horde of watchdogs. The group moved shallower and returned towards the bow over the upper deck and pilot house where AJ led them through for a turn at the large wheel still mounted in the middle of the room. From there they exited on the upper side of the listing ship at around thirty feet and headed across the open water to the reef in time to spot a hawksbill turtle cruising over the coral head and dropping down the other side into the depths of Sand Chute.

As AJ hung with her group at fifteen feet for their safety stop, allowing their bodies to dissipate excess nitrogen they'd built up over the dive, she admired the great ship before her. Always a breathtaking view. The moorings were now alive with boats and divers descended from all directions; AJ was glad they'd hustled to miss the rush on the popular site.

It was hard to believe two days before she'd been inside the wreck of a seaplane in the midst of a storm and now the wreck of an historic navy vessel on a perfect blue sky day. Thoughts of the Cessna brought her back to the men at the dock. Paranoid or not, she knew the safest thing would be to move the fugitives and the hard drive.

42

———

The north side had lain down calm enough to move the police boats outside the reef and moor to the dive buoy on Pinnacle Reef, close to the crash site. Floating next to them was a large flat barge with a crane mounted on one end of the deck and a small wheelhouse at the other end. Roy Whittaker sipped on a coffee and watched his two divers prepare their gear.

"What do you think we can strap to on the wreck, fellas?" he asked casually.

Reg looked up from mounting the first tank of the day to his BCD. "All the weight is up front where the motor is so I'm thinking a strap around the nose, forward of the windshield, and one behind the doors. What do you think, George? Should pull her up pretty square?"

George nodded. "I reckon. The roof is mostly torn away where the wing ripped off so we can't strap around there."

Roy sipped some more coffee and took his time. "Alright, I'm sure you two will figure out what's best."

Reg rubbed some anti-fog in his mask and dipped it in the ocean to wash it out. He could sense Roy was playing with small talk but had something more on his mind.

The detective looked out over the water where the wreck of the plane still lay on the bottom. "You know what's a bit odd to me?"

Here we go, thought Reg. He hated misleading Whittaker. They were friends, but he also knew the man was sharp and very perceptive; he couldn't pull the wool over his eyes for long.

"What's really odd is we haven't found anything personal yet." Another thoughtful sip of coffee. "If you were stealing a plane and flying to another country wouldn't you throw in a spare pair of underwear and maybe a shirt or two?"

He glanced back and forth between the two divers. "I mean, he had to know there was only one way he was going back home to Cuba and that would be in handcuffs, right?"

Reg and George knew the questions were rhetorical and let him keep going on his train of thought.

"If you were leaving your homeland forever wouldn't you take something with you? A family picture, your favourite baseball hat, some toiletries, something, right?"

Reg nodded slowly. "I guess. Maybe he was in a big hurry." Pangs of guilt ran through him for surreptitiously pulling the watch out but overpowering that was the knowledge Whittaker was on the right path. Reg wasn't worried about Carlos being confirmed – they all knew he was the pilot – but in theory no one yet knew Sydney had been on the plane.

"Could be, Reg, could be," Roy countered. "Just keep an eye out for me down there, be nice to confirm the ID of the pilot. Right now we only have the word of the Cubans that Rojas is our man; I'd like to corroborate that with some evidence."

"We can do another sweep once we hook up the fuselage," George offered as the two divers moved to the stern, ready to splash in.

Roy nodded. "Sure, that would be good. As I say, just keep an eye out for me."

The mooring pin was at forty feet and using a compass heading the two men made quick work of the 200-yard underwater swim to the wreck, lying exactly where they'd left it the day before in shallower water. With the seas calmed, the pieces of the plane now rested serenely in their new undersea world with plenty of curious critters and fish moving in, sizing up the new housing opportunity. Each man brought a large rolled-up nylon ratchet strap and they quickly began wrapping them around the fuselage as best they could. Once they were tightened around the beaten aluminium fuselage, fore and aft of the cockpit, Reg eased up to the surface and waved the barge over.

The sixty-five-foot vessel, usually used for moving containers around in the harbour, slowly chugged over. One man operated the crane while another ran the barge and they communicated back and forth by radio. Reg hoped they were good at doing that as he was a speck bobbing in the water and the wrong signal would have him run over by thousands of tons of steel. The barge came to a stop twenty feet from Reg and the crane operator swung the boom around off the bow and lowered the cable. Hung from the main clasp were two short steel cables with large hooks on the ends and Reg let the heavy lines drop past him and watched them lower towards George and the seaplane. George signalled when they were near to him, which Reg relayed to the crane operator, who then halted the powerful winch.

Reg dropped back down to join George and the two divers manhandled the bulky hooks around each strap. Slowly returning the twenty-five feet to the surface Reg signalled for the crane operator to start winching. With regulator in mouth Reg looked down at George, who continued to signal, indicating when the slack was taken. With his hand clear of the water Reg passed the signals to the boom man. When the tension came on the lines the winch motor strained noticeably and the barge's bow dipped slightly in the water. The barge was used for moving shipping containers so it had plenty of muscle for this operation. The plane wasn't that heavy but the weight of the water was immense and the key was to move slowly or the straps would break or rip the plane apart. George eased back a bit as the cables quivered under the strain and the plane moved off the sea floor and swung away from the coral head a few inches. Painfully slowly the winch eased the wreck through the water, Reg keeping his eye on it the whole time, with a thumbs-up to the crane operator to keep winching. George followed the fuselage up, staying about six feet back in case something gave way, watching the straps and cables for signs of trouble.

Reg poked his head out of the water and gave the operator a nod and okay sign, letting him know it was going well and to keep that pace. When he ducked his mask back under George was gone. A stream of regulator bubbles slithered around the fuselage and a fin swooshing in the water revealed George was below the plane where it had been lying on the bottom. Reg was about to signal for the crane to halt when George reappeared, swimming back up level with the rising wreckage. He excitedly gave Reg an okay signal and held up a black rucksack. The bag had obviously been thrown from the cockpit and trapped under the wreck. Reg signalled back okay. But it was not okay – he had a good idea what they'd find in that bag.

43

The last of the customers splashed in and, after flashing a big grin at AJ, Thomas took a giant stride off the swim step and followed them down. AJ dropped the weighted regulator on a long hose off the side which would hang at fifteen feet in case anyone was low on air for their safety stop. She then fussed about and tidied up around the boat. They were moored on Royal Palm Ledge and at a depth of forty feet the divers would spend a solid hour enjoying the reef and the large overhanging coral.

Satisfied all was in order on deck, AJ scaled the ladder to the fly bridge and scanned the view to her south towards George Town harbour. Despite the longer run from the Kittiwake to Royal Palm Ledge, passing many great shallow dive sites along the way, she'd offered the group their second dive here as an excuse to get another look at the Cuban boat. It was a great dive site so the sacrifice was hers in extra burned fuel. She wasn't sure what she could learn by staring at the moored trawler but like a Christmas present under the tree she couldn't help but look. She was retrieving her binoculars from under the console when her phone buzzed, indicating she had a text.

It was Reg: 'Found a bag, guessing it's their clothes, not good.'

AJ swore to herself. This whole thing felt like they were trying to hold water in their hands – whatever they did it poured out. All they needed was a little time for Jackson to get Sea Sentry here and prepared but everything and everyone around them seemed to have a different agenda. They were stuck in the middle between the good guys and the bad guys and both were closing in. She lifted the glasses and focused on the Cuban boat. All appeared still and quiet aboard, no movement. She slowly moved from bow to stern along the railing, studying the layout, looking for something. What was she looking for? AJ shook her head, setting the binoculars down. She'd felt a nagging urgency to get here to see the boat but had no idea why when she really thought about it. What did she expect to see? Bad guys with big guns patrolling the decks? More than anything she sensed a lack of control; maybe looking at the trawler made her feel like she was doing something rather than waiting for pieces to fall in place. Waiting was not her forte. What she wanted to do was march over to Whittaker with Carlos and Sydney in tow and lay out the whole story so he could protect them both and send the Cubans and their Russian muscle packing. But she knew it wasn't that simple and the detective had rules he had to follow which meant everything would be pushed through red tape, which took time. Meanwhile the explosives would be set on Monday and nothing would stop them blasting the reef to pieces. No, they had to push on and hope to hell Jackson could convince his people to make a big enough splash in the world media that the fuses wouldn't be lit.

She lifted the glasses back up and scanned again, this time a little higher, looking at the cabin and wheelhouse structure. Standing out the back of the wheelhouse on some metal stairs running to the stern deck was a man. He also had binoculars, and he was looking directly at AJ.

44

Pavlo took a long draw on his cigarette and held the breath in his lungs while he kept the binoculars steady on the dive boat. The girl on the bridge was slender and shapely with a great tan, but he wasn't sure about the tattoos. He wasn't used to tans or tattoos on the women in Russia, or the whores he occasionally frequented in Cuba. She looked pretty good from here so maybe he liked the edgy, rebellious look and hadn't known it until now? He blew the smoke out of his nose and played with the focus, wishing the glasses were stronger so he could see her more clearly. From downstairs in the dining area he heard his computer ding an alert. Grumbling, he reluctantly ducked back inside handing Silvio his binoculars back before heading down the steps from the wheelhouse to the main deck. Silvio took the glasses and watched the Russian hustle down to check on whatever they were monitoring or watching with all their fancy computer gear.

Silvio stepped outside and tried to figure out what Pavlo had been interested in. He trained the lenses on the closest stationary boat, maybe a half a mile or more north. It struck him as odd that the girl on the boat was also looking at him.

45

Roy Whittaker looked across the water at the flat barge a hundred yards away. On its deck lay the forlorn-looking fuselage of the Cessna seaplane and its crumpled wing section, buckled in the middle. At the stern of the police boat the divers were preparing to get back in the water to retrieve the pontoons. On the bench before Roy lay a sodden wet rucksack.

"It was right under the plane itself, just lying there," George gushed, pleased to provide his boss something to work with. "As soon as we lifted the plane up, there it was."

Reg continued getting ready, hoping by some miracle the bag didn't reveal anything useful.

"Well, let's see what's in this thing," Roy slipped on a pair of pale blue nitrile gloves to examine the evidence and started by unzipping the main compartment. Water poured out and the detective was careful not to let any contents spill with it. Clothes were stuffed inside and he removed them as one soaking wad and flopped them on the bench. Both divers had now turned to watch the process, fascinated for different reasons, forgetting about the pontoons for the moment.

Roy pulled the garments apart from each other. A pair of blue jeans, a grey tee shirt, a pair of shorts, socks, more socks, boxer shorts which Roy held up to the divers with a slight smile.

"No man travels without spare underwear."

Another tee shirt, another pair of jeans and a beige brassiere… Roy held the bra in front of him and couldn't hide the surprise on his face.

"That's a new twist," he mumbled to himself.

Roy placed the bra down and separated the last two garments, a pair of women's panties and a lightweight windbreaker.

Reg tried to suppress any outward reaction but inside his stomach turned. He knew Roy was like a bloodhound once he had a lead and moments for Reg to come clean about what he knew were stacking like bricks about to topple over.

"There was someone else on board the plane," George finally voiced the obvious conclusion.

Roy smiled. "Or this young man liked to wear women's clothes. Or he was bringing clothes to a friend. But, yes, most likely I'd say there were two people on that plane." He looked over at the battered fuselage. "Two people, it is appearing more and more likely, who survived this crash."

Reg stayed silent; as much as his conscience screamed, he hung on to the chance nothing left in that bag would actually identify the female passenger. Roy unzipped the second compartment at the front of the rucksack to a cascade of more salty water. Reaching his gloved hand inside he retrieved a thin brown wallet which he opened to show a Cuban driver's licence and a handful of currency. The licence bore the name Carlos Miguel Rojas.

"Positive ID on our pilot, Mr. Rojas," Roy relayed, "and the money is Cuban pesos." He held up a bank note. "Local money, not CUC, the tourist money they use in Cuba."

Setting the wallet aside he peered in the compartment again and pulled out two more items, which he examined. He set down a blue Cuban passport belonging to Carlos Rojas and opened the second similarly blue-jacketed passport. Reg could see the cover sported the coat of arms of the United Kingdom, but below were the words

'Cayman Islands', identifying the owner as a British Overseas Territories citizen.

"Regina Sydney Bodden," Roy read aloud. "Well I'll be damned."

Roy stared dumbstruck at Reg. "Isn't that Thomas Bodden's sister? The lad that works with AJ?"

Reg nodded reluctantly, "I believe you're right Roy, uses her middle name Sydney, goes to school in Miami if I'm not mistaken."

"What on earth would that young lady be doing on a stolen seaplane from Cuba?" Roy mused.

Reg struggled to think of a further diversion. "Maybe this Rojas kid stole the girl's rucksack? Would explain her stuff in there."

Roy pondered a moment. "Still doesn't explain what she would be doing in Cuba to give him the chance to steal her bag. Well, I guess I'll call young Thomas and ask him if he's seen his sister lately, perhaps he can shed some light on this. Do you have Thomas's number, Reg?"

While Reg retrieved his mobile from his gear bag to get the number, Roy tapped the passport on his other hand, deep in thought.

"The Cubans didn't mention a word about anyone else on that plane," he pondered. "Means either they didn't know, or they're hiding the fact. Funny how they didn't mention the plane was even missing until we found it, yet they had a boat and an unfriendly Russian representative already in our harbour."

He put his hands on his hips and nodded wistfully. "This keeps getting more interesting. Sure seems like the Cubans and their Russian fellow are keen to keep something covered up. Can't say I approve of that when they bring their problems to our little island."

46

AJ glided the Newton alongside the dock in West Bay and Thomas skipped onto the pier and tied her to the cleats. Their boatful of happy divers began passing their gear to Thomas and making their way up the dock, ready for some lunch after two great dives. AJ cut the motor and slid down the ladder to help folks as they left and to stow the gear for those returning tomorrow. Thomas caught her eye and nodded towards the public dock next door. Another dive operation's boat was just docking and there on the deck was Billy, the Australian kid. He was dropping bumpers over the side and getting the lines ready but they could also tell he was looking around the car park nervously.

AJ passed some gear over to Thomas. "How about we have a little word with Billy once we're sorted here."

"That's what I was thinking," Thomas echoed.

One of Reg's boats was tied on the far side of the jetty and when Pearl was done greeting their passengers and squaring away payments, she joined AJ and Thomas, who were unloading empty tanks.

"Haven't heard any more from Reg, I think he's back in the water," Pearl offered.

AJ subtly looked over towards Billy's dive boat that was now docked and unloaded. "That's the kid I was texting you about over there."

Pearl checked him out without being obvious. "Yeah, I know him, nice enough kid but likes his night life a bit too much; Reg passed on hiring him last year."

"Let's see what he has to say about this morning." She beckoned Thomas along. "Be right back, Pearl."

They walked around to the public dock and found Billy loading a couple of tanks into the dive company's van.

"Hey Billy, how are you?" AJ asked in a friendly tone.

Billy stacked the tanks and turned around. "Oh, AJ, how are ya?" Billy looked around; he was jittery and they'd only said hello.

"I'm good, thanks," she smiled at him. "Who were your friends this morning, Billy?"

His face turned ashen and he stumbled, "Who do you mean, I mean, what friends..?"

AJ stepped a little closer and kept smiling. "You know, the blokes in the car you got into and drove off with. You must remember? You were yelling at them pretty good before that."

Billy made to head back to the dock. "I gotta unload the boat..." Thomas stepped in his way and blocked his path. The young Caymanian had the friendliest manner and everyone knew him for his ever-present smile, but when he took on a stern face his tall, broad-shouldered presence could be slightly menacing.

"What the hell, guys?" Billy complained. "I don't know who they are, but they're mean bastards and they told me to keep quiet so that's what I plan to do – I don't need another beating."

"Why would they beat you Billy, what do you have to do with them?" AJ persisted. She was impressing herself with her interrogation skills.

"Nothing! I don't know who the hell they are. One of them stole my bloody bike yesterday so I was telling them to give it back! Arseholes told me they'd take me to it but drove me down the road and give me a thumpin'. Threw me some dough for the bike and made me swear not say anything, so I'm not telling you this alright? Or I'll get beat again. The one guy is big but the other one, bugger me, he's mean."

"But you don't know who they are? Are they local, foreign, accents, you must have got something, Billy?" AJ softened her voice for some sympathy.

"I got a long walk back and yelled at by the boss, that's what I bloody got!" Billy calmed a little. "Yeah, they got accents, eastern European I'd say. But please, I ain't telling you any of this, alright? Seriously, I don't want to ever see those blokes again."

"Don't worry, Billy," AJ assured him, "We won't ever mention you. We think these guys may be bothering another friend is all. Thanks for the info, take care of yourself."

Billy was relieved to carry on with his work and AJ and Thomas ambled back to their boat. Thomas pulled his phone from his pocket. "I missed a call here." he looked at the number but didn't recognise it and hit play. "Oh shit boss!" he quickly hit speaker and restarted the message.

"Hello Thomas, this is Detective Roy Whittaker of the Royal Cayman Islands Police Service. I had some questions about your sister, Regina, I believe she goes by Sydney? If you'd please call me back at your earliest convenience I'd appreciate it."

AJ and Thomas stopped in their tracks and looked at each other.

"Reg said they pulled a bag up, guess they found her passport," AJ said quietly.

"Yeah, got a text here too from Reg, says just that," Thomas added despondently. "Looks like she's wanted by the Cayman Police and the Russian now. This is crazy."

AJ put a hand on his shoulder. "We gotta move them."

47

———

The flat barge slowly motored its way back through the cut into the North Sound with its cargo of broken seaplane parts. Reg and George had helped them winch up the two pontoons separately and then took a third dive to recover some smaller debris and sweep one more time for useful evidence. Still moored on Pinnacle Reef, the two divers now packed their gear and turned their attention to Detective Whittaker, curious if they were still needed.

"What do you think Roy, we diving some more today?" George quizzed.

Roy stepped from behind the small wheelhouse where he'd been conversing with the boat captain.

"Hear me out fellas, see if you think I'm figuring this correctly." He rested one foot on a bench and pointed out across the North Wall. "Weather came out of the north the other night, plane was slammed up against the reef, a few smaller pieces made it over into the sound, right?"

The two men nodded their agreement and Roy continued, "So, anything or anyone going in the water that night would end up here against the reef or make it over the top and be inside the sound, am I still making sense?"

More nods.

"Puts our missing pair, as we now must assume there was two aboard when she went in –" he held up two fingers "– puts our missing pair inside the sound, because we've searched the whole stretch outside the reef and there's no bodies. Still good?"

"They gotta be inside the sound," George agreed.

"Well, we've had six boats, between the marine units and some borrowed craft, combing the shoreline and found nothing. We've performed a search pattern with the same boats and canvassed the whole sound and seen no bodies." He ran his hand across the horizon of the North Sound. "Be floating by now too. See bodies, they sink when they drown as the water fills the lungs and replaces the air so they're now heavier than water and down they go. But especially in this shallow, warm water, decomposition starts pretty fast and the body emits gases inside and pop, up they come again. A day or at most two and they're bobbing on the surface. It's been two and a half days and the boat's just finished another full sweep of the shoreline and the whole sound with nothing."

Reg knew where Roy was heading but stayed quiet, letting George do the talking.

"If I follow what you're saying then maybe they did survive the crash and made it out," George surmised.

Reg saw an opening. "You think they may have survived the plane crash, okay, that could have happened, the fuselage was fairly well intact. But then to make it to shore in the middle of a tropical storm from out here on the North Wall that seems like a stretch to me."

Roy nodded. "You're right there, no question, they'd have dodged death twice. Seems rather implausible I have to agree."

Reg breathed a sigh of relief; maybe he'd got Roy doubting again.

"Unless someone helped them," Roy offered.

Reg was mortified. He felt like a kid caught with his first girlie magazine; he was sure he was flushed red and had big shiny 'guilty' signs pointing at him.

"Who would be crazy enough to come out here in the middle of that storm, and besides, how would they even find them?" George asked doubtfully.

"Another good point," Roy responded, "But what if it was all arranged?"

He let that sit with the two men a moment and shouted towards the boat captain, "Call them all in, we're done looking out here." Turning back to Reg and George, he said, "Those two were picked up by someone out here, crazy as that sounds, and then they scuttled the plane to hide it. Hiding from the Russian too; there's got to be a reason they ran here but haven't turned themselves in for the lad to seek asylum. I don't have all the pieces put together by a long shot but I'm pretty damn sure those two are on dry land, and alive."

Reg couldn't believe his friend was figuring this out so quickly – he had some details wrong but he sure was on the right track.

"Who from here could be involved in all this? Be quite the conspiracy wouldn't it?" George chuckled.

Roy seemed to look squarely at Reg. "Hard knowing, but someone on this island knows more than what they're telling."

Reg visualised the shiny signs starting to blink in bright neon like a Vegas Strip wedding chapel. He looked down and needlessly fussed with his gear bag to avoid any more eye contact with Roy.

"Heading in then?" George confirmed.

"Yes sir," Roy answered. "While I'm waiting for young Thomas to call me back I believe I'll wander over and see his mama; lovely lady, haven't seen her in a while, be nice to catch up. Reckon I'll ask her about her daughter while I'm there."

48

———

AJ paddled the kayak towards the dock from where she'd left the Newton tied to its mooring, away from the shore. At the end of each day and to begin each new day, either she or Thomas would paddle the two hundred yards to or from the mooring as they couldn't keep the boat tied to the dock overnight. Sometimes she chose to swim and get the extra exercise. AJ enjoyed the few minutes of peace it allowed her to prepare for the day ahead or process the morning and organise her thoughts for the afternoon. Normally that meant arranging the tasks in her mind and running through a daily mental checklist of jobs to ready herself for the next day of diving. Today her mind was speeding like a racing car, bouncing around the chaos happening since Thomas had received a call from his sister two nights ago.

She was convinced Billy's friends were the Russian Reg had met and a crony. That meant the dock was being watched, which meant the Russians, or Cubans, knew Sydney was on the plane and were watching her brother to see if he'd lead them to her, and subsequently Carlos. The question was how long had they been watching? Had they already followed them? If they had then they probably knew Carlos and Sydney were at Reg's house. A wave of terror coursed through her as she realised they may have found them already, perhaps this morning while no one was with them. She shook off the thought and focused on next moves; she had to assume they were still safe in the house. She tried to convince herself of that but she felt a tug of urgency to get over there and make sure.

Reaching the dock she hauled the kayak up and dragged it to the little storage building where she met Pearl finishing up her paperwork. Thomas closed the van doors, having finished loading the empty tanks, and joined them.

"I think we have to move them to a safer spot and do it now, don't you agree?" AJ started, getting straight to business.

"Agreed," Pearl concurred. "Reg texted; Whittaker's called off the search out north. He's figured out they were picked up and had help, so now we've got the police hunting for them too. When do you think Sea Sentry will get here?"

AJ shrugged. "I'm not completely sure, sounded like tonight some time. They still don't have Internet on their boat so we won't hear anything more until they arrive. Jackson's email just said we have to keep them hidden until tomorrow, they're setting up a press conference for then."

Pearl turned to Thomas. "Whittaker was heading to your place to speak to your mum and dad by the sound of it, should we warn them?"

Thomas shook his head, troubled his mother would be bothered again. "Best to not say anything; I don't want to lie to her any more and she doesn't know anything so she can't tell him anything useful. She'll say Sydney's in Florida, 'cos that's where she thinks she is. Pops is likely still on the water or at the market selling his fish."

"So where are we going to move them to that's better than our house?" Pearl asked.

"I've been going crazy thinking about that," AJ said, concerned. "I figured my place, but if the Russian arsehole is following us around he may end up tailing me home. Besides, we don't know how many of them there are; their boat is still moored outside the harbour, they could have brought half an army on that thing. Maybe they have a tail on each of us and it's not like we have safe houses lined up around the island."

"All this is way out of our league, man," Thomas sighed. "I feel really bad we've got all of you involved."

Pearl put her arm around him. "Livened up our week I'd say. We'll figure it out, don't fret about it lad, we're all in it together when it's family."

AJ punched Thomas softly on the arm. "It's not like I've ever dragged you into anything crazy before," she laughed. "Now what the hell are we going to do with those two?"

They all thought for a moment until Thomas jumped. "What about the 'Rum Runner'?"

AJ and Pearl looked at each other. "Perfect," AJ blurted.

"Agree," Pearl added.

"I really shouldn't involve the Flemings but I'd say these are special circumstances, and it's only one night, right?" said AJ.

She hesitated a moment, thinking about the couple who owned the house her apartment belonged to. They'd been so good to her and their forty-one-foot Bertram deep-sea fishing yacht was his pride and joy. One night, she thought, they'll crash there for one night and no one will be the wiser.

"Good thinking Thomas, it's perfect."

She lowered her voice a little. "I need to take our tanks to get filled, but first, let's get Reg on the phone, I have a plan."

49

A small convoy of vehicles pulled into the car park of the Instituto de Estudios Geológicos in Jucaro, joining Silvio's beaten-up old Lada and Julio's equally decrepit MZ motorcycle. The procession was led by a military lorry with two rows of armed soldiers lining the benches in the back, who quickly disembarked and formed a perimeter around the car park. A slightly overweight, well-dressed man with a substantial moustache stepped from an air-conditioned Mercedes and stretched for a moment, easing the tension built over the six-hour journey from Havana. He'd already made a phone call with regard to road improvements needed in the Jucaro region for tankers to travel to and from the town.

Salvador Barrios was second in command at the Cuban Ministry of Energy and Mines, reporting directly and exclusively to the minister himself. A subordinate hurried around and unlocked the front door of the building, turned off the alarm and held the door for Barrios. Behind him men stepped out from four unmarked vans and began unloading gear. The first items carefully stacked by each van were large metal crates. Each crate was clearly marked with red explosive warning labels.

Barrios took a quick tour of the offices while his assistant preceded him, turning lights on and opening doors. Stepping out the back door onto the dock they were greeted by the imposing mass of a large military boat moored in the inlet. Sailors could be seen on deck and several stopped to look down at the two men. They immediately snapped to attention and saluted. Barrios nodded in their direction before returning inside the building and making his way to the nicest office he'd seen.

"Have them load the explosives and other gear, but take it around the outside, I don't want them traipsing through here." He barked at the other man who scuttled away to bark at the next man down the food chain.

Barrios took out his mobile phone and dialled a number, waiting while it rang.

"Señor Barrios, how are you today?" came the gruff voice, the voice of the man Mikhail had spoken with.

Barrios raised one eyebrow. "I'm in Jucaro, where I see your man is not. You told us this business would be resolved, where is he?"

The man at the other end took a moment in replying, "I indeed told you it would be resolved and so it will be. Gurov knows what he's doing and he's aware of the timing. He'll make this whole problem go away, don't worry."

Barrios scoffed, "This whole problem began under Gurov, forgive me if I doubt the man."

The Russian fired back without pause, "This problem began with a Cuban national who was placed under my man, by your people, and now Gurov is forced to clean up the mess. If there's a publicity problem over this it's Cuba's problem. We don't give a shit what an American paper says, we just want the oil, and we expect you to start construction on Monday."

Barrios leaned back in his chair and chewed his lip. "We don't care about the press either, but we do care about our partners in the northern oil fields, and they care about bad press regarding their suppliers when their markets are effected by it." He relaxed his tone a step. "We have everything here in Jucaro, ready to begin on time, don't worry. Please, let's just get this problem resolved today so we can move on."

"It will be," the Russian retorted. "I'll call you when it's done."

50

Detective Roy Whittaker strode up the path and rapped firmly on the front door of the West Bay bungalow. It took Wilma Bodden a few moments to set down her sewing project and make her way through the house to answer the door, but she beamed when she saw Roy on her doorstep.

"Roy Whittaker, well aren't you a welcome sight, been a while eh? Probably nearly a year since I sewed some curtains for Rosie," she babbled excitedly, waving him into the house. "How is your lovely wife, Roy? She still keeping the postal service running? I guess so, get my post everyday rain or shine."

They made it all the way to the living room before she drew breath and Roy got a word in.

"She's doing well Wilma, thank you."

"Well sit down Roy, sit down, I'll fetch some ice tea, you like ice tea don't you?"

She was already in the kitchen and pouring before he could answer, "I'll take a glass, that would be fine, thank you."

She bustled back in and set a glass brimming with ice tea in front of him. "What brings you by in the middle of the day, Roy?" The notion struck her that a policeman visiting may not mean good news and a moment of panic struck her. "It's not Jeremiah is it? Is he okay? Has something happened, Roy?"

He held up his hand and shook his head, almost spilling the tea he was about to sip, "No, no, nothing like that Wilma."

She plonked into the chair and put her hand on her chest, "Lordy, gave myself a fright for a moment."

Roy set the glass down in case she got excited again, "I have no reason to think she's not fine but I did come to ask you about your girl, Sydney."

Wilma looked perplexed. "What in the world is going on with that girl? Just yesterday I had some strange fella coming to the door asking about her, saying he was some Cuban official of some sort but I didn't know him and he sure didn't look Cuban to me so I sent him packin'."

That got Roy's attention. "A man you say? Came asking about Sydney?"

"Sure did, I didn't like him one bit, told him come back with someone I know, like you, and I'd talk to him then."

Roy texted something from his phone before carrying on, "Okay let's come back to that fella in a moment. So, where is Sydney at the moment, Wilma?"

"She's at school in Florida. After that fella came I had Thomas get hold of her to make sure she's okay and he said she was fine."

"And this all happened yesterday?" he asked politely.

"Sure did, mid morning yesterday I'd say."

Roy's phone buzzed and he checked the text. "Here," he said, holding up his mobile phone screen for her to see, "this your man at the door?"

"That's him alright, ornery fella, weren't no Cuban though. So what on earth is going on with my little girl Roy? Why is everyone asking about her?"

Roy smiled. "Nothing to worry about I'm sure, especially if Thomas spoke to her and she's okay. Some possessions of hers were in that plane we found off the north side, you may have seen on the news? I'd like to talk to her and tell her I have some things of hers so I can get them back to her."

Wilma stammered with a mix of concern and confusion, "In that plane that crashed? You don't think Sydney was in that plane do you? Oh my God!"

Roy quickly moved to settle her down, "No Wilma, we know a young Cuban lad, Carlos Rojas was flying the plane."

Wilma put her hands over her mouth in shock. "Carlos?! That's Sydney's boyfriend!"

"I figured he might be. I believe he may be fine Wilma, we haven't recovered any bodies and I don't know, but I suspect, whoever was in that plane survived the crash. If you're sure Sydney is in Miami then we know she wasn't on it at least."

"I've never met the boy but Sydney started dating him in university, best I know he went back to Cuba to work but they still been dating. Lord, I pray he's okay. She sure thinks the world of him, I do know that."

"Why don't we call Sydney and ask her what she might know about all this?" Roy offered. "Let's call from your phone so she knows who's calling."

Wilma looked unsure. "I don't normally call as it costs too much, we just have the local plan you see."

"Then we'll use mine," Roy conceded. "What's her number Wilma?"

She took a minute to fumble through her old flip phone and find her daughter's mobile number which she read to the detective. He placed his phone on the table between them and put it on speaker. Without a single ring it went straight to voicemail and as Sydney's greeting played out Roy suggested Wilma leave her a message.

"Hey honey, it's mama. Been worried about you, got people here at home asking about you, give me a call as soon as you get this. Love you."

Roy ended the call, thanked Wilma for all her help and assured her repeatedly that he felt everyone was okay. She saw him to the door and after reminding her to call him if the Russian came by again, they said their pleasantries and he walked towards his car.

As a detective he was used to people omitting pertinent details, twisting the truth or outright lying to him. He didn't usually let it bother him, it came with the territory. But apart from Wilma, who clearly didn't know anything, he was getting the distinct feeling everyone else around was leaving out all the key details, and it was starting to irk him.

51

———

AJ drove her van slowly up Reg's street, carefully keeping an eye on either side of the narrow road for out-of-place vehicles. She saw none, to her surprise. She pulled up in front of the house and backed into the driveway to the garage door, which opened as she approached. She kept reversing until the tail of the van was inside the garage before stopping. Hopping out, she went into the unlit garage and opened the rear doors of the van. Carlos and Sydney stood in the shadowy corner at the back of the garage by the door into the house.

"You ready?" AJ asked.

"We're ready," Carlos whispered back. "Thomas told us; scared the crap out of us when he sneaked in from the back though!"

"Yeah, sorry about that, no way to reach you otherwise," AJ apologised.

She walked back to the driver's door and got in the van, starting the engine. As soon as the back doors of the van had closed, she pulled out, leaving the overhead door closing on an empty garage. Turning left out of the driveway she sped back down the street and wiggled her way out of West Bay to Esterly Tibbetts Highway, the dual carriageway that ran behind the Seven Mile Beach shops and businesses. Just when she thought she had slipped away unnoticed she picked up a grey mid-size car in her rear-view mirror, a couple of hundred yards back. It looked a lot like the car from the West Bay dock car park that morning. It was tempting to stand on the accelerator a little harder and try to pull away but she resisted, her pulse quickening and her eyes flicking from the road ahead to the car behind her. Through the Camana Bay roundabouts the car drew closer but dropped further back on the stretch between the hospital and the AL Thompson's roundabout. She took North Sound Road until the next roundabout, where she turned right on Elgin into the back of George Town, hoping the traffic wouldn't be backed up. Sure enough the car followed; she had no doubt now she was being tailed by the Russian and she noticed her palms getting sticky with sweat, despite her air conditioner pumping in the van. Grabbing her mobile from the centre console she hit send on a text and returned her attention to the road.

What am I doing, she thought, this is madness. Calming herself down, she made it to South Church Street, a narrow-frontage road in town, and headed left past the tourist shops and restaurants. There was now one car between her and the grey saloon and she pushed the throttle down to speed away and get a gap. Half a mile out of downtown she braked hard and hung a right turn into Sunset House Hotel and Dive Resort on the waterfront, taking the first parking spot she could find. Looking back to the road she saw the car that had been between them go by, then nothing. She paused a moment, breathing like she'd run across town rather than driven; still nothing. Leaving the van she strode into the hotel office and made for the window overlooking the car park.

"They see you come in here?" Reg asked from behind her.

"I think so, they didn't go past at least," she replied without turning around.

The two waited anxiously, scanning the car park.

"Where were they watching from?" Reg asked.

"I've got no bloody idea," AJ said, discouraged. "They're good. I didn't see them until they appeared behind me on the bypass."

"There he is!" Reg growled, seeing Mikhail already at the back of AJ's van. "That's him, that's the Russian, Gurov."

"See what I mean?" AJ gasped. "Where the hell did he just come from? It's like he dropped out of nowhere."

Mikhail peeked in the back of the van then tried the door. It opened and he checked the interior quickly before closing the door again and moving around the far side of the van, out of their view.

"I tell you, he's no diplomat or official or whatever other bollocks the Cubans claim he is, that bloke's military."

They waited some more but Mikhail didn't reappear.

"Where did he go?" AJ looked all around from the window but he was nowhere to be seen.

Reg let out a sigh. "I tell you kid, this guy worries me, we're playing with fire. Whittaker knows we're involved, I can tell. We're better off coming straight with him and letting him help."

AJ turned and looked at Reg, registering the concern on his face. "I promised Carlos we wouldn't, Reg. Believe me, I'm terrified we're digging ourselves a hole but I promised I wouldn't turn him in. He's convinced they'll hand him over to the Cuban government or at least hold him so he can't get this to the press."

They both froze at the sound of a monotone accented voice from around the corner at the hotel front desk.

"I'm looking for the young couple that just checked in, friends of mine, we're supposed to meet here."

Reg pointed at the door and they both quietly squeezed out as they could hear the receptionist tell him, "No one has checked in sir, in fact we're full all week. Perhaps you have the wrong hotel?"

AJ ran to the van while Reg split along the back of the hotel building and ducked into Cathy Church's camera shop. AJ fired up the van and backed out. Putting it in gear she swung around to leave just as Mikhail stepped out the door they'd escaped through. Their eyes locked for a moment. His was a cold steel stare, void of emotion, and she knew hers had to be a look of complete terror.

52

Pearl pulled out of her driveway with Thomas in the passenger seat of her Jeep. Huddled down on the rear seat and floor were Carlos and Sydney, a blue rucksack wedged beside them containing nothing they actually owned. The clothes were borrowed, the food supplied and the much-sought-after hard drive belonged to the Republic of Cuba. It had seemed like forever waiting for AJ's text telling Pearl it was clear to pick them up from the house, but they'd agreed they had to be sure the Russian had taken the bait. Now, as Pearl sped down the road heading for the yacht club, she was filled with a mix of adrenaline and fear. Thomas's head was on a swivel watching for any suspicious vehicles following them as they had no idea how many people the Russians had with them. As AJ had noted, the boat they arrived in had room for a hundred agents and the airport had opened after the storm so who knew how many more had arrived. The more they spun scenarios around in their heads the more paranoid they got but they'd agreed the only fact they had was two Russians in one car... and possibly a bicycle, which they felt confident the Jeep could outrun.

It only took a few minutes to reach the yacht club marina where the Flemings kept their Bertram, a few piers down from Reg and

AJ's north-side berths. Pearl drove slowly through the marina car park making sure no one was following or watching them. The marina had been quiet all week, firstly with the storm and then the RCIPS had the North Sound restricted while they'd been investigating the plane crash. Access had been reopened that afternoon so a few recreational boaters and dive boat operators were busy coming and going. Confident they weren't followed, Pearl parked the Jeep at the top of the jetty leading to the Rum Runner and she and Thomas got out and unlocked the security gate. Pearl continued down the deserted pier to open up the boat while Thomas retrieved the two fugitives and hustled them after her.

The Rum Runner was a beautiful boat, about seven years old but maintained to look like it was fresh in the water last week. A service had already been by and cleaned her exterior after the storm and the interior was cool and dry from the shore power running a tickle of on-board air conditioning a few times a day. Pearl turned on the lights but left all the curtains closed on the windows so no one could be seen moving around inside. Thomas brought Carlos and Sydney in through the sliding door from the stern deck.

"Wow." Carlos looked around at the luxuriously appointed stateroom with fine wood cabinetry and plush carpet. "This is someone's fishing boat?"

Pearl chuckled, "Yup, but it's their pleasure yacht too, pretty nice huh?"

Carlos just nodded slowly, speechless. Sydney went forward past the galley to the cabins and found a main stateroom in the bow with an en suite bathroom, a guest stateroom and second bathroom.

"Check this out," she called back, setting their bag on the bed as Carlos joined her.

"My God, this is nicer than any home I've ever been in," he whispered.

Thomas checked the water was working in the kitchen sink and the fridge was cold, letting Pearl know it was all working. Pearl asked the two to come back to the lounge so she could run through the plan.

"Okay guys, you have running water and power so you can shower, water's drinkable and the stove, microwave and oven will work. What you can't use are the marine toilets, as the owners don't have the pump-out service come around when they're not here. There's a bathroom in the building in the car park and it's quiet around here in the evening and at night except for the traffic coming to and from the two restaurants down the end. Just be careful and don't be seen. Carlos, your picture has been all over the news and a lot of people know Sydney on the island."

"We don't know if they'll release your picture as well now Whittaker is pretty sure you were on the plane," Thomas added, looking at his sister.

"We'll stay inside and out of sight; if we have to use the bathroom we'll be quick and make sure we're not seen," Sydney assured them.

"Thank you, again," Carlos said, the burden of what he was responsible for showing in his eyes. "I promise you saving the Jardines de la Reina is worth all you are risking for us."

Sydney wrapped her arms around her boyfriend from behind and kissed him gently on the back of his neck.

"Come on Thomas, let's leave them alone," Pearl said, smiling.

"I'm ready, I can't handle seeing my sister getting all lovey and stuff!" he said as he opened the door, laughing.

53

———

Mikhail watched as AJ's van disappeared down South Church street back towards town. Most men would be angry getting duped by a young girl but Mikhail wasn't most men. He was annoyed, not that you could tell from his blank expression, but his analytical mind simply registered that the locals were not to be underestimated. More importantly they were actively hiding Carlos, which meant he was up against a wider group. The thought occurred to him, as he joined Anatoly in their hire car, that the detective could be collaborating with them too. The man seemed too 'by the book' for that, but they were all being a pain in the arse.

"Where now?" Anatoly asked.

"The girl's apartment," Mikhail ordered as his mobile rang from a local island number.

"Gurov," he answered sternly.

"Hello there Mr. Gurov, this is Detective Whittaker of the Royal Cayman Island Police Service."

"Can I collect my cases?" Mikhail snapped.

He sensed Whittaker was grinning when he replied, "We're almost done with them Mr. Gurov but I did have a few questions for you. Could you meet me at the police station – we can chat there and see about the cases?"

Mikhail glanced at his watch. It was a few minutes after two o'clock. "Three pm, I'll be there."

"Thank y—" Mikhail hung up before Roy had finished.

Anatoly looked at his boss expecting a new plan but Mikhail just growled at him, "What are you waiting for? Girl's apartment, let's go."

54

———

AJ stepped from the shower and grabbed a towel. The main reason she wore her hair shorter was drying time. Her life was a constant stream of getting soaking wet, either in the ocean, a pool or showering after one of the other two. Short hair, combined with her decision to only wear make-up for evenings out, reduced her turnaround time considerably. She hurriedly towelled off and ran a brush through her hair before pulling a few drawers open on her dresser trying to decide what to wear. She rarely wore underwear during the day. It made more sense to wear a bathing suit under her clothes as she often had a change of plans, an extra dive or a swim to the moored boat required. She found a clean two-piece, threw a tee shirt over it and pulled on some cotton shorts that she'd only worn once since laundry; they'll be fine, she decided. Fifteen-minute turn-around, not many boys can match that, she thought proudly. Slipping into her Rainbow sandals, she grabbed her van keys and shot out the sliding door that doubled as the cottage entry.

Standing under the warm shower had finally washed some of the tension and stress from earlier away. She breathed easier knowing Carlos and Sydney were hidden away somewhere no one could find and the plan was to stay away from the yacht club so none of them could be followed there. Tomorrow they'd pick them up and take them straight to wherever Sea Sentry had figured out to have this press conference. Later, she thought, maybe I'll swing by Yacht Drive, across the water from the marina, and check in from afar. She had no idea how that would help but figured it would rest her mind at ease to at least take a look, much like staring at the trawler.

Crossing the garden between the guest house and the main building, she passed through the front gate to her van parked out front of the house on Boggy Sand Road. With errands to run and a part to pick up for the boat she headed out, careful to watch for the grey rental car on her street or following her down the road. She saw no sign of it.

She didn't see it because Mikhail had Anatoly park it in the Fosters supermarket car park off West Bay road, and the two had walked around to Boggy Sand, where they hid in the bushes watching AJ leave. Once the coast was clear they easily opened the lock on the sliding door and stood inside her apartment. They had ten minutes before Mikhail needed to leave if he was to meet Whittaker on time but the apartment was small and they were both trained professionals. They knew two ways to perform a room search depending on what they were trying to achieve. The first was a warning or threat where they'd turn the place over, leaving it obvious you'd been there, designed to scare the resident. The second, which was more common, was the opposite: you left everything exactly as you found it. The two men carefully and efficiently worked from either ends of the home and checked every possible hiding place that may house a computer hard drive. They wore gloves, made sure their shoes were clean and left no marks and paid detailed attention to the position of every item so it would be restored to its original place. They passed over anything that wouldn't relate to or contain the one thing they were looking for and in nine minutes closed the slider in full confidence the evidence was not in AJ's apartment.

Instead of returning to the road through the front of the property they chose the rear that backed onto Seven Mile Beach. Slipping their shoes off they left though the gate to the white sand beach and walked to the pathway by the cemetery that led back to West Bay road. From there they walked briskly back to Fosters, dripping with sweat by the time they reached their car. Mikhail had already come to a conclusion, hence the search they just performed, but his disciplined character forced him to be on time to his meeting with Whittaker where he'd verify his suspicion. He was sure the hard drive was not in the cases.

55

Detective Whittaker entered the reception area of the Royal Cayman Islands Police Services central police station on Elgin Avenue. Mikhail Gurov was standing to one side, arms folded, sternly observing all movement in the room, waiting for him. Before Roy could greet the man he was straight to business.

"Where are my cases, Detective?"

Roy halted in front of the Russian and smiled politely, refusing to be baited by his ill manner, "All in good time sir, perhaps you would follow me and we'll discuss a few items first?"

Without waiting for his response, Roy turned and walked to the door and held it open. Mikhail hesitated but decided to follow without further protest. Roy directed them into a small interview room with four chairs around a table. "Please, have a seat," he offered calmly.

Taking the chair, Mikhail insisted, "Hopefully this will not take long, the Republic of Cuba would like their property back. I assure you they are eager to have it returned."

The detective took his time getting settled before responding, "They may well be sir." He returned the Russian's cold, blank stare with a warm smile, "But to be clear, you are here on a visitor's visa as a Russian citizen, you do not hold diplomatic status or immunity as no paperwork was filed before your arrival and your tie to the Cuban government is a document stating you are authorised to receive any items recovered from the Cuban-registered and owned plane that crashed in our waters. That appear accurate to you, Mr. Gurov?"

Mikhail held Roy's stare for an eternity without changing expression. He finally responded but didn't look away, "This is all correct, which is why I agreed to this delay. Perhaps you can hurry up with your questions so we can expedite this process as my return was expected today."

Roy smiled a little wider as though he appreciated the Russian's position. "Absolutely."

He carefully opened his notebook and took a pen from his shirt pocket, taking his time again. "So, according to you, Carlos Rojas, a young lad from Cuba, was the pilot of the plane?"

"According to the Republic of Cuba he was, I am relaying what they tell me," Mikhail corrected.

"I see, so you don't know this Rojas fellow or anything about him?" Roy probed.

"Only what they provided in a report."

"Okay, anything in this report that may help us find Rojas? He is still unaccounted for," Roy continued.

Although he was more familiar with being the interrogator, Mikhail was well aware of interview techniques and could tell Whittaker was setting him up for something but he wasn't sure exactly what. His whole presence on the island was a lie from the beginning so there was a string of details the detective may have found suspicious or conflicting. All he could do was follow along, not say too much, and think quickly.

"I would share the report with you, Detective, but it is the property of the Republic of Cuba, so without their permission I'm afraid I cannot."

Roy noted he didn't answer the question. "I understand. But you're confident he was acting alone?"

"I am confident my contact with the Republic of Cuba tells me he was acting alone," Mikhail replied without hesitation.

"Perhaps then, you can tell me why you're looking for Regina Sydney Bodden, a Caymanian citizen?" Roy hit him with the key question and studied the man's face and posture, looking for any tells or indications.

There it is, Mikhail thought, remaining expressionless and answering promptly, "She's been dating Rojas for over a year, we thought she may know something; he flew to her home country after all."

Not a single quiver, tic, tensing, relaxing, nothing. This guy is really good, Roy realised. "You don't think that would have been pertinent information, contained in the report I presume, that would have been useful for our investigation? Not to mention we frown upon individuals conducting interrogations with our citizens."

"I assure you there was no interrogation, I simply asked some questions. But more to the point detective, can you account for the girl's whereabouts in the past three days? She is a Caymanian citizen after all," Mikhail fired back.

Roy kept the volleys flying, "We do not track our citizens Mr. Gurov, we are a free country after all, but for the record we show Miss Bodden exiting Cayman several months ago on a flight to Florida, where she goes to university."

"We identified Miss Bodden entering Cuba earlier this week and her whereabouts appear undetermined," Mikhail countered.

Roy stopped smiling. "So when you say you're confident Rojas was acting alone that is in fact not true, you suspect Miss Bodden of involvement?"

"As I said, my contact with the Republic of Cuba tells me he was acting alone, I suspect nothing and no one," Mikhail deftly deflected.

"So you're a marine biologist on a visitor's visa to our beautiful island, asking questions around town about one of our citizens and choosing not to share key information that may assist our investigation of a very suspicious plane crash in our waters? That about sum it up?" Roy threw everything at the Russian to see if the man would give anything away.

Mikhail's mouth turned at the corners in a hint of a smile. "You have my assurance I will not ask your people any more questions, Detective. May I retrieve the cases now?"

Roy leaned back, studying the Russian. The man appeared to be enjoying this. Roy had interviewed a lot of people, it came with the job; occasionally he came across fast thinkers that could twist and turn, artfully lying, but never had he questioned someone that seemed to enjoy the challenge. He knew Mikhail was too nimble to give anything much away but at least it was now clear that his frail cover was blown and the police would be watching him.

"Sure. Follow me, we have them in another building." Roy rose to leave.

Whittaker wasn't the sort of man to have personal grievances or missions against suspects; the facts were the facts and they separated the guilty from innocent. He wasn't the judge, his job was to provide the proof either way. But in this case he had to admit, it would feel good to put handcuffs on this guy.

56

———

Sydney pulled the edge of the curtain back and peeked outside towards the car park of the yacht club. There were four jetties extending from the land into the marina with berths separated by short piers on either side like a ladder. Each berth fitted two boats except the third jetty which had longer piers to accommodate bigger boats such as the Rum Runner. The bathrooms were at the top of the first jetty so she had to walk almost the entire length of the car park to reach the building. She couldn't see anyone along her jetty but further up the car park was a small group of tourists unloading from a tour boat that had just returned from Stingray City. She'd been watching for half an hour now and this was the quietest it had been. She really needed to go.

"I'm going," she said to Carlos and opened the deck door slowly and checked around again. He moved over to the window to keep an eye on her.

She'd found a baseball cap on the boat which she now pulled down low to hide her face as she briskly strode up the jetty. She was a little self-conscious wearing a hat with 'World's Best Hooker' emblazoned on the front next to a logo of a fishing hook, but she hadn't been spoilt for choice. Her nerves felt like tightly stretched violin strings ready to scream at the slightest touch. She checked up at the gate leading to the car park and scanned around again; the tourists were filtering to their cars, excitedly recounting their trip, otherwise all was clear. Through the gate she walked to the far side of the car park away from the marina and broke into a jog towards the buildings to her right about two hundred yards away.

Sydney caught something moving quickly in the corner of her eye to her right from behind a parked car. She instinctively flinched and broke into a sprint but what ever it was dove for her feet and she leapt over it like she was clearing hurdles in track back at school. It was a toss up who was more scared, the cat or Sydney, but they both kept moving at full speed in their respective directions with hearts racing. Realising a girl at full sprint across the car park was probably drawing attention, she eased down to a jog and looked back at the cat now sitting under another car licking its paw like nothing had happened. Bullshit, she thought, you were more scared than I was.

She slowed to a walk as she reached the bathrooms and looked for the ladies' room sign. This side was the men's of course, which meant she had to walk further around to the other side. She glanced over her shoulder before turning the corner at the building and when she turned back, exiting the men's room was a young man. Quickly looking down, she skirted around him and kept going but could sense he'd stopped and was watching her.

"Sydney? That you?" came the voice behind her.

There was no time to think; she reacted purely from instinct as adrenaline spiked again and her heart raced.

"Yo no hablo inglés," she blurted and ducked into the ladies room, rushed into a stall and locked the door behind her. She stood absolutely still and listened. Silence. She'd looked away so quickly she hadn't registered a face but the person had appeared to be around her age so she presumed it was a classmate from school or a friend of Thomas's. She was out of breath and trying desperately not to breathe heavily, each lungful drawn in and exhaled sounded like an echoing torrent of noise amongst the stillness. She heard a foot shuffle outside. Was he waiting for her? She held her breath. Finally she heard footsteps, starting slowly but getting quieter, as the person walked away. She let out her breath in a surge of air and relief and quickly sat down, her urgent need to pee returning rapidly.

Joshua Ebanks worked in the boat repair yard behind the marina where their bathroom was suffering a plumbing problem. He ambled back towards work mulling over what just took place. He'd been on the same track-and-field team as Sydney Bodden at John Gray High School, although it had been a few years since he'd seen her. It was a fleeting look as they'd passed by and he didn't get a good look at her face with a baseball cap on but that walk and her lean, athletic build sure looked familiar. He took out his mobile phone and opened Facebook. Looking in his friends list he found Sydney Bodden and went to her page. He paused and thought a moment, studying a few of the pictures. Going back to her timeline he typed, 'Ran into your twin at the yacht club! Made me think of you. How are you doing?' He chuckled and hit send.

57

Whittaker led the Russian out the main office building to a smaller structure at the far end of a yard where the police parked their vehicles. They entered a secure room with benches around the perimeter, an open area large enough for several vehicles in the centre and a roll-up door leading from the yard. The sign on the door read 'CSI No Unauthorised Persons'. Spread across the floor were the remains of the seaplane. The cases were set on the benches and laid open with the contents inside.

"Everything has been examined by our team and returned as they were found to each case. Here's a list of the contents contained in each one," Roy handed some paperwork to Mikhail, who was eyeing the wreckage.

Reluctantly turning away from the plane, Mikhail systematically read each item and inspected the matching case contents, verifying the inventory. Roy waited patiently while the man checked every single item regardless of how meaningless or small. When he was done he turned to Roy. "You confirm this is everything removed from the seaplane and the surrounding area?"

"Yes sir, this is it. Were you expecting something else?"

Mikhail ignored the question. "We will arrange for the items to be collected as soon as possible."

Roy looked surprised. "I thought you were in a big hurry to get these back to the Republic of Cuba?"

Mikhail folded his copies of the inventory and put them in his back pocket. "I need to arrange a vehicle to move them."

Roy smiled. "I'll be happy to deliver them to your hotel, where are you staying on the island?"

Mikhail lied, "We're not, we're staying on our research vessel."

"No problem then, I'll have a van deliver them to the dock and a marine unit can take them out to your boat." Roy took out his mobile phone to start making arrangements.

"Please, delivery to the dock is adequate, we have a skiff we use to go back and forth," Mikhail quickly added; he had no intention of letting Whittaker snoop around the trawler – the customs and immigration guys were enough.

Roy paused before dialling his mobile. "Fair enough, I'll get a van pulled around now."

While Roy called dispatch and organised a van, Mikhail closed all the cases and carried them to the roll-up door. Each time he walked beside the wreckage he scanned it intently and took a slightly different path. Two minutes later a vehicle could be heard outside and the door went up. A constable helped Mikhail load the cases and arranged where to drop them at the steps in the harbour that led down to the water. Before Roy pulled the door down behind them he stopped Mikhail.

"Mr. Gurov, now you have the cargo returned may I ask how much longer you'll be staying on the island?"

Mikhail half turned but didn't face him. "Aren't we still missing something, Detective?"

"As I said, that's everything we pulled from the plane and we have to wait for the Air Accidents Investigation Branch from the UK to examine the plane itself; they'll be here in a few days but that will take weeks to complete." Roy replied.

"You're forgetting Rojas, Detective – you have, as of yet, failed to recover the pilot." He turned the rest of the way and stared at Roy to punctuate the failure.

Roy nodded slowly. "I wouldn't wait around, bodies can take a while to show up and often never do. All kinds of ways they get carried off; as a marine biologist you would know that better than I."

Mikhail paused, deciding his next play. "Tomorrow, Detective, I expect we'll leave tomorrow." With that he turned and walked away.

Roy called after him, "Guess we'll see you when you come back to do your research then?"

Mikhail faltered a moment but then continued across the yard without answering.

Roy almost chuckled as he closed the roll-up door and secured it. Taking out his mobile he dialled a number. "Spalding? It's Whittaker, do me a favour, find where Mr. Mikhail Gurov is staying on the island please. It'll be on Seven Mile Beach, odds are the Marriott, everyone from off island knows the Marriott. Thanks."

He hung up and dialled another number. "Judge, it's Detective Whittaker, would you happen to be in George Town this afternoon? You are? Perfect. Can I trouble you for a small favour?"

58

Pavlo hit the space bar on his laptop as the screen went into sleep mode and it woke back up, displaying an array of scrolling windows and data. He needed waking up, he thought; this was as tedious as surveillance could get. Stuck inside this stinking hot, smelly boat that constantly reminded him of puking even when it wasn't rolling around, staring at his computer program and listening to the police scanner. The excitement from the Royal Cayman Islands Police Service today was two cars bumping into each other in George Town, a small group of drunks being escorted back to their cruise ship and early this morning a bicycle reported stolen in West Bay. According to a later report the owner had found said bicycle.

The Russian Foreign Intelligence Service's scanning software trolled the worldwide web for hits on any keywords Pavlo asked it to. Yesterday he'd churned through hits on existing articles from the names he'd supplied as search keywords. Bodden, as one of the original families on the island returned an unmanageable number of articles, but filtering down to Thomas and Regina Sydney had reduced it to a couple of hours of checking. The bulk of the Internet references was from Sydney's track-and-field success in high school and subsequently university in Miami. Thomas came up from two years ago in a flood of news about a German U-boat discovery off the coast of Cayman. Mikhail had added AJ Bailey and Reg Moore to the search keywords that morning, which brought up many of the same articles. None of them had had much activity in the past week – a couple of social media posts on Mermaid Divers' and Pearl Divers' business pages, all innocuous pictures tagging happy customers and drawing comments about their dives.

He sat back and sipped his lukewarm coffee, the fifth cup of the day, and contemplated another cigarette, the daily count he chose to ignore once it surpassed 'too many'. The laptop dinged an alert. Pavlo leaned in and clicked on the recent Internet hit from his keywords. The program opened a new window showing the activity while not letting the website know it was being seen or allowing a cookie. Someone had recently posted something on Sydney Bodden's Facebook timeline.

"Shit!" Pavlo exclaimed at the first decent lead in two days. Fumbling for his mobile he excitedly texted Mikhail with a screen-shot of the post.

Silvio strolled into the galley where Pavlo was set up at the table. He nodded at the Russian. "How's it going?" he asked, for something to say more than interest.

"We've got them," the Russian declared proudly. "It was just a matter of time." He smiled smugly.

Silvio looked slightly surprised. "That's good." He responded before he had contemplated what that really meant. At the end of the day it probably meant that his friend Carlos would be locked away for the rest of his life, or more likely he'd be executed. He didn't think that was good. But what could he do?

59

———

Carlos alternated between looking out the window, checking his watch and swearing in his native tongue. It had been forty-five minutes since Sydney left and no sign of her. His mind raged with scenarios from Mikhail abducting her to the police picking her up to Sydney being suddenly struck with good sense and leaving him. God knows he deserved it, he thought; who in their right mind would put up with this madness, risking everything for his crazy stand to save a reef and some fish? He paced around and had an extra bout of foul language, digging deep in his repertoire of Spanish swear words. The door from the deck slid open and Sydney shot in, closing it quickly behind her. Carlos pounced on her, throwing his arms around her and squeezing her as tightly as he could.

"I was so scared, so scared, I thought they'd got you," he babbled half in Spanish, half in English.

She relaxed in his arms and soaked up the moment, savouring the urgency and safety of his embrace. After the tension and fear she'd just been through his arms felt like a fortress around her. Involuntary tears rolled down her face and dampened his shirt.

"Someone saw me," she managed. "I hid in the bathroom."

She tore herself away from his arms and carefully looked around the curtain to the jetty and car park; all looked clear.

"Who saw you?" Carlos asked urgently.

"I don't know, I think it was someone from school or maybe just from town, but he called my name."

"Shit, what did you do?" He put a hand on her shoulder as she stepped away from the window.

"I pretended I didn't speak English and ran into the bathroom." She laughed at how silly that sounded.

"What did he do?" Carlos persisted.

"He waited a while and then walked off, I think, I mean I couldn't see but I heard his footsteps. I didn't see him when I came out and ran back."

He softly wiped a tear from her cheek. "It'll be fine, hopefully he thinks he was mistaken. It's okay my love, you're safe now." He drew her close again and held her.

She whispered in his ear, "If we run out of food there's a cat out there I'm okay frying up."

<h1 style="text-align:center">60</h1>

Whittaker marched through the expansive lobby of the Marriott Hotel on Seven Mile Beach with a constable in tow. Guests in bathing suits or shorts and golf shirts milled about heading for the pool and the golf course. Roy grinned at the constable as he was distracted by a couple of young ladies in particularly skimpy swimsuits. He flashed his badge to the receptionist before she could start her greeting monologue.

"Detective Whittaker and my associate Constable Spalding. I talked to your manager on the phone, a Mr. Johnson, is he available?"

The young lady smiled although she was clearly alarmed by the police showing up. "One moment please, Detective, let me check for you."

She scuttled off to the offices behind the lavish reception desk and quickly returned with a smartly dressed Caymanian man who looked equally concerned.

"Hello, I'm the manager, you must be Detective Whittaker?" They shook hands and Johnson made his way out from behind the desk.

"Nice to meet you Mr. Johnson and thank you for helping us at short notice," Roy said, smiling.

The manager glanced around the lobby, probably worried how the police presence might affect gift shop sales and beckoned the men to follow him, seemingly eager to get them out of sight. Whittaker held out some paperwork. "Here's the search warrant." Johnson didn't even look back to see it.

"I'm sure you have everything in order, Detective, let's just get this done as quickly as possible."

Whittaker shrugged his shoulders, put the paperwork back in his jacket pocket and followed the man down a hallway until they arrived at the room they were looking for. Johnson knocked loudly on the door.

"Hotel manager, may I have a word sir?"

No response. He knocked again and paused a moment before swiping his master key. "I'm entering the room sir."

Whittaker put a hand on his shoulder and stopped him entering. "Best you wait out here, we'll let you know when we're done."

Disappointed, the manager stepped aside and let the two policeman enter the hotel room. Whittaker proceeded cautiously but announced his presence, "Royal Cayman Islands Police Service entering, please show yourselves if you're present."

The room was clear and the constable checked the bathroom and announced it was clear as well. The men relaxed a notch and, donning nitrile gloves to preserve any evidence, they began their search of the room. It was a twin room with two queen-size beds and Roy noted two duffel bags indicating the Russians were sharing the room. He lifted the first bag onto the bed and began examining the contents. Spalding checked in the bedside table drawers, under both beds and the dresser drawers, finding nothing belonging to a visitor. He moved to the second duffel bag. Roy found nothing but clothes in the bag he'd searched and after checking the duffel thoroughly for hidden pockets and double lining he returned the garments.

"Sir!" Constable Spalding blurted, reaching in the bag he was searching. "You'll want to see this."

Spalding carefully held up a revolver by the barrel, staying well clear of the trigger.

"Well I'll be..." Roy muttered.

Shaking out a clear plastic evidence bag Spalding asked, "Surely they know we don't allow firearms on the island sir?"

"Indeed, I'm sure they know," Whittaker calmly commented, "but on the positive side, one –" he pointed at the revolver "– he doesn't have his gun with him, and two –" he smiled at the constable "– we can now arrest the arsehole."

61

Neither Carlos or Sydney had slept well for days so it didn't take much for them to fall asleep on the comfortable sofa, her head snuggled against his chest. Coming down from her excitement from earlier, Sydney drifted off quickly while Carlos faded in and out. With tired eyes half open he traced the line of her arm with his hand; her skin felt warm, smooth and comforting. His fingers came to rest at the watch on her wrist and he smiled as his eyes closed again. He hadn't been able to afford an expensive watch but apparently it was waterproof to at least forty feet, as it was still working. The water lapped at the hull and the gentle breeze made a soothing whisper as it softly rocked the boat. The floating pier system creaked and groaned in a low tone that seemed to have a slow rhythm in time with the water brushing the boat. And then it didn't. The creaking went out of rhythm. Subtly and quietly, the sounds were out of phase and Carlos's senses went on high alert. He gently placed a hand on Sydney's shoulder and squeezed firmly. "Wake up."

She mumbled but didn't wake so he lifted her head from his lap. "Sydney, wake up." She stirred awake and started to speak but he put his finger to his lips, "Be silent. Let me get up."

She sat up and he turned around, very carefully moving the curtain enough to see the jetty. He did not recognise the man who was slowly walking towards the Rum Runner, slacks, button-down shirt, polished black shoes, close-cropped haircut, but he had the same look as a Russian he did know and that was enough.

"They've found us!" he whispered frantically. Sydney was mortified and froze for a second.

"To the stateroom, quick." He led her to the forward main bedroom and grabbed the rucksack that still lay there. He unzipped the top and pulled out everything except the hard drive then stuffed a shirt back in around it for padding.

"There's no where to run Carlos, what can we do?" she stammered, looking over her shoulder and expecting the door to burst open any second.

"I won't be running, I'll be swimming," he smiled reassuringly at her.

She looked at him, confused. "You can't take the hard drive in the water."

"I'm not. As soon as he comes in the water after me, you will run and take this." He slipped the rucksack over her shoulder and held the other strap for her to put her other arm through.

"Carlos no, I'm not leaving you, we can't be separated!"

He leaned in, giving her a firm kiss and then reached up and sprung open the window hatch in the ceiling that opened to the bow of the boat, forward of the bridge. "You must, my love. He can't chase us both and he will not outswim me and once you are clear he can't outrun you."

A soft thud came from the stern and the boat rocked slightly, which they knew had to be the man stepping down to the deck. He was moments away from opening the door. Sydney swung around to look and Carlos used the bed to step up and pull himself through the hatch.

"No, Carlos, this is crazy!" she whispered desperately. He crouched and looked back down at her through the hatch. His eyes sparkled and pierced to her very core. "I love you."

With that he stood up, took one step towards the railing and leapt over, shattering the afternoon quiet with a loud splash as he hit the water.

Sydney froze. They'd gone from asleep to complete chaos in a matter of seconds and now the man she loved was in the water and a Russian agent was twenty feet away from her on the rear deck. She hadn't heard a second splash. She urged herself into motion and softly stepped as quietly as she could towards the stern through the lounge. The rear glass was tinted so no one could see in during daylight but she could see out. She brushed the curtain slightly aside. There he was on the starboard side trying to see who or what had made the splash in the water.

Anatoly scanned the surface where big ripples waved out from where whoever it was had dived in but was yet to surface. He had no idea if this was the boat they were hiding on so it could be a kid playing around or some big bird diving for fish; shit, he thought, could be some weird creature he'd never seen before on this sweaty damn island. A head popped up about fifteen feet from the boat towards the open water and the man turned and looked straight at Anatoly.

"Rojas!" the Russian yelled and instinctively reached for his revolver in his chest harness as he'd been trained to do, and practised endlessly. Nothing there. "Damn it," he cursed and reached behind his waistband where he'd been hiding it from Mikhail. Nothing. Unbelievable, he thought to himself, here I have an easy kill I can do in my sleep and that bureaucratic idiot Mikhail makes me leave my weapon at the hotel. With his hand behind his back and his body rotated awkwardly he was completely caught off guard by the missile that launched from the door of the boat and hammered into him.

• • •

Sydney charged with all she could muster and dropped a shoulder to catch the Russian on his left side at the ribcage. His legs buckled over the low side of the boat and he tumbled awkwardly over and into the water with a huge spray and crash. With outstretched hands she just caught herself from following him into the bay. Without hesitation she turned, took one long stride, leapt from the deck to the jetty and accelerated in a full sprint towards the gate, the rucksack slapping against her back. Relieved the Russian had left the gate open she hesitated to look back but could see neither man. She forced her concern for Carlos aside, knowing he was a strong swimmer; she had to believe that with a head start he could lose the attacker. Her focus had to be on getting the hard drive as far from the agent as possible. She turned right into the car park and ran down the pathway behind the fence.

As overwhelming as the last few days had been, adrenaline and fear kept her focused and rising anger and frustration powered her long muscular legs along the path at the head of the jetties. Eight hundred metres was her speciality in track but she regularly ran five miles or more for endurance training and five miles on Grand Cayman covered a lot of ground. But where should she go? She had time to figure that out as she ran; there was only one way off this spit of land and it would take a few minutes to reach the highway.

It felt like she had hit a brick wall. Someone stepped from behind an SUV and Sydney slammed into him at full speed. Stunned and dazed she had no resistance as the man expertly tie-wrapped her hands, removed the rucksack and manhandled her into the open boot of a car. The boot lid closing felt like a hammer falling on a verdict of failure and she was plunged into darkness. All she could feel was the utter despair of letting Carlos down.

62

————

Yacht Drive came off a roundabout on the dual carriageway and threaded through the mangroves towards the North Sound. A turn to the right wound around to the yacht club marina, a boat yard and a couple of restaurants on one spit of land. Straight ahead led to another spit with a warren of small neighbourhoods sporting high-dollar homes on the water. AJ drove her van straight and followed the narrow road around past smaller streets leading off either side into enclaves of huge homes on the inner waterways behind the sound. She pulled over on the right and parked at an opening in the mangroves that opened into a piece of land that had been cleared but not built on yet. From there she walked in the cover of occasional shrubs and small trees towards the end of the land which looked directly across at the yacht club.

She didn't feel an urgency to hide her presence; she was confident no one had followed her, but everything felt cloak and dagger at the moment so unconsciously she was staying near cover. As she approached the water's edge she picked out the Rum Runner in its slip about a hundred yards across the bay; nothing looked out of place. Then she noticed a man walking away along the jetty towards the gate to the car park. He wore slacks and a white shirt and, as she looked more closely, he appeared to be dripping wet, carrying his shoes in his hand.

"AJ!" an accented voice whispered urgently from nearby. Surprised, AJ swung around and tried to identify the source but couldn't see anyone.

"AJ! Over here, behind the bushes!" A hand waved from behind some scrub.

"Carlos?" she asked nervously before approaching any closer. Carlos leaned out so she could see him. He looked worried and he too was clothed and soaking wet.

"My God, what happened? Why are you over here?" She rushed over to him and ducked behind the bushes next to him.

"Did they see you?" he asked urgently.

"I don't think so, I saw a man leaving the jetty though, looked like he had been in the water too. Where's Sydney?" They both peered around their cover to watch the marina.

"I diverted the Russian while Sydney ran – she has the hard drive. She shoved him in the water and I took off swimming over here. He tried coming after me for a bit but gave up at the end of the jetty. By the time I climbed out here he was on the back of the boat. Looked like he went through the boat and searched it. He was just leaving when you showed up." Carlos wiped away the water that was running down his face from his wet hair.

Across at the marina the Russian made it through the open gate as a car pulled up and stopped. "That's the same car that followed me earlier this afternoon, that must be the Gurov guy driving." AJ blurted.

"So where's Sydney?" Carlos muttered in a worried tone.

The wet Russian got into the hire car and the car took off imme-diately.

AJ jumped up, "Run, quick!"

Carlos followed, puzzled. "Where are we going? We have to find Sydney!"

AJ yelled back over her shoulder in full sprint to her van, "Where do you think they're heading right now?!"

"Oh shit, of course!" Carlos put his head down and tried to catch AJ, surprised at how fast she ran.

They reached the van and AJ fumbled the key into the ignition and fired it up. Slamming the transmission into gear she took off just as Carlos closed the passenger door. Flooring the throttle pedal she shot down the road and flung the big van around a couple of turns before slamming on the brakes, much to Carlos's surprise. He pitched forward, stopping himself with a hand on the dashboard.

"Hang on!" AJ yelled.

"I figured that out," he quipped, grabbing for his seatbelt as she turned hard right through a gap in the mangroves onto a tiny dirt path. With shrubs scraping down both sides of the fifteen-passenger van AJ popped over a kerb and landed on an asphalt street with large houses fronting another part of the bay beyond. Cutting to the left she ran parallel to Yacht Drive, hidden by the bushes and trees separating them. She pulled the van to a stop, powered down the windows and shut off the ignition. They both sat still and listened carefully. Except for the sound of their heavy breathing, from the run and the sudden excitement, and a few birds twittering in the shrubs, it was silent. Finally, the low drone of a car's engine rose as it approached along Yacht Drive and faded as it kept going past them in the direction they'd come from.

Mikhail cruised slowly, glancing from the map on his phone to the road and surrounding terrain. Anatoly, pissed off and bedraggled, scoured every piece of open terrain, keen to exact revenge on the kid that had helped sucker him into the water, for which Mikhail had rewarded him with a good arse-chewing. The girl had thumped on the inside of the boot a few times but stopped when Mikhail growled at her to shut up, threatening to wrap her head to toe in duct tape. Mikhail had been searching boats on one of the other jetties when he heard the commotion and saw Sydney run; all he had to do was lie in wait and she literally ran into him. Now, on the back seat sat the rucksack containing the hard drive, fifty percent of what they'd been sent to retrieve. The other half of their mission was somewhere on this spit of land, hiding. Take care of that problem and they were heading home.

Mikhail's phone rang and he stared at the caller ID, deciding whether to answer or not.

He hit accept. "Detective, how can I help you?" Mikhail answered and pulled the car over, listening to Whittaker.

"Mr. Gurov, we have some news on the case, could you please come back to the station so I can brief you?"

Mikhail's monotone showed a hint of annoyance. "I was just with you, can you not tell me this information over the phone? I have a lot to do if we're to leave tomorrow."

Thumps and muffled groans echoed from the boot of the car and Mikhail quickly opened his door and stepped out. Figuring the girl must have heard he was speaking with the detective he made sure he got out of earshot and pointed at Anatoly to go back and take care of it.

Anatoly watched his boss walk away, unsure exactly what was expected of him. Making his best guess he took the keys from the ignition and gathered the duct tape from the back seat. Checking around to make sure no one could see them, he popped the boot and the girl immediately went quiet and stared up at him, blinking at the bright sunlight pouring in. Mikhail had bound her wrists with plastic tie-wraps and put tape across her mouth. She lay motionless, staring up at Anatoly looking terrified and for a second he felt a tinge of shame. He also remembered the verbal lashing he'd just received for letting Carlos get away, which started when she embarrassingly bowled him over the side of the boat. He started peeling off a strip of tape to wrap her legs together but as he went to tear it off the roll a movement caught his eye a moment before he felt a stinging blow to the side of his head. He staggered back, stunned, dropping the tape as Sydney wriggled to her knees and threw one leg, the one that had kicked him, over the back of the car to climb out. Shaking off the ringing pain he stepped forward to grab her but before he could get to her a fist swept in and punched Sydney in the jaw, sending her sprawling back into the boot. Mikhail snatched up the tape and roughly bound her ankles, closed the boot and shoved the tape back into Anatoly's hands.

"Get in the car before you screw something else up," Mikhail barked.

Carlos and AJ ducked back behind the shrubs as the grey car shot past. It had been everything AJ could do to hold Carlos back when he saw Sydney in the boot and Mikhail strike her. She clung to him and held him down so he'd have to drag her with him, which he tried to do at first. They were no match for the two Russians and they both knew it but Carlos didn't care, he simply wanted to fight for his girl. He'd finally sat back with tears of frustration streaking his cheeks.

They rushed back to the van and AJ grabbed her mobile phone as she started the engine. "Carlos, I have to call Reg for help, I don't know that I can catch them now, we have to get out of this neighbourhood and they have a straight shot to the main road." She pulled away as soon as Carlos was in and accelerated hard again.

"Reg will insist we involve the police," she continued. "Honestly Carlos, I think it's time, we need their help."

"I don't care any more, whatever we need to do, Sydney is more important than anything to me," Carlos replied desperately.

AJ took the winding paved road back to Yacht Drive and turned right towards the highway, but the grey car containing the two Russians and Thomas's sister was long gone. She slowed down and dialled Reg on her phone, putting it on speaker.

It rang twice before Reg picked up. "Hey, did you check on them?"

"The Russians have Sydney," AJ got straight to the point. "I don't know how they found them but they did. I have Carlos but they grabbed Sydney and the hard drive."

"Oh shit! Any idea where they headed?" Reg sounded ready to give chase.

"We lost them – they chased us but we managed to hide. The Gurov guy got a phone call and then they left in a hurry. I'm worried they'll take Sydney and the hard drive to the boat and leave," AJ said, continuing slowly down Yacht Drive.

Carlos added, "We have to find Sydney, she's innocent in all this, I dragged her into it and now she's been taken. Whatever we have to do to stop them and get her safe, Reg." Carlos was beside himself.

"Alright, we'll find them, it's a small island, but I have to call Whittaker and tell him, we need to tell him everything now," Reg warned.

"Whatever we need to do to get her back, police, trade me for her, whatever," Carlos begged.

"It won't come to that, I'll call him now," Reg assured them and hung up the phone.

AJ rolled to the end of the road and stopped the van, unsure what to do or where to head next. They looked at each other. She could see the desperation in his eyes, the disbelief that his noble effort to save a beautiful stretch of reef could lead to the current mess they were in.

"We'll get her and the hard drive back, Carlos, we just have to figure out what their next moves will be. If we were them what would we be trying to do now?" AJ asked, trying to think it through.

"That's simple I think," Carlos said in a wavering voice, "They have the hard drive, now all they need is me out of the way."

"Agreed, so why did they leave when they knew you had to be around here?" AJ puzzled.

"I can't figure that out either. Maybe they think the evidence is enough, no one will listen to me without something to prove what I say?"

"Perhaps," AJ said, mulling it over, "but I have to think they'd be in a hurry to get the hard drive safely to the boat, or just destroy it, right? You said they have backups of everything? They don't need the hard drive, they just need to make sure you don't have it."

"I guess that's true," Carlos agreed. "But what about Sydney?"

AJ thought carefully about how to reply. The truth was she couldn't think of any good reasons they'd want to hang on to her, unless they planned to trade her for Carlos, as he'd mentioned. But the logistics of that didn't fit: the Russians had no open line of communication with Carlos, and where could they hide her? Where could they meet? This was not a big island and wasn't the Russians' home turf. No, she wasn't part of their plan, she just happened to be holding the hard drive when they grabbed it, now she was another problem they had to deal with. AJ couldn't believe she was thinking about this like they could do anything against a group of Russian agents or whatever these guys were; certainly they weren't geologists. They didn't need Sydney or the hard drive. But they couldn't leave loose ends on the island that led to them, and Sydney would be a loose end. But no one officially knew she was on the island.

AJ felt the urgency rising within her, as Carlos became more defeated and overwhelmed, she became more determined. The answer was the Cuban boat. If both the hard drive and Sydney needed to disappear the obvious place was the vast ocean surrounding them. How do you dump things in the ocean? You take a boat and head away from land.

"We have to get to their boat, that's where they'll take her." She sounded more convincing than she felt but he needed hope and she was hell bent on doing something more than sitting in her van by the side of the road.

"How do we get to the boat without them knowing?" Carlos asked, perking up at the suggestion of a plan.

"I don't know but let's get to the harbour and we'll figure something out. Hopefully Reg has got Whittaker arresting the Russians right now and it'll all be over before we get downtown."

AJ hoped with all her heart that Roy could have Gurov and his buddy in handcuffs by the time they were to the port, but something told her it wouldn't be that easy.

63

Roy Whittaker sat down at his desk, placing the gun from the hotel room in front of him, safely wrapped in an evidence bag. He took a deep breath. Firearms unfortunately made their way onto the island occasionally but it wasn't every day he prepared himself to put a Russian agent in custody for possession of one. Or for any other reason. He wasn't sure exactly what role Gurov played in this pantomime but he was certain the man wasn't a marine biologist, all of which made this more complicated. He needed to make sure he aligned all the details correctly or this could be an embarrassing episode for the RCIPS, played out in the scandal-hungry press. Roy didn't crave attention, and whenever possible actively avoided getting his name in the papers, but more important in his mind was upholding the good name of the police service and representing it appropriately. If this whole business became wrapped up in politics and went sideways it could certainly reflect poorly on the department. But that aside, he'd found an illegal weapon and his job was to react appropriately, so act he would. If he did his job correctly everything else would take care of itself.

His mobile phone rang and he checked the caller ID. Reg Moore. He pondered a moment. Gurov should arrive any moment and he had arranged to meet him in the police yard behind the station; he wanted to be waiting when he got there. His curiosity was too much – deciding he could talk and walk he answered as he headed for the door, putting the evidence bag in his jacket pocket.

"Hey Reg, I've only got a couple of minutes, how can I help you?"

Whittaker stopped midway down the stairs at Reg's opening line, "Roy, you have my sincerest apologies but I've not been straight with you and now we have a big problem."

The detective's shoulders dropped. He'd known there was something Reg was holding back but this sounded bad. "I assume it has something to do with our Russian friend Mr. Gurov?"

"It does," Reg replied, "and your missing pilot, but more importantly right now it involves Thomas's sister Sydney Bodden."

"Start with the Gurov part Reg, he's on his way here right now, then tell me about the Bodden girl." Roy asked urgently.

There was a pause on the line. "The Russian is coming to you?"

"Yes, I had a matter to discuss with him, he may be waiting downstairs; I was on my way down." Roy decided until he heard Reg's full story he wouldn't mention the gun and his intended arrest.

"Open the boot of his car and you should find Sydney tied up in there."

Roy was incredulous. "What? Are you serious?" He started back down the stairwell in a hurry. "My God, do you know if she's okay?"

"She was alive and kicking ten minutes ago," Reg relayed.

Whittaker reached the lower floor and waved over Constable Spalding. Holding the phone aside he directed the policeman, "Spalding, get me three more constables to the yard and find any detective in the building and have them come down immediately." He shouted after Spalding as the constable took off to round up people, "Tell the detective to come armed!"

He returned the phone to his ear and stepped out the back into the empty yard, trying to process the barrage of new information. "Where's the pilot, Rojas? I assume he's alive?"

"He is," Reg admitted, "He and Sydney were in the plane, they both got out okay. Carlos is with AJ, they're the ones that saw Gurov grab Sydney."

"Damn it Reg." Roy tried to stem his frustration, but why did everyone choose to make his job more difficult? "Why the hell didn't you all just come to me from the beginning? If the kid wants asylum we could have worked with him."

"I know, I'm sorry Roy, but it's more complicated than that, it's not about asylum, he has information on the Cuban government and the Russians' involvement that needs to be known."

Roy cut him off as a detective and several constables poured out the door into the yard. "He'll be here any moment, I need to hang up, but Reg?"

"Yes Roy," Reg answered hesitantly.

"Bring Rojas to the station, now."

64

It wasn't just dark in the boot of the car, it was ink black, not a sliver of light anywhere. As if being kidnapped, bound and gagged and stuffed in the boot of a car wasn't terrifying enough, the complete darkness added another element of fear. The only thing it helped was the claustrophobia. Sydney felt something against her when she moved in any direction and she was sure if she could see how confined the interior of the boot was it would put her over the edge. The 'edge', she thought laughingly. If anyone had asked her three days ago what her limit was, what would be too much too handle? Where was her 'edge'? She would have stopped the ride sometime during the flight in the storm, well before the plane crash – or 'harsh landing', she could hear Carlos saying. Before the ride to the sea bed, before the desperate escape and subsequent mayhem on the surface. Definitely before the kidnapping by Russian thugs. Maybe she hadn't reached her 'edge' yet? Maybe she could take more than she thought? She shifted uncomfortably and her arm, foot and head all bumped a confining surface simultaneously. She fought down the overwhelming urge to crumble into total panic. No, she was teetering at the cliff of her personal 'edge'. Her jaw throbbed. Thinking about the pain distracted her from the panic and she made note of that. She needed something to focus on.

They'd bounced down the road and then made a curve on a smoother surface; she'd barely noticed in her state of shock and fear but now she tried to focus on anything she could pick up from her other senses. She felt the car turn left then right then left again – that must have been the roundabout where the redirected West Bay Road met the dual carriageway, they'd gone straight over, staying on the bypass. Another roundabout, this would be the one by the cut price market, same thing, they'd stayed straight on the bypass. Should be some bumps ahead where the pavement had been poorly repaired. She waited and sure enough the car bumped and rumbled over the uneven surface, jolting her around in the boot. Forgetting her anxiety, a little excitement crept in as she felt connected again to the outside world just knowing where she was. Another roundabout, that would be the one with no other exits which no one knew why they'd ever built.

A voice from the car. They hadn't said a word since they'd driven off but now she could hear the muffled voice of one of them speaking in excellent Spanish. The sound was dulled but she could make out what he said.

"Bring the skiff to the port, same place, we'll be there in five minutes." The voice paused, presumably listening to whoever was on the other end of the line.

He continued, "Just you, and bring a cover or blanket, you need to hurry."

Back to silence. The car had been curving slightly back and forth and now took a bigger arc left, right, left, which she determined was the roundabout at the north end of Camana Bay. She was amazed how much information was streaming into her senses, she was confident she knew where she was and fairly sure where they were going. The fear rose again like an evil serpent wrapping itself around her throat and tightening its hold, constricting her breathing, quickening her pulse and closing the world in around her. What would happen when they got there? She worked her jaw back and forth causing a searing pain to jolt though her skull and drag her consciousness back from the brink. I have to stay focused and alert, she demanded repeatedly, as a swaying left then long right forced her to visualise the road she knew and figure out the turns. Left again. They'd turned towards Seven Mile Beach off the dual carriageway. A short distance and then slowing to a stop. Edging forward. Left turn. They must be on West Bay Road now behind the hotels and condos on Seven Mile Beach. These guys didn't know the twists and turns you had to take through the back of George Town to the harbour so they'd joined the tourists on the front road.

The voice she heard earlier spoke again, but this time in Russian, which she couldn't understand. The second man appeared to acknowledge what the first one said, he was clearly subservient in his manner; he must work for him she presumed. The first man spoke some more, monotone, deliberate, unfriendly. He sounded businesslike, giving commands. What were the instructions he was giving? Were they the specifics of how she would be dealt with? Disposed of? She shivered at the paralysing thought. Silence again. They rolled to a stop. She heard traffic moving around them so maybe a red light? That would mean Lawrence Boulevard or were they already at the edge of George Town at Eastern Avenue?

Time was running out, they'd be at the dock soon; she tugged and pulled at the plastic ties wrapped around her wrists but they were tight and dug in painfully when she tried to twist them. Her watch strap dug into her wrist as well and she wondered if she could use the strap to cut the tape. She shifted focus to her ankles that were wrapped in tape. She tried to bend backwards to get her hands that were strapped behind her back to her ankles but her knees hit the front of the boot and she was wedged in place. Sydney wriggled and twisted but her height was against her in the confined boot and she couldn't get her fingers to the ankle tape. If she could get her feet free again she'd take another swing at them, she had a chance at surprise as they expected her to be trussed up. Maybe she could cause enough ruckus to get someone's attention.

She stretched and reached and squeezed her body into a painful arch with parts of her body shoving against parts of the car. Her fingers extended until it felt like her tendons would tear themselves apart and finally touched the edge of the duct tape. She scraped her knees hard against the side of the car, which moved her ankles a tiny amount closer enough to get the nail of her index finger firmly on the tightly stretched edge of the tape. She nicked the tape and felt it give. The car stopped. She couldn't hear any traffic. She was out of time and options to get free as just then she felt her watch strap come undone. The engine cut and the doors opened. She made her last attempt at survival. The boot lid opened and strong hands roughly dragged her out and before she could focus in the flash of sunlight she was tossed into the bottom of a small boat and everything returned to darkness as a smelly canvas sheet was thrown over her.

65

AJ pulled the van into the narrow parking next to a dive operator's office on the north side of Casanova restaurant. The building shielded their view of the harbour but walking around to the concrete pier, extending a hundred feet into the water, revealed the Cuban trawler moored outside the port. Carlos followed AJ down the pier, nervously looking around in case he was recognised. This was the first time he'd been in the open since landing in Cayman three days ago.

"Hasn't moved." AJ pointed to the trawler.

"I can't believe they brought the Explorador de la Reina all the way here; that poor old boat struggles back and forth to the islands off Cuba, that must have been quite a trip in the storm," Carlos sympathised.

They both stood staring at the old trawler-turned-research vessel resting idly in the flat, calm water. From behind the concrete structure of the port a small skiff appeared slowly chugging towards the Cuban boat.

"Look," AJ alerted Carlos.

"That's our skiff!" Carlos immediately recognised the little craft, "And that's Silvio driving it."

The skiff had a small outboard with one man at the tiller and a second man sitting in the bow.

Carlos continued, "I don't know the other guy but it looks like one of the Russians doesn't it?"

AJ strained her eyes at the little boat a thousand yards away. "Yeah, I'm pretty sure that's the one that we saw open the boot." She pictured the man standing there stunned from Sydney's kick. "Where's the other Russian, I wonder?"

Something moved between the two men, a cover of some sort. "Did you see that?" Carlos shouted.

AJ did, but was it fluttering in the wind or was there something else there? The cover moved again as the skiff disappeared behind the trawler, pulling up along the starboard side, the far side from them.

"They have her! They have Sydney! We must get to the boat before they leave!" Carlos looked at the water between the pier and the trawler as though he was contemplating swimming across right now.

"Wait, wait," AJ grabbed his arm, "You can't go there, if they catch you they have everything they need!"

Carlos paused and looked at her, his eyes frantic. "I swear that was her they have in the skiff, they've taken her to the Explorador, I'm sure the hard drive too. They're going to leave, we have to stop them! Once they go we lose everything; I cannot let them take Sydney!"

AJ had been thinking all along about getting to the boat and every time she'd convinced herself it was a crazy idea. They had no clue who was on that boat but she was nearly as convinced as Carlos that Sydney was on the skiff, which probably meant they'd pull anchor and leave. Why wasn't the other guy with them? She looked at Carlos.

"Of course, the other Russian stayed." She waited for him to figure it out.

"To find me," Carlos caught on.

"I'll go to the boat, you have to stay hidden." AJ started back towards the van.

Carlos trailed her. "No way, you can't go alone, I have to come too, you don't know the boat. Besides, how can you get to the boat without them seeing you?"

AJ opened the back door of her van and dragged out her dive kit and a tank. "Don't worry, they won't see me coming."

"Shit," he said, surprised, "that might work. But you still don't know the boat, I have to come with you." He reached in the van to grab another kit but there wasn't one, only tanks.

AJ smiled. "Sorry. Tell me all about the boat, I need to know the layout."

She hauled the gear to the pier, questioning her sanity all the way, but every other option seemed to have the same dead-end answer. If they called Whittaker he'd need proof before searching a foreign boat, she'd learnt this before. Besides, hopefully Reg had him chasing the other Russian and in case they were wrong and Sydney was still in his boot, he needed to catch him. They could go get her boat but by the time they got her boat in West Bay and came back the trawler could be gone, and if it wasn't they'd see her coming anyway. If she didn't act now the Cuban boat would leave, she was sure of it, and they'd never see Sydney or the hard drive again. The Gardens of the Queen would be destroyed and she could have stopped it. Well, tried to at least. She had to at least try.

She realised Carlos was telling her about the boat and pushed her mental debates aside to pay attention.

"There's not many cabins and only three levels so it's not too complicated but everything's quite small and tight. The top level you can see," Carlos pointed to the trawler, directing AJ to the wheelhouse. "Stay away from there. You have to go up the outside stairs behind it or inside from the main deck and there's no reason to go there. The main deck level is the galley and the dining area which is most likely where people will be. Problem is you have to go in the back of that section to get to the stairs down to the lower deck. When you go in the door, which enters from the stern, the stairs down are on your right, but the hall ahead opens into the galley and then the dining room. Once down the stairs there are only cabins and doors to the engine room and storage. Most likely they will put her in a cabin down there." Carlos made the sign of the cross and put his hands together. "I pray they do this."

AJ finished preparing her gear and jogged back to the van with Carlos in tow. "Okay, so I need to go through the door in the back, down the stairs to the right, and there will be some cabins and she should be in one of them?"

"Yes. And the guy who was driving the skiff, that's Silvio, he's a good man. I believe he would be helpful if you ran into him and told him you were with me; we are friends. He's doing what he's told by Gurov but at heart he doesn't want to hurt anybody. The other Cuban that's probably on the boat is Julio – he's younger, I don't know about him, he doesn't care about much except having a good time so I wouldn't trust him."

AJ took off her tee shirt and shorts and slipped a wetsuit top over her bathing suit, relieved she made the decision to wear a swimsuit. She didn't have a full wetsuit in the van but at least the top would give her some coverage; she really didn't want to lay siege to a Cuban trawler in a two-piece bathing suit.

"Okay, so I'm going to try and avoid anybody but if I do run into somebody, let's hope it's your friend." She closed the van door.

"So what exactly is your plan?" Carlos asked with more than a hint of concern.

AJ walked back down the pier to her gear. "That's a good question."

She dipped her mask in the water and washed it out, thinking, what is my plan?

"I'm going to get Sydney and leave. If the hard drive is handy I'll take that too. Mind you, as we'll be back in the water when we leave I doubt that'll help. Beyond that I think I'll have to make it up as I go." She attempted a smile but she knew it wasn't convincing. After all, if she couldn't convince herself, how would she convince

Carlos? She sat on the side of the pier and slipped into her BCD and buckled it, the base of the heavy tank banging on the concrete pier.

"I should be going with you," Carlos said solemnly.

AJ slipped her fins on and looked up at Carlos. "I know you want to but you need to stay hidden, I'll be fine. Hide in the van; the keys are in the ignition in case you need to move but just stay out of sight if at all possible." She pulled her mask down.

"Thank you AJ, be safe, I will see you both shortly," he managed, though his voice was cracking.

AJ gave him an okay sign. "Be right back, oh and check my phone, it's in the van, maybe Reg will call with good news. But whatever you do don't tell him or anyone I've gone to the boat. They'll send in the cavalry and if we're right the trawler will take off." She turned and looked at Carlos, hoping he could see her serious expression through the lens of her mask. "Promise me Carlos, you can't tell them. Well, let's say for one hour; if I haven't come back by then I'd say send the cavalry, I probably need them. Promise?"

"Okay," Carlos muttered reluctantly, "I promise."

AJ pushed off the pier into the clear blue warm water to a scatter of small fish. Before she could second guess herself any further, she descended and kicked away from shore.

66

Whittaker looked up as a grey four-door saloon rolled slowly through the open gates into the police yard and pulled up next to him. He could see Mikhail scan the yard but if he was alarmed at the constables and detectives waiting for him his face didn't betray it. Roy smiled and waited patiently for the Russian to weigh his options.

Mikhail shut off the engine and stepped from the car. "What is so important that I had to come here, Detective?"

The armed detective kept his weapon concealed but moved to keep a clear view of Mikhail without Roy blocking his vantage, Mikhail's eyes calmly tracked him. Roy noted the man's every move was slow and predictable; his eyes weren't darting about but slowly took in all around him. There was no doubt in Roy's mind Mikhail was a highly trained agent well versed in keeping situations calm.

Roy extended his hand to the Russian. "Thank you for indulging me, just a few loose ends I'd like to clear up."

Mikhail shook his hand firmly. "Fine, I'm here, what are your loose ends I can help you with?"

Roy maintained his smile. "I must have been mistaken yesterday, I thought you told me you weren't staying on island?"

Mikhail paused, clearly processing but his expression never changed. "Why is this important? Surely you have more pressing concerns than where I sleep?"

Roy's smile widened. "Indeed I do sir, your sleep is of no concern to me." His smile evaporated. "But I prefer to be told the truth Mr. Gurov, that is a concern to me."

Now Mikhail laughed, which he managed without any sign of joy. "And I prefer my privacy detective, so I omitted to tell you I took a hotel room. Again, how is this important enough to interrupt both of our busy days?" He looked around him at the other policeman all watching him or looking at his car, "And tie up half your police force it appears."

Roy's reply was all business. "Are you aware, sir, that it is strictly illegal to bring a firearm to the Cayman Islands?"

Finally Mikhail's expression changed, his face tightened and his jaw set. They were all subtle signs but Roy could tell he was angry.

"Is it normal in the Cayman Islands to search the rooms of foreign diplomatic guests, Detective?" Mikhail's voice was now tense and his eyes were darting from Roy to the other detective.

"Only when they act suspiciously and a judge agrees to issue a search warrant," Roy calmly replied. He knows he has the Russian trapped and can tell Mikhail has come to the same conclusion. Trapped is when a man like this could be the most dangerous but Roy cautiously assumed Mikhail was smart enough to know his options were limited.

"I had to do some searching to find an MP-443 Grach in our database, we don't see too many guns here." Roy looked Mikhail squarely in the eyes. "Other than the ones we carry." He wanted to make sure the Russian knew their little island police force weren't just going to yell stop if he ran. "A Russian-made gun issued to Russian military and the Foreign Intelligence Service of the Russian Federation. Seems strange for a marine biologist to carry a weapon in the first place but certainly one issued to soldiers and agents, Mr. Gurov?"

Mikhail relented, appearing to accept his cover was blown. "How would you like to proceed, Detective? Obviously my government will be eager to secure my exit from your island so why don't we contact our nearest embassy, which will be the one on Cuba?"

Roy pointed in the direction of Constable Spalding, away from the car. "Please join my constable over there, Mr. Gurov; he will check you for any other weapons and we will now search your car."

Mikhail walked towards Spalding with his hands in clear view. The armed detective stayed out of reach but tracked him carefully.

"Is there anything you'd like to tell us before we search your person and your vehicle?" Roy continued, making a point of looking at the boot of the car as Mikhail stopped and turned around by Spalding.

"I do not have anything to hide from you, Detective, you will find nothing," came the Russian's smug reply.

67

─────────

As the sun lowered in the western sky with evening approaching its intensity dropped, although the temperature didn't change much. Inside the van was hot and humid and Carlos rolled the windows down to catch the light breeze off the water. He settled on the floor between the front seats and the second row bench seat to remain out of sight. The quiet and stillness after the frantic events of the afternoon seemed surreal and he felt detached and helpless. He should be the one heading to the Explorador de la Reina to find Sydney, not a stranger he'd met a few days ago who was risking everything to help him, and for what? Why would she leave the safety of the island, alone, and head straight into harm's way on the trawler? Because AJ recognised Sydney didn't deserve any of this chaos he'd brought down on them? That was certainly true and he expected everyone to shun him when this was over. Including Sydney.

He held his head in his hands. All this over a stretch of coral reef that most people didn't even know existed. But it was not just a stretch of reef, it was miles of reef that had taken thousands of years to grow, evolve and flourish and would be destroyed over the course of a few weeks. Carlos could picture the barges and heavy equipment descending on Jardines de la Reina as he sat there, helpless, doing nothing. In two days' time the blasting would begin. The destruction of life would be unimaginable as the beautiful coral was blown apart and replaced with massive concrete pedestals to house the Goliath rigs. The delicate balance of the ecosystem established over lifetimes would be destroyed and another chunk of the globe's precious reefs will be lost as we humans rapidly wipe out the natural growths that keep the air we breathe in balance.

He slammed his fist on the seat beside him, his mind overwhelmed with frustration and above all fear for Sydney from the avalanche of events he'd created. He'd completely forgotten to check AJ's phone so it startled him when it rang, dancing on the centre console of the van. He picked it up and saw 'Reg' on the caller ID. He tentatively answered the phone, "Hello?"

After a pause, "Who's this?"

Carlos was relieved to recognise Reg's voice, "It's Carlos. Have the police found the Russian? Do they have Sydney?"

"Whittaker is on it, Gurov should be at the station now. Where are you?" Reg sounded serious but Carlos didn't know the man well enough to gauge his mood.

"I am by the water next to a restaurant called Casanova, you know it?"

Reg chuckled without amusement. "Yeah, I know it, stay put, I'll be there in five minutes."

Carlos hesitated, wondering how he could explain AJ's whereabouts. "You are coming here?"

"I'm only a few minutes away, is AJ with you?" Reg finally asked.

"No, she's..." Carlos stumbled, trying to get the words right in his second language. "She's away for a moment."

"Okay, I'll be right there, hopefully Whittaker will call any second with Gurov in custody," Reg finished and hung up.

Carlos was left pondering how he could explain why AJ wasn't there and where she had gone. From the van he couldn't see the trawler and he dare not step outside any more in case he was spotted. He pictured AJ under water navigating her way across the front of the harbour; it was quite a distance and he prayed she was good with a compass. She'd been gone only a few minutes and he wondered how long it would take to reach the trawler. Twenty minutes? An hour didn't seem like much time to get there, find and free Sydney and get back. How was Sydney getting back? There was only one set of Scuba gear. She could breathe off AJ's reserve regulator but it would take a lot longer swimming back without fins. He kept churning over the myriad of scenarios in his mind and none of them made him feel any better. He was convinced Gurov no longer had Sydney and she was on the boat. Which meant everything was riding on AJ and her cursory plan.

68

AJ was usually calmed as soon as she submerged, with all sound becoming dampened and limited to the air passing through the regulator. She found it soothing and the rhythm of her steady, even breathing relaxed her even further. This evening she found it a little harder to settle down as the stillness focused her attention on what she was about to attempt. The first problem was finding the trawler from underwater starting from nearly half a mile away. It was easy to underestimate how tricky navigation could be when above the water looking clearly at the destination. Once underwater with limited visibility and the scale and distance distortion of the human eye looking through water from behind a mask, it was easy to get disorientated and horribly lost. She'd taken a compass heading from the pier but decided to rely more heavily on her knowledge of the local terrain. This area to the north of the harbour wasn't frequented very often by the dive boats. The cruise ship snorkellers tended to cover the waters as it was walking distance from the terminal and several tour companies guided them to this spot. But she had done some open-water class work with students here and there were some key underwater landmarks she knew could be used.

Using her compass heading she finned across the shallow pan and found some scattered coral leading into more reef formation at around ten feet depth. Turning slightly to her right took her to where the reef dropped into more of a sandy bottom, where she turned back south-west to follow the edge of the reef. The coral landscape consisted of little peninsulas and recesses where the fingers of reef extended and retreated towards the deeper water and she connected the peaks of the outreaches staying on her compass heading. Curious tarpon with their long silvery bodies and strange hinging jaws hung by a coral head and watched her pass with mild curiosity. A stingray belched sand from under its wings in the flats to her right as it burrowed down to a tasty shell-fish meal. On a normal dive AJ would linger and enjoy the sights of the undersea world, revelling in the privileged moments spent observing life below the surface, but today she passed by with nothing more than a fleeting glance. Too much was riding on her and while she'd formulated a solid plan to find the trawler, she was a long way from knowing what she would do once there. They'd taken the skiff alongside so there had to be a ladder or some means of getting from the surface to board the boat – locating that would be task one. A shiver ran through her when she thought much beyond that.

To her right in the sand and scattered coral heads appeared some dark shapes on the sea floor. As she closed in, the shapes could be identified as coral and growth-encrusted metal sections of the landmark she'd been looking for. The wreck of the Balboa had been outside the harbour since the storm in 1932 that had smashed her against the sea wall of the docks and sent the 375-foot freighter to the bottom in forty feet of water. Blown apart to clear the obstruction when salvage was deemed too expensive, she remained a scattering of twisted metal carnage and pieces of hull. Diving the wreck was by permit only and strictly prohibited when cruise ships were moored outside the harbour. With three of the expansive floating hotels in port today AJ was confident she'd be alone at the wreck.

Cutting to deeper water she followed the wreckage west, scattering the shoals of chub and snapper that frequented the wreck. Under a large overhanging section of metal lay a grey hulk trying to blend with the sand and the shadows. The seven-foot nurse shark had no interest in the noisy bubble-maker passing by and remained still except for its willowy gills pumping water through its own, natural breathing system. The larger pieces of wreckage thinned as she met forty feet of depth, leaving more sand flats and smaller remains of the ship ahead. AJ paused and searched the water to the south and west for signs of a hull but was still too far away. Working from her original compass heading she continued across the front of the harbour, scanning ahead for a glimpse of the trawler. As she methodically finned her way forward, occasionally checking her compass to make sure she was on course, AJ mulled over her plan, or more appropriately, her lack of plan for when she found the Cuban boat.

69

———

A loud rap on the side of the van made Carlos jump and he instinctively slid down lower on the floor.

"Carlos?" came Reg's gruff voice.

Carlos scrambled up and peeked out the window; sure enough it was Reg staring back at him with a smile. Reg opened the passenger door and sat down, turning to face Carlos who lifted himself up to sit on the bench seat.

"AJ still not back? Where'd she go?" Reg enquired, looking around.

Carlos had been rehearsing his answer while he was waiting. "She said she had to see someone and would be half an hour or so."

Reg looked puzzled. "She say who?"

Carlos had hoped his first answer would be enough but apparently not so he kept it simple, "No."

Reg looked around again like he was trying to figure out where she may have gone. "Odd place to park... Don't know who she came to see here..."

It wasn't phrased as a question so Carlos took the opportunity not to answer and change the subject. "Have you heard from the policeman? Does he have Gurov? Did he still have Sydney?"

"I haven't heard back from him yet." Reg still looked confused. "So she left her phone here and said she'd be back?"

Carlos couldn't decide if he was doing a crappy job lying or if Reg was naturally inquisitive, but he was clearly suspicious. "She said to watch for you to call as she might not be able to talk if she was around other people."

Reg shrugged. "Alright, well we can't wait for her, let's get over to Whittaker and hopefully he's got Sydney by the time we get there."

Carlos felt pretty good he'd finally satisfied Reg's curiosity but he certainly didn't want to leave the van. What if AJ made it back with Sydney and he was now gone? Besides that, if he went to the police station he was probably not getting to leave.

"I can't go to the police, Reg; if they arrest me I can't do anything. I'd rather stay here and wait for AJ. Can't you call me when he has Sydney?"

"Don't you want to see her yourself," Reg countered, suspicious again.

"Of course I do but what's to stop them deporting me and all of this will be for nothing?" He spun an extra air of desperation into the statement.

Reg shook his head. "He ain't gonna' arrest or deport you. Whittaker's a good bloke, he'll help us. He's arresting Gurov, not you."

Reg stepped out of the van and waved for Carlos to follow, standing outside the open door. "I'll text AJ and tell her where we went, she'll see it on her phone when she gets back."

He closed the door and walked towards his van that he'd pulled in close by.

Carlos sat in a quandary, unsure what he could do. He felt he could trust Reg – the man had been incredibly kind and accommodating so far – but he was genuinely concerned that once he set foot in a police station he wouldn't be allowed to leave. He tried to convince himself this wasn't Cuba and they did things differently here but he had stolen a plane and landed it illegally on the island.

Well, near the island. Either way he'd broken laws on Cayman as well as Cuba; he couldn't imagine they'd let him walk away and go about his day. Reg had reached his own van and was looking at Carlos, expecting him to follow. What choice do I have?, he thought, I'm not going to run from this man too. He slid open the side door and exited the van, once again putting his fate in the hands of another person.

70

———————

Constable Spalding finished his pat-down on Gurov and nodded he was complete to Whittaker, who had moved to the back of the car. Mikhail stood with his hands still held up, a mobile phone in one hand and his wallet in the other. His blank stare held a hint of a smile. Whittaker released the lock to the boot and took a small step backwards, tensing in anticipation. The boot lid swung open to reveal an empty space and Whittaker breathed again, relieved but equally disappointed. He looked over at the other two constables and directed one to search the interior of the car and one the boot. He walked back over to Gurov, who'd finally dropped his hands and returned his mobile and wallet to his pockets.

Roy considered how to approach the Russian now; he'd expected to find a young Caymanian girl in the boot based on Reg's call but of course it didn't make sense for Gurov to drive into the police station with her. That would certainly be a ballsy move. His accomplice was also missing so a stop had been made on the way here.

"You look surprised, Detective, what were you expecting to find in my car?" Mikhail prodded before Roy had formed his next line of questions.

Roy ignored the taunt. "Where is your associate, Mr. Gurov?"

Mikhail shrugged his shoulders nonchalantly. "On our boat. I'm alone on the island, Detective."

Roy shook his head despondently. "Come along now, Mr. Gurov, surely we're beyond this aren't we? Your hotel room contained the personal items of two men. You were seen earlier today with another gentleman in this car. So, where is your associate now?"

Mikhail lost all trace of a grin and spoke aggressively, "We have diplomatic status detective and your questions and accusations are becoming offensive. We are prepared to leave so I suggest you allow me to return to our boat and be on our way."

Roy's tone matched Mikhail's toe to toe, "You don't have diplomatic anything Gurov, as you showed up unannounced. As far as I'm concerned you're a tourist bringing a firearm to the island which puts you in hot water. You're not going anywhere except our jail cell." Roy inched closer to the Russian and continued, "So how about you help yourself out and start explaining where your associate is and while you're at it where Sydney Bodden, who you had stuffed in the boot of your car half an hour ago, might be!"

Mikhail considered his response. "These are preposterous allegations, Detective, I assure you the Russian Federation does not look kindly on such threatening behaviour."

Mikhail trailed off as a van pulled into the yard and parked. Reg stepped out. The constable searching the interior of Gurov's car ducked out and stepped towards Reg with his hand up.

Whittaker called over to him, "It's okay, I asked him to come." Roy scanned the van but the sun was glaring off the windscreen and he couldn't see inside. "Have someone with you Reg?"

Reg turned back towards his van and beckoned with his hand. Carlos cautiously stepped out from the passenger side and nervously looked across the yard at Gurov. The Russian glared at him and started towards him but Spalding immediately grabbed his shoulder and the detective reached for his gun inside his jacket, ready to draw at any second. Mikhail stopped but never took his eyes from Carlos, his cold-steel stare locked on the terrified young man.

"Sir!" Came a voice from behind Gurov's car. Whittaker frowned at the constable. What could possibly warrant an interruption at this moment?

"Sir, you should see this," the constable urged.

Whittaker walked over as the constable pointed in the boot. Hanging from the curved hinge mechanism of the boot lid was a woman's watch. Reg and Carlos trotted over and Carlos's eyes got wider. "Sydney's watch!" He stared back at the Russian with equal venom and Reg grabbed him before he could bolt towards the man. "What have you done with her?!" Carlos screamed across the yard.

"Is that her watch?" Whittaker quizzed, "Are you sure?"

"Absolutely sure! Look at the inscription on the back!" Carlos wriggled in Reg's grip but the big man held him firm.

The constable reached in with a gloved hand and rotated the watch to see the back. He read off the inscription, "Todo mi amor, Carlos."

Whittaker whipped around and pointed at Gurov. "Put him in cuffs, Spalding. And Gurov, you'd better tell me right now where the girl is."

Before Spalding could restrain Gurov he pulled his mobile phone from his pocket and hit the send button. The phone slipped from his grasp as Spalding got hold of his arm and Mikhail didn't resist as the phone clattered to the ground. Whittaker stepped over and picked it up but the text message he sent was in Russian and he couldn't understand it. Spalding had his hands cuffed behind his back and Whittaker poked the Russian in the chest with the phone. "Where is she, Gurov? A firearm offence and kidnapping are one thing but if that girl's harmed, believe me you're never leaving the jail on this island!"

Mikhail gave Roy his blank, disdainful look and said nothing.

"They took her to the boat! The other Russian took her on their skiff. AJ is heading there now!" Carlos blurted.

Roy turned to the young man in disbelief, "Seriously?"

Carlos reiterated, "I saw them in the skiff myself."

Roy shook his head. "That part I'd figured when she wasn't in the boot." He turned his attention to Reg. "But why on God's green earth is AJ going to the trawler?!"

Reg shrugged. "Beats me, he told me she'd stepped away!"

"We figured they'd run if they saw a boat approaching and once they left you wouldn't be able to stop them," Carlos admitted sheepishly.

Roy was speechless for a moment before gathering his wits and forming a plan. "I don't read Russian but I'm pretty sure this text says 'leave now' so that hasn't worked out very well, has it?" Without waiting for a response he barked orders, waving a hand at Gurov. "Take him inside and lock him up. He pointed at the constable who'd found the watch. "Secure this vehicle and tell CSI to go through it from top to bottom. Detective," he pointed to the armed man, "with me. Reg, drive us to the harbour. I'll call the marine unit on the way."

Carlos looked at the detective quizzically as Reg released his grip.

"You're coming with me, I'm not letting you out of my sight." He put his hand on Carlos's shoulder, directing him towards the van. "I can't wait to hear how you crash a plane off the north wall in the middle of a storm and survive."

Carlos looked at Roy earnestly. "No, no, I didn't crash the plane, Detective, I landed it."

<h1 style="text-align:center">71</h1>

Anatoly read the text on his phone and jumped up from the table in the galley. Pavlo looked over his laptop at him expectantly.

"We're leaving," Anatoly announced in Russian. "Secure your equipment, be ready to take only what's absolutely necessary. We're switching to Plan B."

Pavlo looked confused. "Going where? What's Plan B?"

Anatoly paused on his way out the room. "Offshore. Plan B means you have whatever you need to take off the boat ready, we may have to leave the boat when we get out there."

As Anatoly left, his compatriot looked none the wiser but slowly closed his laptop lid and looked around, assessing what he needed to pack up.

Anatoly flew up the stairs to the wheelhouse and made Silvio, who was resting his eyes, jump. "I told you to be ready," Anatoly barked in poor Spanish. "We're leaving, quickly, so pull the anchor and fire up this piece of shit."

"I need to warm the engine for a while and then pull the anchor," Silvio said calmly.

"What?" Anatoly asked, his faced contorted in annoyance and only partially understanding what he'd said.

Silvio repeated patiently, "The engine, I must warm it up for a while and then we can pull the anchor."

"Listen you idiot," Anatoly yelled back in pidgin Spanish, "Start the damn engine and get us out of here right now, no warming, no screwing around, I told you earlier to be ready, let's go."

Silvio shrugged as Julio came in the wheelhouse having heard the commotion.

"What's up?" Julio enquired.

"Our friend wants me to blow up the engine trying to leave the harbour so apparently this is what we will do," Silvio said nonchalantly and turned the big diesel over waiting for it to splutter into life. "Head to the bow and watch the anchor for me, Julio."

The whole boat shuddered as the old motor coughed into life.

Anatoly swore in Russian and stomped out behind Julio, leaving Silvio with a wry grin. He made sure the motor had settled down at idle and walked to the back of the wheelhouse. The other two had gone down the interior stairwell which Silvio stepped around to open the rear door of the wheelhouse, overlooking the rear deck. The davit was swung over the side with lines running down out of view. The skiff was on the other end of those lines. He decided it would be fine to drag it a few feet while they hauled the anchor up then he'd have Julio winch it up as he turned the boat to leave.

Making it back to the console, he could see Julio upfront give him a thumbs-up and point in the forward direction. Silvio engaged forward drive with a loud clunk from below decks and the big boat very slowly began to move. Julio pulled back on a lever which ran the winch for the anchor. The old electric motor groaned as the lodged anchor initially tried to pull the boat down to the bottom of the ocean. Julio held his hand up as the boat came over the top of the anchor and Silvio selected reverse with more grinding and clunking. The electric winch slowed and groaned until just as it sounded like it would stop turning all together it managed to wrench the anchor free from the sand and whirred back up to its normal lethargic pace.

72

The drone of a diesel motor starting reached AJ at the same moment she saw the dark shadow of the hull of the trawler. She finned harder, now confident in the direction she needed to head. Shallowing to thirty feet, she kicked until making it under the large mass from where she could see the anchor line extending to the sea floor from the starboard side of the bow. The motor note changed and the propeller spun into life adding a higher pitched buzz to the deep tone of the diesel. Damn it, she thought, they're leaving! I'm too late by a few minutes! Rotating upside down she scanned the barnacle-ridden hull as it slowly edged forward above her. She watched the line to the anchor slacken as the trawler released the strain and another motor sound started from the boat, which she guessed was the anchor winch.

AJ desperately searched for any option to get herself aboard that didn't involve going near the stern and the prop violently crushing water through its blades. To the starboard side was another outline alongside. The skiff! She ascended as fast as she dare without risking the bends as the trawler slowed its forward motion with more changes in engine note and the prop wound down to a stop, before reversing and churning the other way. The trawler came to a stop just as AJ reached the skiff and the prop went to neutral with another clunk.

She slowly peeked her head above the surface and prayed no one was looking over the side. She came up behind the skiff so she could tuck in by the outboard, figuring if anyone was looking they'd be focused on the anchor that was now winding up through mid-water. She could just see a head glancing over the side towards the bow but the man was indeed watching the anchor. AJ swiftly pulled herself up the side of the skiff to roll inside but as soon as the bulk of her air tank came out of the water the mass dragged her back down. Shit! She hadn't considered manoeuvring above the surface with a Scuba rig weighing close to fifty pounds when wet. She inflated her BCD so it would float, unbuckled the waistband and slipped it off her back. The BCD and tank bobbed in the water and the tank slapped against the skiff with a loud clunk. She quickly pulled it away and checked the man up front but he was busy with the anchor that was now clearing the water. She was running out of time. Pulling herself up again she easily hauled herself into the skiff and turned around to grab her BCD. The rocking of the skiff as she'd rolled in caused a small wave which had pushed the rig away and she lurched as far she could reach to just catch a shoulder strap.

Clonk. She looked to the front to see the anchor was set against the hull. She guessed next job would be to bring the skiff aboard. She dragged her BCD and tank up into the skiff and looked up at the side of the trawler. A wooden ladder hung from the side rail of the boat's hull. She slipped her fins off and scrambled up a couple of steps until she could just see over the top. Halfway to her from the bow was the man she'd seen; he was now heading back towards the stern. She scrambled back down and looked about her. Scrunched up in the front of the skiff was on old canvas cover. Shoving her rig under one of the two seats that ran across the skiff she grabbed the cover and dragged it over herself just as she heard the scraping of the ladder being pulled aboard. She held her breath and hoped she'd managed to cover herself completely. Silence.

Then she heard some movement and a man's voice barely audible shouting something in Spanish. The only word she understood was 'Julio'. The Cuban to be avoided, according to Carlos. The man she now presumed to be Julio shouted something back that she didn't understand at all, but could only hope didn't involve her. She had to let the air from her lungs and take another gasp, which sounded infinitely louder than she desired, echoing around under the cover. Salt water dripped from her body and the steamy humidity under the canvas was stifling. Finally, with a jerk the skiff started rising out of the water and the davit winch whined as it steadily lifted it clear of the rail. AJ was coming aboard the trawler whether she wanted to or not.

73

From Elgin Avenue, Reg made a left on Sheddon Road and shot down the narrow street to the stop sign at Harbour Drive with the little island museum on their left. Across the road in front of them the harbour opened up into the Caribbean Sea and three cruise ships sat idle waiting to start their overnight voyage to their next destination. To the right was the small commercial dock out front of which the Cuban trawler had been moored. It was no longer moored and had turned and appeared to be under steam, heading out to sea by the small wake its slow progress stirred up.

Carlos pointed at the boat. "They're leaving! We're too late, we must stop them!"

Roy already had his phone to his ear. "This is Detective Whittaker, put me through to the Marine Unit." His voice was calm but urgent.

After a pause waiting on the transfer, "This is Whittaker. I need a marine unit to the harbour right away, we have a trawler under the Cuban flag we need stopped from leaving immediately."

The surprised dispatcher stumbled out her response, "Sir, I'm afraid everything we have on west side is tending to an incident."

A frown crossed his face as he listened. "All the boats are being used?"

"Yes sir they are, called out thirty minutes ago."

Roy held his hand over the microphone of his mobile and looked at Reg. "Can we take one of your boats?"

Reg nodded. "Sure, but we'll have to get to West Bay dock and I don't know if we can catch them from there."

Reg turned right and accelerated along Harbour Drive as Roy replied with his hand still covering his phone, "I don't want the marine unit to have to stop here to pick us up; they can beat us to the Cuban boat, we'll catch up."

Reg sped through George Town, glancing at AJ's van still sitting next to the dive shop by Casanova's while Roy barked a few more orders over his phone at the police marine unit dispatcher. He hung up and drummed his fingers on his knee. "The two marine units on West Side are down past Jackson Point at Sand Cay – someone ran their yacht up on the Cay with the tide going out. Our other boats are still in North Sound." He turned and looked at Carlos with a slight grin. "Guess I can bring them back around now we've found our downed pilot."

Carlos looked sheepish. "Sorry sir."

Roy chuckled. "Anyway, one of the units will leave Sand Cay and head to intercept; they have some ground to cover but that old trawler can't make much speed, we'll get them."

Carlos leaned forward from the back. "And when they catch the trawler how will they stop it?" he asked innocently.

Reg swung around a slow car, identified as a tourist by the white licence plate, then looked at Roy curiously. "I was wondering that too."

Roy shifted uncomfortably in his seat. "I'm not completely sure to be honest, we can point some guns at them but these Russians don't strike me as men that are particularly bothered by that."

The three fell silent as Reg continued to weave around traffic heading north on West Bay Road.

74

———

AJ lay perfectly still well after the skiff had been lowered to the deck and she had heard footsteps on the decking fade away. She wanted to be certain the coast was clear but also her vague plan of 'get Sydney, leave boat, swim back to shore' was now out the window as the trawler chugged further away from the island. Under the sweltering hot canvas she could tell they were moving and there was no doubt where they'd head initially; the shortest route to twelve miles offshore into international waters. Deciding it was better to face the problem nearer, if not close to land, she took a few calming breaths and eased the cover back. The sun was fading in the sky but obscured by the wheelhouse forward of her, which confirmed they were heading due west. AJ blinked a few times to clear her vision after the dim light beneath the canvas. With no one in sight she took a moment to study the layout and orientate herself from Carlos's description. She was on the stern deck and ten feet ahead was a two-storey structure with steel steps to a door at the second level and another door underneath the steps on the main deck level. From Carlos's briefing the deck door led to the galley, dining area and the stairs down to the cabins.

The skiff was hanging from the davit but resting on the deck so she stepped out and pulled the canvas back over her rig and fins to hide them in case anyone wandered by. Her heart was pounding in her chest. What on earth did she think she was doing playing Navy SEAL trying to singlehandedly rescue a kidnapped girl she could still only assume was on board? Against trained Russian agents. She felt woefully ill-equipped to tackle any of this. But what if Sydney was being held on board? She couldn't do nothing. In fact, as she had effectively now put herself captive on the trawler, the only option was to escape the boat undetected. Might as well take Sydney with her. If Sydney was even here and it wasn't canvas flapping in the breeze they'd seen. She'd feel pretty dumb getting caught by the Russians trying to rescue someone that wasn't even on the boat. She pushed that ironic and embarrassing thought aside.

She stepped carefully across the metal deck towards the lower door. The trawler was old and showed the rough finish of years of paint slapped over layers of earlier paint with grime and dirt built up in nooks and crannies. The door was a heavy steel marine door with rounded corners and a flange that overlapped the opening to keep the weather out. The door had a small window and the cabin had a window either side of the opening but they were too dirty to see through. She stayed low in case anyone could see out. AJ noticed her hand was shaking as she reached for the handle, her movements slow and heavy as her nerves tightened her muscles and made her feel stiff and clumsy. As her hand touched the handle the door above her banged open and someone shouting in Spanish started down the metal stairs with a clanging ring from each step. Before she knew it she'd opened the door and slid through the opening, bringing it to a close behind her as softly as she could manage. She froze, half expecting the man outside, who had sounded like the Julio guy, to burst through having seen or heard her. When no one came she realised she had her back to whatever lay inside the room and slowly turned. Her heart stopped. Through a doorway ahead was what appeared to be the dining area and standing by the table was a man placing electrical equipment into a large case. His back was to her and he appeared not to hear or didn't care someone had come through the outside door. The big diesel engine droned on, shuddering through the whole boat and the hull thudded against the water yet her breaths and heartbeats felt like they drowned out all other sounds. Her mouth was dry. She forced herself to look away and in the dimly lit hall she saw to her left the stairs up to the wheelhouse and to her right the stairs down. Her bare feet felt the harsh grit of the non slip texture on the steel floors as she made for the stairs taking her down below deck, deeper into the boat. The steps went down half a level then turned ninety degrees to the left and continued to the lower deck where a hallway stretched out thirty feet before her, lit by a series of small portholes in the hull. On the left of the passageway were a series of doors that she assumed were the berths.

From above she heard a man's voice urgently barking in Russian and another replying, "Da, da."

She froze at the base of the stairs listening for footsteps. When none came she stepped forward and peeked into the first door that was cracked ajar. The smell gave it away before she saw it was the head. The remaining five doors were all closed but she noticed the farthest one had keys hanging from the lock in the handle. That has to be it, she thought. Why lock a cabin door from the outside with the key left in it unless you're keeping someone from leaving? She glanced out the first porthole as she passed by and noted they were well clear of the island and by the swell picking up a little they must be beyond the drop-off and in deeper water. Arriving in front of the last cabin she paused and considered knocking to alert Sydney she was there. The way Sydney had fought the Russian from the boot of the car she wouldn't be surprised if she attacked whoever entered. But what if it wasn't Sydney inside? AJ settled on stealth and, after confirming the door was indeed locked by trying the handle gently, she turned the key and this time the handle rotated down and she eased it open.

The cabin was lit by a single porthole and laid on a cot against the wall was Sydney, her hands and feet bound by large plastic tie-wraps and tape across her mouth. Her eyes were wide and fierce but instantly gave way to relief as AJ stepped inside the room and closed the door.

75

Reg swung the van into the little car park by his dock and the three men hurriedly unloaded. Young Carlos led them at full run down the pier, where Pearl was just pulling up in one of their Newtons. Reg had called her on the way, sending her rushing over to paddle a kayak out to the mooring and retrieve a boat ready for them when they arrived. Without even tying up they leapt aboard and Pearl reversed straight out, swung around and laid the throttle back, ignoring the usual no-wake courtesy around the dock area. They all scampered up the ladder to join her on the fly bridge and Roy headed straight for the marine radio. Selecting the police channel he clicked the handset open. "Marine Unit in pursuit, this is Detective Whittaker, how's your progress? Over."

Reg pulled up GPS on their navigation screen while they waited for the response.

Finally the radio crackled, "Detective Whittaker, this is Marine Unit Three in pursuit, making good time, anticipate intercept in ten to fifteen minutes, over."

"Unit Three, this is Whittaker, understood, keep me posted, over." Roy hung up the handset and looked over at Reg, who was figuring a heading to meet the trawler offshore.

Reg pointed to the GPS map which he had zoomed out to show the western portion of the island and the open water. "Taking a best guess here on heading but I'd rather be out in front than behind them; we can do more coming at them that way than chasing them."

Roy nodded in agreement and they all hung on as they cleared the shallower water, meeting the light chop beyond the wall. Below them the sea floor dropped from around eighty feet to over six hundred in a matter of moments and kept getting deeper from there.

Once the boat settled on plane Roy turned to Carlos. "Before we get out there how about you give me the whole story, young man? Perhaps there's something you have to say that'll persuade me from arresting your friend Reg here for obstructing justice?" Roy threw a look at Reg, who frowned at his friend.

Carlos shook his head. "Please, sir, Mr. Moore didn't tell you before because I insisted he didn't. I can explain everything to you in a moment." He leaned over to Reg. "I am still worried what we can do to stop them Reg."

Reg shared his concern. "Nothing I'm afraid, but maybe we can help redirect them and slow them down so Roy's guys can come up with something."

"We just have to keep them inside the twelve-mile mark, outside that things get more complicated," Roy reminded them, "And right now we're on track to do that."

"But how do we do this, they have a much bigger boat?" Carlos persisted, his anxiety level clearly not receding.

"Well," Reg paused thoughtfully. "We play chicken, I guess, see who flinches."

Pearl looked at Reg. "You'll take the helm for that part, dear."

76

———————

Julio plodded back up the steps to the wheelhouse, annoyed; Silvio was getting as bossy as the Russians. He'd folded the canvas and stowed it so it didn't fly away out the back of the boat as Silvio had nagged him to do. He opened the door and contemplated going down to the galley to avoid being given more stupid jobs to do but the Russians were down there and they were in a fouler mood. The whole thing seemed like a complete shambles to Julio and he couldn't wait to get home. He ambled forward to the wheelhouse and gazed out the window at the vast blue ocean ahead: certainly more pleasant waters than their outbound trip. Standing next to Silvio, he rested is hand on the console and leaned against the second chair. Something felt different about the boat. He touched the console top and then the window itself.

"The main bearings," Silvio mumbled dejectedly. "I told that arsehole we'd kill the engine taking off like that, but he didn't want to hear it."

Julio nodded. "She gonna make it?"

Silvio looked at him glumly. "It's got steadily worse and Anatoly won't let me slow up, so no, I doubt it'll make Cuba but it seems all he cares about is making international waters; maybe it'll stay together until then."

Julio wanted to ask about what happens when they're stuck offshore but decided he wouldn't poke the bear and make things worse for himself. Then he remembered the canvas cover.

"Hey, can I have the scuba gear you brought back with the girl?"

Silvio looked at him, puzzled. "What are you talking about?"

"The scuba gear in the skiff. I figured you brought it back when you picked Carlos's girlfriend up." Now Julio was confused.

"We didn't bring any gear back, just the girl. You sure the Russians didn't put something in there?" Silvio tried to reason.

"I haven't seen any scuba tanks on board, have you?" Julio said and thought more about it. "We took all the gear we have off the boat last time into Jucaro; besides, this stuff is nice, not like the old crap we have."

Silvio shook his head. "Take the wheel and stay straight on this heading, let me go look."

Julio stepped over and took the wheel as Silvio disappeared out the back door and loudly clanged down the steps outside before the door swung closed. Julio looked over the gauges. The engine was hot and the rpm needle was fluttering from the motor's vibration. He really hoped it didn't come apart while he was at the helm, he'd catch all kinds of shit from everyone.

Silvio stared at the scuba rig in the skiff. Julio was right, this was much nicer stuff than he'd seen. He ought to go ask Anatoly if it had anything to do with them, but he'd had enough of that prick today and none of it appeared to be Russian made or military style. He felt the vibration from the straining engine through the decking and knew the propeller shaft bearings must be taking a beating. He looked up and scanned off the stern while he considered what to do. He could still see the island and easily picked out the three hulking cruise ships about six miles behind them. Slightly south he could see a small boat kicking up a good wake heading out in a similar direction to them. Pretty late for a fishing trip, he pondered, but the scuba gear was nagging on his mind and he looked back down at the wet gear. Wet gear? Gathering up the BCD he whipped around and strode back towards the main deck door.

77

After getting the tape from Sydney's mouth and helping her sit upright, AJ whispered a quick synopsis of how she'd ended up on the trawler while it headed what appeared to be straight out to sea. While she explained, she searched for something sharp enough to cut the tie-wraps but, needless to say, they hadn't been stupid enough to leave blades or cutters around. For once she wished she was one of the macho divers with a machete-like knife strapped to her leg.

"I'll have to find something in another cabin," she whispered. "Have you heard anybody down here recently? I don't want to walk in on a sleeping Russian."

Sydney shook her head. "No, I've heard them on the next deck but no one down here since they locked me in."

AJ winced, looking at the knotty red shiner swollen up on the side of Sydney's face. "At least the guy that did that to you isn't on board, pretty sure he stayed on the island. I'll be right back with something to cut those ties."

She eased the door open and checked the hall. The keys jangled in the lock and she gritted her teeth and held still. The diesel engine noise drowned out most sound but she couldn't help being over cautious. At least her nerves had calmed a little since she'd found Sydney; if nothing else it meant she hadn't come aboard for nothing. She kept noticing the engine didn't sound too healthy and the old tub shook a lot but for all she knew that's how it had been for years. She slipped out the room, closing the door behind her and moved down the hall to the next cabin. The door was unlocked and she held her breath while she carefully looked inside. There was nothing in the cabin except a small travel duffel on the floor next to the bed. Very neat, very military. She closed the door behind her and knelt by the bag to go through it. Carefully removing the meticulously folded garments on top, she ran her hands around the inside, hunting for a useful object. She felt something that seemed the size of a passport, a paperback book and then a smaller bag that she grabbed and pulled out. Unzipping the top she discovered a wash kit and further rummaging produced a pair of nail clippers. She'd been hoping for a Swiss Army knife but clippers would do in a pinch, and a pinch she was certainly in.

Sydney's pensive look dissolved to a smile when AJ re-entered the cabin and held up the clippers with a grin. It took some snipping and working but she was able to cut the plastic tie-wraps and Sydney sat rubbing her wrists and ankles for a few moments, massaging the angry red marks where the ties had been.

"What do we do now?" Sydney asked in a low voice.

"I guess we still need to find the hard drive, right?" AJ queried, hoping the answer wasn't yes.

Sydney shook her head. "No, that's not important now, we need to get out of here."

Relieved, AJ laid out her best plan. "We sneak back out to the stern, drop the skiff overboard and jump in after it."

Sydney nodded apprehensively. "Okay, and pray they don't see us, right?"

"Correct, if we're spotted, we'll be a rowing boat with a tiny outboard against a trawler. I'd say they'll run us over and move on." AJ managed a weak smile.

Sydney forced a grin. "Par for the last few days. Well, doubt it'll get better if we wait so let's give it a go."

They both rose to leave as the door to the cabin jerked open and a man stepped into the room.

All three stood motionless unsure what to do.

It wasn't the Cuban she'd seen on deck so she took a guess. "Silvio?" AJ asked quietly.

The man looked puzzled. "Sí." He softly closed the door behind him.

"Inglés?" she asked, stretching her own Spanish vocabulary.

Silvio shook his head. "No muy bien."

Sydney touched AJ's arm. "I speak Spanish, do you think he'll help us?"

AJ shrugged. "Carlos said he might, tell him Carlos told us he was a good friend and would help us, see what he says."

Silvio watched them carefully and it was hard to tell if he understood more than he'd let on.

Sydney addressed him in Spanish. "Silvio, Carlos told us you are a good friend and you would help us if we saw you. These Russian men are bad people, we need to get off this boat."

Silvio listened carefully and nervously double-checked the door was closed properly before quietly replying, "Carlos has caused a big mess, you two shouldn't be here. I don't like these men either but I don't know how I can get you off the boat, we're way out to sea now."

AJ tried desperately to understand odd words but they both talked too fast for her to recognise anything beyond names.

"We were going to drop the skiff in the water and take that, we just need to get back to it without being seen," Sydney explained.

Silvio nodded slowly, clearly thinking it through. "Okay, wait here, let me see if it's clear. I'll be back."

He turned to open the door but AJ stepped forward to stop him. "Wait, what did he say, what's going on?!" She looked at Sydney for answers.

"It's okay, he's going to make sure it's clear and he'll come back," Sydney assured her.

AJ relaxed a notch but looked squarely at Silvio, trying to read the man's eyes, "You sure we can trust him?"

Silvio held up his hand for them to stay and put his finger to his lips for them to keep quiet as he opened the door.

A loud clanking noise came from the diesel motor and the boat shook violently. Silvio's expression changed to panic and he hissed in Spanish, "Stay here, stay here, I have to fix the motor, I'll be back as soon as I can!"

He shot out the door with the noise from the motor growing so loud it drowned out the thud of the door closing.

78

Silvio stepped around the scuba gear at the base of the stairs and strode up the steps two at a time to meet an extremely upset Russian stomping out of the dining area.

"What the hell is happening with the engine?!" Anatoly yelled in his pidgin Spanish. "This is no time to break down, fix the damn thing!"

Silvio desperately wanted to point out he'd warned him about this before they left port but he knew it would only bring more wrath upon him. Instead he ignored the man and continued up the next stairs to the wheelhouse leaving Anatoly switching to his native tongue to deliver what he presumed was a string of insults. Rushing into the wheelhouse, Julio saw him coming and shrugged, stepping aside, letting Silvio see the gauges and take the wheel. The temperature was pegged in the red and the rpms were well down.

"This is bad," Silvio mumbled. "These stupid Russians think because they demand things they can happen regardless of mechanics and physics."

Julio rolled his eyes, "We're gonna be stuck out here and we have a kidnapped girl on board. We're all going to jail."

Silvio glanced at him. "Two girls on board, that diving gear belonged to a friend of Carlos's who sneaked on the boat to save the first one!"

Julio slapped the outside wall of the wheelhouse. "You have to be kidding? What the hell is going on? This will end badly, we're screwed!"

Silvio eased the throttle back to half, stepped back and indicated for Julio to take the wheel again. The engine noise reduced but still sounded like it was rattling to pieces.

"I have to go to the engine room and see if there's anything I can do, keep it at half throttle for now." Silvio turned to leave.

"What about the girls? Are they both downstairs? Does Anatoly know about the other one?" Julio blasted off a series of questions.

Silvio paused. "I told them to stay put and I would go back to help them."

Julio looked surprised. "So you haven't told Anatoly?"

Silvio shook his head. "Everything went crazy at once, I couldn't think what to do." He continued out the back of the wheelhouse to the stairs. "First I have to try and fix the engine."

"Silvio!" Anatoly yelled at him as he crossed the back of the main deck level. He really wanted to keep going to the engine room but he also didn't want Anatoly following down and seeing the scuba gear he'd brought in from the skiff. He had figured on stuffing it in his cabin but after checking on Sydney and finding the other girl all hell had broken loose. He stopped. Both Russians were huddled over one laptop Pavlo hadn't packed yet and he could hear radio transmissions coming from the speakers.

Anatoly waved at him to come over, still listening to the radio message. "Can you fix the engine?" Anatoly asked quietly for once.

"I'm going to look now but it sounds bad, maybe we can limp along on low power," Silvio offered, keeping his voice low so they could hear the radio. "But no way can we make Cuba like this, it needs a major repair."

The transmission stopped and the Russians both looked troubled. Anatoly left the table and headed to the door to the rear deck. He looked out the window. "They're catching us. Come on, let's look at the engine and see if there's any chance." Before Silvio could catch up to him the Russian was bounding down the stairwell to the lower deck. He caught up with him at the base of the stairs where Anatoly had halted, staring at the pile of scuba gear.

"What the hell is this?" he barked.

Silvio froze, his mind whirring through the options of how to respond and more importantly the ramification of each answer.

He stammered, "I found…" Before he could finish his sentence the engine made a final death throe of metallic clanking and grinding before stopping altogether. Silvio leapt past Anatoly and ran down the hall to the engine room door at the far end; flinging it open, he stepped inside the dark engine room only to be met by a wave of putrid smoke billowing out into the hallway. Behind him Anatoly coughed and sputtered as the fumes engulfed him. They both retreated, closing the door as fast as they could.

Silvio managed to wheeze out some words, "The big end bearings are fried, it has seized everything now, we're dead in the water."

They staggered back down the hallway, catching their breath. "My Spanish is not that good, I didn't understand all of it, but I'm guessing you said we're screwed?" Anatoly gasped.

"Sí," Silvio nodded, "we're screwed."

He looked down at AJ's dive gear still resting by the steps and knew he couldn't dodge an explanation any longer. He had to decide on his story right now.

79

AJ and Sydney huddled low on the floor in the tiny cabin. The fumes had leaked in around the old metal door jamb but had risen to the ceiling and stopped coming in after they heard the door in the hall slam shut. Quiet hung over the boat now the engine had expired and they were desperate to not cough on the fumes and alert the men they could hear in the hallway. The small porthole was the only illumination in the room now the light in the ceiling had died along with the engine, but unfortunately it didn't open to release the noxious gases. Sydney stood and, keeping her head below the slowly dissipating fumes, tiptoed over to the door. She gently put pressure on the handle but it didn't budge at all. She turned and frowned at AJ. "He locked it," she whispered.

"Maybe in case the Russian came down and checked?" AJ said optimistically.

Sydney nodded. "Maybe, I guess."

They sat back down on the cot and listened intently. They could hear two men talking quietly but couldn't make out what they were saying. Then footsteps up the stairwell. The echoed foot falls sounded like one person to AJ but she couldn't be sure. She could hear movement on the main deck above them but it seemed like there were only a few crew on the boat and Sydney had said she'd only been aware of two and maybe heard a third. AJ wondered what they could do now, she felt even more helpless knowing they were locked in the cabin. At least before they tried the lock she had the idea that they could try and escape on their own. Now their fate was solely in the hands of this man Silvio. Carlos obviously thought a lot of him so she clung to the hope he'd return as promised.

"He'll come back," Sydney whispered, clearly thinking the same thing. "Carlos spoke well of him, said he can be grumpy but was a good man. Has a daughter he doesn't get to see much but talks about all the time."

AJ glanced at her dive watch. "Carlos should be raising the alarm about now anyway so hopefully there'll be someone coming for us shortly. We're dead in the water so we shouldn't be hard to find."

The key turned in the lock and the handle rotated down.

"He's back," Sydney said quietly, relieved.

AJ recognised the man that stepped into the cabin as the second Russian from the car and the skiff. In his hand and squarely pointed at her was a gun. Growing up in England, AJ had never even seen a handgun in person and had been shocked by their prevalence in America when she lived in Florida. Now, facing the barrel of one aimed right at her in a confined environment she was paralysed by the instant realisation of her lack of options. In the movies she'd sweep in and knock the gun aside or trick the man into pointing the gun away. But in this moment the glaring truth she faced was a trained professional who wouldn't hesitate to take her life, and even on her best day she couldn't move faster than a fired bullet. All he had to do was squeeze one finger. Pointed directly at her was a device efficiently designed for a singular purpose: killing. All the bravado and daydreams of being Lara Croft were out the window, her legs felt like lead and a wave of fear seared through her stomach.

Her moment to act would have been the second he opened the

door but she hadn't been prepared for an armed aggressor to step in. He on the other hand was fully prepared and showed no sign of fear or even concern.

"You came alone?" the man asked calmly in heavily accented English.

"Yes," AJ heard herself say and immediately realised her next mistake.

The man looked around the room, seemingly assessing his options. AJ choked back the fear, her anger at not giving him the concern of others with her spurred her into action, if only in words.

"Why are you holding us here? We have nothing to do with whatever you have going on. Let us go, we can take the skiff and be out of your way," AJ said hopefully, in the back of her mind thinking this was the part where the bad guy spills the beans on his intentions and makes his big mistake.

The Russian simply stepped back out of the room and locked the door without a word. She really needed to stop watching stupid movies.

"Hey!" Sydney shouted and banged on the door but they could hear his footsteps already on the stairs.

"Damn it," AJ mumbled dejectedly. "I'm really sorry Sydney, I screwed this whole thing up."

Sydney sat down next to her on the cot and hugged her. "You shouldn't even be here, it's Carlos and I that started this mess. I can't believe you tried to save me. Seriously AJ, you've been amazing, I'm the one who's sorry for getting you and your friends involved."

Sydney's words were nice but didn't stop AJ feeling like a total failure. She should have gone to the police and not tried to do it herself with some half-baked plan. Now they were both in deep shit with whatever destiny the Russian bestowed upon them.

80

―――――――

Anatoly stood out the back of the wheelhouse at the top of the steps and focused the binoculars on the approaching boat. It was still probably two miles away but it was moving fast and was clearly a police boat. He stepped back in and faced Silvio and Julio, who were waiting curiously to know what the plan was now.

"Mikhail told me you have explosives on board?" Anatoly asked sternly.

The two Cubans looked at each other in surprise. "We have a little, yes, we had it for test blasts," Silvio replied tentatively.

"Show me," Anatoly snapped and stood aside for Silvio to show him the way.

Silvio didn't much like the idea of anything being blown up anywhere near the boat but figured he didn't want to see that gun of Anatoly's pointed at him, so he'd better comply. He led Anatoly back down the stairs to the storage area through a narrow door behind the stairwell in the stern of the boat. The room was incredibly hot and steamy and reeked of a strange mixture of diesel, fish and decades of stale air. Various crates and old boat parts were scattered around the space lit by one porthole on each side. Silvio walked over to a wooden crate, leaned over and pulled out a smaller canvas bag.

"Here." He handed the bag to Anatoly. "This is everything we have."

Anatoly opened the bag and examined the contents: eight black and yellow cartridges with protruding wires, a control box and a large coil of thin wire.

"What are you going to use that for?" Silvio cautiously asked.

Anatoly looked at him as though he was simple. "Sink this piece-of-shit boat, and we need to do it now so you and your helper better gather up anything you want to take with you, you've got three minutes."

Silvio was stunned into silence. Anatoly hustled out of the storage room with the bag in his hand. Over his shoulder he added, "And we'll be leaving in the skiff so whatever you bring better fit on your lap."

Silvio had no great love for the boat but he had spent many days and nights aboard her and the thought of scuttling her didn't sit well. He pulled himself together and left the storage room. Anatoly was opening the engine room door and ducking under the smoke as it wafted out. Silvio could hear the girls banging on the cabin door and shouting at the person they could hear in the hall-way. He wondered what Anatoly's plan was for them, but he already knew the answer to that question. He crossed himself before grabbing his small kit bag from the tiny cabin he shared with Julio, stuffing it with a few personal items and rushing up the stairs.

Julio was pacing around the wheelhouse when Silvio came in. "What's going on? What are we doing?" Julio asked as soon as he saw him.

"Get your things from our cabin right now, we have to get off the boat," Silvio told him, out of breath.

Julio looked out the window at the vast sea around them, "Leave and go where?!"

"Quit asking questions and grab your gear unless you want to stay on board when they blast this thing apart!" Silvio snapped.

"Holy Mother… They're blowing up the ship?" Julio blurted out, dumbstruck and still not moving.

"Yes, now hurry or I swear they'll leave you here," Silvio persisted.

Julio's jaw dropped open. "What about the girls?"

Silvio shook his head with a pained expression. "They're not our problem Julio, get your stuff or you'll end up with them."

Julio turned and banged his fist on the steel wall. "This is crazy Silvio, we're not killers, I don't want any part of murdering anyone, especially women!"

Silvio grabbed him by the shirt. "Listen you fool, do you think I want their blood on my hands? But I want to see my daughter again and if we don't go along with the Russians we'll end up on the sea floor, or in jail back home. And by the way, we're in two thousand feet of water right here so what goes down will be lost forever which I'm sure is what they're counting on! Now go grab your bag and meet me at the stern."

"Okay, okay, you know I don't want to make any trouble," Julio reluctantly succumbed, grumbling and swearing all the way down to the lower deck.

Silvio went down a level and almost ran into Pavlo, who was lugging his cases out the door to the stern deck.

"Get those other two," Pavlo ordered and nodded towards a couple more cases in the dining area.

Silvio obliged and followed the Russian to the skiff still hanging from the davit in the stern. Silvio looked at the little boat and then the pile of gear cases. Four adults plus this gear was not going to fit but Pavlo starting lifting the black waterproof cases into the skiff seemingly determined.

"Don't just stand there you idiot, help me load these," Pavlo snapped, sweating in the humidity.

Silvio helped lift the remaining cases in without a word and then grabbed the wooden ladder and draped it over the side, hooking it to the railing. Walking over to the davit controls he turned a switch and pulled a lever to raise the arm. The motor whined and very slowly lifted the arm.

"What's wrong with it?" Pavlo demanded.

"It's running on the battery which is draining now the engine isn't charging it," Silvio answered absentmindedly as he wondered if there was enough power to get the skiff over the railing. He thought about telling Pavlo his stupid cases were weighing it down too much but wisely refrained. Julio appeared through the door and dropped his bag on the deck, closely followed by Anatoly, who was streaming with sweat and running out wire all the way.

"Get that boat over the side, we need to go!" Anatoly yelled, looking over the railing in the direction of the oncoming police boat that was now less than a mile away.

"The battery is dying," Silvio remarked, as he switched levers having lifted the boat high enough to clear the railing. The davit started swinging out over the water painfully slowly.

Anatoly removed the control box from the rucksack he carried and attached the wires he'd been playing out. Behind them off the bow the sun was approaching the horizon in a vibrant display of bright orange and yellow but none of them noticed. The skiff finally hung over the sea and Silvio returned to the first lever and lowered the boat to the water, gravity doing the work instead of the electric motor. Pavlo immediately scrambled down the ladder and positioned himself in the bow. Silvio looked around at the ex-trawler he'd become attached to, trying not to think about what was about to happen to her and the two people left on board. Without warning or ceremony Anatoly pushed two buttons simultaneously and a low boom shuddered through the boat which rocked violently. Anatoly staggered to the railing as the boat settled and stepped down the ladder into the skiff taking position at the tiller. Silvio and Julio looked down at the two Russians and both hesitated. Anatoly pulled the starter rope and the little outboard came to life on the back of the skiff as Pavlo unhooked the davit lines.

Anatoly looked up at the two Cubans. "If you want to live, get in the boat." He reached for the pistol holstered under his arm.

81

Sydney shook the door handle, but it was futile: the door might be old but it was heavy steel with a sturdy lock mechanism to match. AJ tried to take the cot apart to salvage something to smash the porthole with, but it was bolted together as well as to the floor. Sydney banged loudly on the door and yelled, but they hadn't heard anyone outside since the explosion. The blast had felt like it was just outside their cabin and had rocked them both off their feet. They couldn't be sure what caused it but the unmistakable sound of gushing water confirmed the result was a hole in the vessel. Without any tools AJ was having no luck with the cot so she sat down to clear her head and think things through. The old trawler had listed a little to the starboard side although she couldn't tell if it had lowered in the water yet. But that was only a matter of time. She also knew these waters well enough to realise they were well clear of the wall and the sea floor was almost certainly thousands of feet below them. Not that it mattered. They were locked in a cabin in the middle of the boat so if it sunk in thirty feet of water they were still going to drown.

AJ scanned the tiny room, looking for anything they might use as a tool to pry open the door or smash the glass in the porthole.

The cot was bolted to the floor and the light cover was screwed to the ceiling. There wasn't anything else in the teeny cabin.

"AJ!" Sydney was still by the door and looking down at her feet.

Water was washing into the cabin under the door. AJ jumped up and looked out the porthole. "Shit, it's going down, the window's only three feet above the water now!"

Sydney's face was streaked with terror, her eyes wide and she violently shook the door handle again. The reality hit AJ like a freight train. This was actually happening. They were helplessly trapped inside the cabin and the boat was going down. There was nothing they could do to prevent their inevitable death which would take several minutes to unfold, and end in a throat full of sea water instead of air. She'd been close to drowning before but the certainty of her current predicament made this far worse in her mind. Here she sat, in good health with plenty of air to breath, knowing that in a few moments she would die. Her legs felt weak and nausea swept through her stomach. Sydney stopped banging on the door and sat down on the cot next to her and they wrapped their arms around each other. Water gushed under the door and several inches up the sides indicating the rising level in the hallway.

"This is awful," Sydney whispered with tears running down her face. Water slapped against the porthole and startled them both.

"It'll be quick once we go under," was all AJ could manage to say. She was a take-action girl who was never one to stand by while life happened around her but she was out of ideas, she couldn't see any way out and if this was the end she was determined to go as gracefully as she could. She'd give anything to be able to write a note to her family, just tell them how much she loved them and how thankful she was. Let Reg and Pearl know how much she cared and appreciated all they'd done for her. Wouldn't get to them of course, the note would end up lost to the world forever at the bottom of the Caribbean Sea, same as the two of them.

Jackson. Her head dropped as she felt his arms around her, his soothing voice and beautiful smile. Every wonderful thing they could possibly be together, the laughter, the tears, the love and passion were about to be snuffed out. The hope and belief that this man truly was her soulmate, her one true and final love was about to drown with her in a few minutes.

The water was up to their ankles in the cabin and rising quickly. Outside, the splashes against the porthole were replaced with the sea itself covering the lower third of the glass. The sound of water gushing and streaming throughout the ship echoed around inside the small steel room. AJ knew once the deck swamped the boat would rapidly drop below the surface and any remaining air pockets would be quickly crushed from the vessel by the increasing water pressure as they plummeted to the depths. The idea that the glass porthole would blow apart in flying shards slashing through the cabin made her shudder.

The cabin door moved. The water poured in around the edge now almost knee high. AJ stared at the door in disbelief: had the water broken the lock? It opened a crack further and she stood up, pulling Sydney with her.

"The door! It's opening!"

AJ reached over and grabbed the handle and pulled with all her might. The door slowly dragged open wider, resisted by the water in the cabin until a face appeared around the edge.

"Date prisa, debemos irnos ahora," the man gasped, still pushing the door. "El barco se está hundiendo!"

AJ squeezed into the narrow gap they'd opened between the steel door and the jamb while the man she recognised from pulling up the anchor kept pushing it open. She reached back and clutched Sydney's hand to pull her through after. "What did he say?" she asked, barely slipping through the gap.

Sydney pushed herself through behind. "He said the boat is sinking."

AJ laughed as she helped tug Sydney into the hallway. "So he noticed then!"

The man made sure they were both clear then smiled nervously. "Hola, soy Julio," he said, tapping his chest.

"AJ. I can't tell you how good it is to meet you, Julio!" AJ replied and pointed to the stairs.

Julio nodded, turned and started wading towards the stairwell. AJ quickly assessed their situation. The hall was getting darker as the ocean covered the portholes and the water was thigh deep and rising visually. Ahead at the stairwell she couldn't see any water running down the steps, which meant the decks hadn't swamped yet, but it couldn't be long. They needed to get up the stairs as fast as they could. She let Sydney go ahead and they shuffled through the water that had already risen to waist height. Julio stumbled as he started up the steps but recovered his footing and by the third step he was clear of the water. AJ watched Sydney trip at the same spot at the base of the stairs and reached down in the water to clear whatever had washed up there. She immediately recognised the smooth curvature of a Scuba tank and, feeling the buckle along its length, realised it was probably her gear.

The boat shuddered and rolled slightly; something had definitely shifted or given way and AJ abandoned her rig and followed the other two up the steps. Julio was pushing against the deck door with all his might to no avail, it wasn't budging. AJ looked out the window next to the door and was shocked to see nothing but the Caribbean Sea and the davit poking through the surface. The decks were swamped, the boat was going down in a hurry and the door, that opened outward, was pinned shut by the water outside. She grabbed Julio by the arm and pointed out the window. He looked just as the water level rose to window level and continued rising at an alarming rate, to their horror. Julio turned to the stairs up to the wheelhouse above and scrambled for them as the water began pouring in through any hole it could find, flowing like a river from the front through the galley and dining area.

"Stay here and hang on!" AJ yelled to Sydney and shot back down the stairs to the lower deck. She met the water at the turn in the stairs and had to plunge underwater to reach the lower deck. Her head careened off something hard and metallic as she swept her arms around trying to locate her gear. Her hand dragged across her BCD and she scratched and scrambled to pull it upright and find her regulator. Tracing the tank up to the first stage on top she followed a hose until it ended and plunged the reg in her mouth, hitting the purge button to clear the water. She sucked down a couple of sweet gulps of dry air and on the third breath the diaphragm went clunk and the air stopped. Damn it, she thought, sometimes I'm too efficient! She fumbled for the first stage and cranked on the shut-off knob until air streamed to her lungs again. She'd turned the valve off by habit when she'd left her gear in the skiff.

The water was moving with force now but she struggled into the BCD and managed to clasp the waistband. She couldn't see a thing submerged but even if her eyes could focus underwater it was too dark now. She fumbled for the steps and half climbed, half swam to the main deck level and stood up. Her head barely broke the surface and it was almost completely dark.

"Sydney?!" she yelled taking the reg from her mouth and trying not to suck in water.

"AJ!" Sydney screamed from close by. They both waved their arms in the direction of each other's voices and grabbed a hold when they touched.

"I've got you!" AJ shouted. "I have a reg you can breathe off, hang on to me, we have to let this level flood above the door before we can open it!"

They both bounced on their tiptoes to be able to keep talking and AJ handed Sydney her spare regulator. "Where's Julio?" AJ spluttered, trying not to gulp the water that was splashing and swirling as the room rapidly filled up. Something bowled Sydney over into AJ and they were both thrown underwater, unable to take a breath before going under. AJ stuffed the reg she had in her hand in her mouth and fumbled to find her octopus, the spare regulator on the end of a long hose used in emergencies. Someone was on top of her as she hit the deck and she fumbled to locate body parts and orientate herself. She found the person's face and collecting her spare reg in her other hand she jammed it unceremoniously in their mouth and purged the reg. By the hair she could feel swirling about she presumed it was Sydney, who stopped flailing and AJ heard her sucking in a big lungful of air. Other hands clawed through the water and swiped at the hose to AJ's reg, wrenching it from her mouth. She grabbed hold of the flailing arm and pulled them towards her, sweeping an arc with her other arm to recover the reg. She found Julio's face and stuffed the reg into his mouth, which stopped him windmilling around and the three lay holding each other on the deck floor as the boat continued down.

AJ needed air and then they needed to get out before they were too deep to survive. She gently held Sydney's head and tugged lightly on the regulator. Sydney instinctively grabbed the hand trying to steal her air but after feeling AJ's hand seemed to get the idea and relaxed, letting AJ take the reg and draw a few breaths. The air felt so good it was hard to give it back but taking a lungful AJ returned the reg and tried to gather the three of them to their feet on the deck. She had to find the door but they'd been knocked away from the rear of the structure and she touched nothing but water.

In the complete blackout she was totally disorientated and the sinking boat had a strange floating feeling as it rocked around; the boat could be inverted for all she knew.

82

Pearl kept the throttle pulled back and the Newton bounced and bucked as fast as she could go. They all hung on to anything they could but no one asked her to slow down. From over a mile away they'd seen the skiff with three people aboard push away from the trawler and start motoring towards shore. Shortly after, the big old boat had begun to lower in the water and list slightly. Half a mile out and it was clear the trawler was sinking and the police marine unit had altered its course to intercept the slow moving skiff. Pearl finally eased back the throttles and the dive boat slowed and glided to where the trawler had recently disappeared below the surface leaving a strange swirling and welling of water behind. Debris and flotsam popped up, bobbing around, and occasional bursts of bubbles frothed the surface.

Carlos dropped his head in his hands. "No, no, no."

Pearl put her arm around his shoulder, squeezing him tightly but she had tears rolling down her cheeks, "Our girl was on there too, wasn't she?" Pearl looked at Reg but all he could do was stare at the water in disbelief.

"We don't know if either of them were still on board, let's not jump to conclusions," Roy tried to offer some hope.

"Sydney was on there, I know she was," Carlos moaned, his eyes filled with tears.

Roy opened the microphone on the marine radio, "Marine Unit Three this is Whittaker, they talking? Over."

After a beat the radio crackled to life, "Detective Whittaker this is Three, two of them swear they were the only ones on board, the third won't say a word, I believe he's a Cuban national sir, but he won't respond to English or Spanish, over."

Roy thought for moment before responding, "Three this is Whittaker, separate the Cuban from the other two and see if he'll talk then."

"There should be two Cubans sir, not just one," Carlos raised his head and spoke, "Silvio and Julio are the two."

Roy looked at the young man. "You could tell us which one we have, you know them?"

"Of course, we all work together," Carlos replied.

"Pearl, can you take us over to them, let's see who we have, maybe they'll talk to Carlos," Roy requested but Carlos wouldn't hear of it. "We cannot leave, please, we have to stay here. They could still be alive, they could appear, there's stuff surfacing still!"

Roy rested a hand on Carlos's shoulder, "Son, if they were in that boat I'm afraid they're gone. Best we can do is hope they weren't and there's three men over there who can answer that for us."

Carlos looked completely defeated but Reg spoke up from behind them. "Give it a minute or two longer. Won't change anything they have to say."

Roy nodded. "Fair enough, we can give it a minute."

83

Total darkness consumed the inside of the trawler and the boat groaned and creaked ominously. AJ could feel a wall to her left, but it could be the ceiling or the floor for all she knew. She moved the entangled group of three forward and felt Julio bump into something. Reaching behind him she felt a horizontal surface. Julio pushed back and she could tell he was guiding them now. He must have recognised his surroundings, which she guessed had to have been the dining area table. Manoeuvring three people, unable to communicate, submerged in water in complete darkness was no easy task. They stumbled and stepped on each other but the two girls could sense Julio thought he'd found his bearings and were happy for him to steer them. AJ really needed another lungful of air so while tripping and fumbling their way across the floor she repeated the exercise with Sydney, who didn't resist the reg exchange. AJ banged into another wall but this time something jabbed her in the hip as the scuba tank made a muffled metallic clang against the steel structure. She took a full inhale of air and returned the reg to Sydney so she could use her hand to feel around. A door handle! She rotated down and the wall felt like it slowly swung outward. Realising it was the door that was opening she pulled the other two into the opening and kept pushing on the door against the resistance of the water. An eerie dim light bathed the stern deck of the trawler and glancing up AJ could make out the faint glow of the surface, which seemed to be falling away from her. She felt dizzy and reached out to stop herself from falling over but as she looked down to catch her fall she could just make out the deck was still below her under her bare feet. Her head spun and she blinked to try and clear her vision before looking up to see the surface light was now gone. It was over her right shoulder. The boat was rolling over, Julio was still inside and her spare regulator was floating in the water on the end of its hose. Sydney stepped clear of the doorway as the door rotated above them shielding the surface light as the boat passed ninety degrees in its roll. AJ grabbed the spare regulator and drew in some clean, dry air while reaching for the door jamb and pulling herself back into the opening. She felt a tug from her first stage which she presumed was Sydney's reg line being pulled tight; she could only hope that Sydney would figure out what was going on. She swept her hand around inside the cabin as far as she could reach but touched nothing.

She knew by the faint light from above they were already far too deep but she couldn't leave Julio inside. The man had come back to save them so despite all instincts screaming at her to ascend she pulled herself back inside the darkened, sinking boat. Still attached to Sydney, who she could feel close behind her, she knew they only had a few seconds to find him before the boat completed its roll and the hull would be between them and the surface. They'd never make it around the structure. She guessed he'd made the wall but missed the door so he had to be either up or down as the boat was now on its side and still turning. Going by nothing more than an instinctive hunch she reached up and swirled her hand around in empty water until she slapped the wall. She could feel the rotation of the boat now with her legs still in the doorway; the door frame was spinning her with it. Her mind was getting hazy and dim from the nitrogen narcosis at depth and she could sense a cloud of paranoia and tension descending upon her. She'd chosen the wrong side, he must be the other way, she'd dragged herself and Sydney back into the sinking wreck and guaranteed their fate. Every regret, mistake and demon her mind could conjure fell upon her in an avalanche of self-doubt and inadequacy. AJ gritted her teeth and lurched one more time into the space above her, fighting back the narcosis, determined to find the man who had come back for them. If they were going to die down here, they'd damn well die together.

Her hand struck a limb and before she could even know what body part it was she pulled down with all her might, hooking her leg around the door opening as an anchor. Julio plunged towards her in full panic, arms flying, free leg kicking, so before he could grab hold of her she took a big gulp of air and with a fistful of his hair in one hand she rammed the reg in his mouth with the other. Pulling violently on his hair she dragged him with her and shoved Sydney back out the doorway. Above them a looming mass blocked the light showing the long smooth silhouette of the hull as the boat continued its roll. AJ kicked liked crazy and could feel the other two doing the same. She angled them up but away from the bulk that was swinging above them, threatening to drag them once again towards the sea floor.

Her lungs were on fire. She'd burned through all the useful oxygen from the last gulp, her heart rate pegged with adrenaline and effort. But still she kicked. Her mind was fading, but still she kicked. The narcosis she'd staved off was crowding in again as her brain craved oxygen, but still she kicked. The hull was above them and felt like it was crushing them, chasing them, relentless in its desire to take them to the bottom. AJ barely hung on to consciousness; as much as her mind told her legs to kick there was nothing left, she was done. What felt like the weight of the world fell upon her legs and she knew it was the Explorador de la Reina. The old boat was taking hold of her, the other two and all evidence of the devastation about to befall miles of beautiful reef. Carlos would be left with no proof. He'd be deported for his theft of the plane and the explosives would be set and the coral blown to pieces along with millions of fish and sea creatures. The world would take another step forward on its own destruction, its seemingly determined path to destroy all that sustains life on the planet. AJ felt a searing pain along her legs like someone was shaving the backs of them with a handful of barnacles. Her arms were pulled tight, stretched painfully taught until finally the barnacles let go of her legs and everything went hazy, her last thought being that death was actually quite peaceful at the very end.

Weird shapes formed in front of AJ's eyes and a strange sound of inhalation and release echoed around her. Her focus slowly formed and she made out two figures in a blurry landscape. She took another long smooth drag from the regulator and like a curtain being raised on a stage all was revealed. Julio and Sydney had an arm each and were pulling her upwards, straining against a pull from below. Her head dropped to reveal a large shadow fading below them as the trawler and the suction from its descent fell away and finally released them. Sydney gently pulled the regulator from AJ's mouth and they began a rhythm of buddy breathing. She looked up and could see the surface still a long way above them. She fumbled around her chest and found her dive watch clipped to a D ring on her BCD. She looked at the screen. The human cornea has evolved to see clearly through air, not the density of water, so no matter how much she squinted she couldn't get focused. The one thing she could see was the screen was flashing, which meant trouble. They were still in deep shit. She pointed her thumb urgently towards the surface and the other two seemed to get the idea. All three kicked harder and AJ hit the inflate button on her BCD to help them ascend. She hated to use the air to fill the BCD instead of breathing but every breath at this depth took massive amounts more air to fill their lungs against the increased water pressure. The sooner they reached shallower depths the longer the air would last. Another minute and they were all desperately tired from kicking and were sucking down air at an alarming rate, all breathing from the same tank. AJ could feel her BCD expanding as the surrounding water pressure lessened and instead of taking her turn on the regulator she released some air through the dump valve on the inflation line and let the escaping bubbles fill her mouth. She took in a little sea water along with it but it saved some of their precious air. She knew they should be making their first safety stop at sixty feet to dissipate some of the large excess of nitrogen they'd been absorbing from the compressed air, but with no way of knowing their exact depth or air left, they didn't have that luxury.

When they reached what she approximated to be twenty feet she halted the group, to their surprise. Julio tugged on her arm to keep going but she pulled him back to her. Without masks none of them could see clearly and with no way to talk AJ was out of methods to communicate. All she could do was hope they'd trust her which by their compliance to hang at this depth they appeared to do. She started counted in her head, one, one thousand, two, one thousand… She looked at her dive watch again and the screen was still flashing. No surprise there, she thought; if she could focus her eyes it would show her the instructions of depth and time to follow to safely release the nitrogen from her system to avoid decompression sickness. Of course it would be wholly inaccurate as three of them had been sharing the tank but her computer didn't know that. She realised she'd forgotten to count as her mind wandered. One, one thousand, two, one thousand, she started over. Holding at the same depth she could no longer take expanding air from her BCD so they went back to sharing the regs, taking turns amongst the three of them. Without knowing how much air was left in the tank and unable to see her computer screen she figured they'd hang here for at least five minutes and then ease up to the surface. She realised she'd stopped counting again, but then it didn't matter. The diaphragm in both regulators clunked closed at the same time, the tank was empty. They all kicked like mad and looked up towards the surface that seemed a lot more than twenty feet away without an air supply.

They burst through the surface and gasped, spluttering and coughing as they swallowed some salt water along with the air. They could just make out the tops of the buildings on the island but they were miles away. The sun was setting and the light fading as they all scanned the water towards Cayman. The thought that they were now lost on the open ocean quickly dawned on them. The swell rolled and lifted them higher and they spotted two boats about half a mile towards shore. They yelled and waved but sensed how difficult they'd be to spot, and impossible to hear, over this distance.

"Need a ride," a soft American voice made them all jump. They turned to face a man in a small boat silhouetted against the setting sun. A hundred yards behind him was a much larger boat. AJ splashed over and with the last strength she had lurched up into the waiting arms of Jackson.

84

———————

Pearl couldn't let AJ go. She struggled to piece together any real sentences; she just muttered and mumbled and cried and hugged. Reg made sure the three survivors were breathing off the emergency oxygen cylinder carried on all dive boats and they passed a second cylinder over from the police boat. They hadn't shown signs of the bends or nitrogen sickness but AJ's dive computer reported a maximum depth of 205 feet, seventy-five below the recreational safe diving limit, so they weren't taking any chances. Carlos endlessly fussed around Sydney, wrapping her in a towel, checking on her oxygen mask and getting her to drink water until she thought she would burst. Once he discovered Julio had been the one to save the girls he gave his Cuban compatriot the same treatment and thanked him repeatedly.

Whittaker had the police boat tied alongside with the two Russians handcuffed to the bench in the stern. They sat silently, refusing to say anything but "contact Russian embassy" with a smug expression. He kept Silvio separated from them, also handcuffed, but seated in the wheelhouse. He'd hung his head when Jackson motored over with the three and had remained that way since. Jackson helped Reg administer the oxygen and squeezed AJ's hand each time he passed when she could free a limb from Pearl's bear hug.

Roy stepped over to the Newton and sat next to Sydney. Letting out a sigh, he scratched his head and spoke quietly. "Would it bother you too much to come over and give me an ID on these fellows? I don't want to put you through any more trauma than you've already been through, so it's fine if you'd rather not, but it would help me expedite things if you're up to it?"

Carlos waved his hand. "No sir, can she do this later?"

But Sydney cut him off, slipping the mask away from her face. "I'm fine, I'd rather do it now."

She stood up and looked over at the two Russians, who stared back disdainfully. "They're handcuffed, right?" she asked.

"Absolutely," Roy assured her, "and strapped to that bench. They're not going anywhere."

Sydney unwrapped herself from the towel, letting it fall, and stepped over to the police boat. "Let me make sure I get a proper look, Detective."

Carlos reached out to stop her and Roy stammered, "Oh, you can just look from over here Miss Bodden."

But she was already on the deck of the police marine unit boat and stood right in front of her assailants. Sydney pointed to Anatoly, "This one and another guy, his boss I believe, are the ones that took me and shoved me in the boot of their car. He also pointed a gun at me and AJ and locked us in the cabin when they scuttled the trawler. The other one," she pointed to Pavlo, "I never saw him."

"I did." AJ escaped Pearl's grasp and stood looking from the dive boat. "I saw him in the dining area of the trawler, he was there."

"Okay," Whittaker began but before he could say anything more Sydney swung a solid right hook and Pavlo's head jolted back. For a second all hell broke loose as Roy jumped over to the other boat and the marine policemen came out of the wheelhouse. They gathered Sydney up before she could get off a another swing. When things settled Pavlo sat looking dazed with blood seeping from his lip and they hustled Sydney back to Reg's boat.

"Well, a positive ID on both then," Whittaker muttered, slightly out of breath. "I'll send the police boat in if, Reg, you're okay with taking everyone else back to the harbour?"

Reg nodded with a smile on his face. "No problem, probably safest for them two."

"Apparently," Roy chuckled and untied the ropes holding the two boats together.

AJ grinned at Sydney. "Nice punch sister, but why did you hit that one?"

Sydney picked her towel back up, "I'd already kicked the other one so I figured I'd work my way around them. It's the other guy I really want, he's the one that punched me."

"I'll remember to keep him away from you," Roy chuckled.

Reg fired up the Newton, and after the police boat had left, they dragged Jackson's dinghy over to the Sword of the Sentry. Jackson stayed on the dive boat and they started the run back to shore with Sea Sentrys' boat following.

"So what happens now, Detective?" Carlos asked Roy politely with a hopeful expression.

"Good question." Roy rubbed his temple and took his time replying. "Not much precedent for these circumstances, I have to say; I'll need statements from everyone of course. You explained to me about your Cuban reef you're trying to save. I suppose that's why these chaps are here?" He pointed to Jackson and the large boat behind them.

Carlos hung his head. "Yes, but I have failed in all of this, the information and evidence I had went down with the trawler; the Russians took it when they grabbed Sydney, now it's destroyed." He looked at Jackson, "I'm so sorry, you came all this way for nothing."

"Not for nothing," AJ smiled and nudged Jackson while she looked over at Sydney.

Sydney grinned. "Nah, not for nothing. I made a flash drive copy you dope."

Carlos's face lit up, "You did? Where is it?"

The girls looked over at Pearl. "Where only one man would ever find it," Pearl said with a laugh and reached into her bra and retrieved a flash drive from her cleavage.

Salvador Barrios stood on the pier out back of the Instituto de Estudios Geológicos and watched as the Cuban naval vessel backed out of the inlet. His mobile phone rang and he retrieved it from his pocket, answering sternly, "Barrios."

"Mr. Barrios, I'm afraid we have a problem," came the Russian voice, sounding less contentious than usual.

"No," Barrios snarled back. "We already had a problem – you're supposed to have a resolution."

The line was quiet for a moment. "I'm afraid it's a bigger problem than anticipated."

Barrios shook his head. "I'm watching the ship leave for Jardines de la Reina now, everything is ready to begin work on Monday. You told me you would resolve this!"

"Tell your boat to come back. When you see the news tomorrow you'll understand why."

EPILOGUE

Sea Sentry, further inspired by Jackson witnessing the attempted murders and suppression of evidence, stayed true to their word and facilitated an impressive press conference, broadcast online to a worldwide audience of eager reporters and public. Carlos overcame his nerves and delivered an impassioned and clear synopsis of the Gardens of the Queen's impending doom with speedily prepared maps and diagrams of his own creation. It was enough. The Republic of Cuba denied all knowledge of the plan and went to great lengths to show their future scheme to drill miles off the coast from deep-sea rigs. The Russians said nothing.

Detective Roy Whittaker had his work cut out sorting through the political hornet's nest in the wake of the sinking of the Explorador de la Reina. The Russians demanded their men be handed over, the Cubans demanded their people, including Carlos, be handed over and the Cayman Islands government were in no hurry to do either. With Carlos not revealing any official Cuban documents and them denying they existed, his crime was stealing the plane. The Cayman Islands court refused the extradition request and granted him asylum and residency on the island, where he planned to marry a Caymanian citizen once she graduated from university in Miami. Silvio, they were happy to hand over. Julio was a harder case but after much campaigning from everyone, including Whittaker, he was also granted asylum with employment secured servicing Reg Moore's dive boats.

All three Russians were sentenced to ten years' imprisonment for attempted murder. The Russian government complained and the Cayman government told them it would be up for discussion in about eight years if the men behaved themselves.

Roy sentenced Reg's wife to play at the RCIPS Christmas party for the next ten years as penance for her husband withholding information from the detective. An arrangement satisfactory to all.

AJ and Jackson enjoyed a few more weeks together before the Sword of the Sentry left port for America. He assured her he would not be a nomad forever and she assured him she'd be on Cayman forever, so he knew where to find her. They chat across the world-wide web whenever they can and he urges his captain to stop by the island whenever possible. Her heart skips when she sees his smile across the airwaves and he thinks he's the luckiest guy in the world. They both feel complete.

ACKNOWLEDGMENTS

This book would not exist without the unwavering support and encouragement from my amazing wife Cheryl and great friend James Guthrie. I'm never alone on this perilous journey. My wonderful Mum and Dad always encouraged my creative adventures and for that and much, much more I'm forever grateful and in their debt. My editor, Andrew Chapman of Prepare To Publish, has been a game changer and an absolute pleasure to work with; thank you so much.

Above all I thank you, the readers, it is your kind words that have opened the door to more adventures for AJ Bailey and myself.

LET'S STAY IN TOUCH!

To buy merchandise, find more info or join my Newsletter, visit my
website at
www.HarveyBooks.com

If you enjoyed this novel I'd be incredibly grateful if you'd consider
leaving a review on Amazon.com
Find eBook deals and follow me on BookBub.com

Visit Amazon.com for more books in the
AJ Bailey Adventure Series,
Nora Sommer Caribbean Suspense Series,
and collaborative works;
The Greene Wolfe Thriller Series
Tropical Authors Adventure Series

ABOUT THE AUTHOR

A *USA Today* Bestselling author, Nicholas Harvey's life has been anything but ordinary. Race car driver, adventurer, divemaster, and since 2020, a full-time novelist. Raised in England, Nick has dual US and British citizenship and now lives wherever he and his amazing wife, Cheryl, park their motorhome, or an aeroplane takes them. Warm oceans and tall mountains are their favourite places.

For more information, visit his website at HarveyBooks.com.